THE LIES We Tell

THE FOUR - BOOK 1

BECCA STEELE

The Lies We Tell (The Four, #1)

Copyright © 2020 by Becca Steele

Cover design by NET Hook & Line Design

Editing by One Love Editing

Becca Steele

www.authorbeccasteele.com

AUTHOR'S NOTE

This book may contain triggers for some readers.

The author is British, and British English spellings and phrases are used throughout.

For Jenny.
I blame you for this.

You may tell the greatest lies and wear a brilliant disguise, but you can't escape the eyes of the one who sees right through you.

— Tom Robbins, *Villa Incognito*

PROLOGUE

Caiden

One year ago...

At Alstone College, we were kings. Untouchable. People called us "the Four." How fucking original. We'd had the nickname since we'd first banded together at school—me, Zayde, and Cassius, all fourteen, and my brother Weston, thirteen. Now, with all of us at university and living together, we were closer than ever. Yeah, only me and Weston were related by blood, but they were all my brothers.

Truth was, I didn't have time for many people, other than my boys. Women were good for one thing, and if it didn't involve a willing pussy or having my dick sucked, I wasn't interested. Speaking of...

"Time's up." I clapped my hands, startling the two topless blondes making out in front of me. They drew apart, heavy-lidded with arousal and the effects of the alcohol and weed they'd been smoking. One of the women continued to fondle the tits of the other, moaning, but my dick didn't even stir. This shit was getting old, fast.

I took another drag of my blunt. "Didn't you hear me? Out. Now." I pointed at the door, and they got the message. Fucking finally.

"You sending away perfectly good pussy?" Cassius wandered in, grabbing the blunt from my hand and taking a huge drag.

"Wasn't that good, believe me."

He raised a sceptical brow. "How much have you had to drink?"

I glanced at the empty bottle of Jack, thrown next to me on the sofa. "Shit. All of it."

"Brewer's droop. Too much alcohol decreases the blood flow to your dick." Cassius nodded sagely, as if he was a fucking medical expert. "That's why you sent them away. Couldn't get it up."

"Fuck off."

"Nah, think I'll stay." He slumped down next to me, throwing his legs onto the coffee table, knocking my phone onto the floor.

"Watch it, mate."

I heard the door slam as I swiped my phone from under the coffee table, as Weston and Zayde burst into the room. Something, a premonition, had me sitting bolt upright, the haze from the drugs temporarily clearing as adrenaline raced through me.

Weston spoke two words, his voice calm and measured, but his eyes showed the underlying worry he was trying to hide.

"Code blue."

Fuck.

ONE

Winter

"Kinslee, I need you to be my guide in everything. What or who do I need to know?" I stood, hands on hips, watching my housemate as she blew out a breath, tapping her lip in thought.

"Nothing specific I can think of right now, but stick with me and you'll be fine. First, and most important, as you well know, there's a big 'welcome back to uni' house party tonight. That'll be our first stop."

"Sounds good." I smiled, pulling my hair out of its messy bun, letting it cascade down my back. "I can't believe I'm really here, about to become an official student."

During the first year of my degree course, when I'd been a normal university student in an ordinary university, the "accident" had happened, and my entire world had been turned upside down. I'd managed to transfer to Alstone College, a specialist business school, after months of back-and-forth, endless paperwork, and assessment of my course credits to ensure I could continue my studies going into my second year, rather than starting the first year all over again

Of course, the money I'd paid hadn't hurt. At Alstone, money talked. That, and connections. A hundred grand, my mother's new surname dropped casually into conversation —as much as I hated to use it, and my enrolment had suddenly been confirmed. Unfortunately, that had used a huge chunk of my insurance money, so I'd need to be careful with my spending.

After my transfer had been confirmed, I was ready. I had enough money to get by, if I was careful. I'd used some of the remaining insurance money to buy a phone, a laptop, other university essentials, and a compact car. My housing was sorted—I'd paid for the entire academic year up front. I'd scoured the online university noticeboard, and after viewing three different sets of accommodation, I'd lucked out with Kinslee Stewart. A second-year student like me, she had a two-bedroom apartment in a block right next to the campus and had advertised for a housemate.

As soon as I'd met her, we'd hit it off. We'd spent the past week getting to know each other, and I felt like I'd known her for years already.

I was beyond grateful that everything had seemingly fallen into place, but, all that aside, I had to keep my end goal in mind. The *only* reason I was now at Alstone College, rather than my previous university, was to investigate my dad's death. And unfortunately, that also meant reconnecting with my mother. We hadn't spoken in person for years, but after my dad had died, my hand had been forced. I didn't, for one minute, believe the accident report regarding his death, and there were too many coincidences surrounding my mother to ignore.

Until I got a chance to investigate everything, I'd throw myself into university life. My dad wouldn't have wanted anything to distract me from getting my degree. He'd been so proud when I'd been accepted to study business—he'd spent hours touring different universities with me and going through the pros and cons of different degree courses and career paths.

Sinking down onto Kinslee's bed, I blinked rapidly as my eyes filled with tears. Fuck. I missed him so much. Not being able to pick up the phone and call or text him...it was like a piece of me was missing. Throughout my life, he'd been my one constant. The person who'd loved me, who had been there for me unconditionally. And now he was gone.

I willed the impending tears to go, concentrating on slowing my breathing. I couldn't afford to fall apart, especially not in front of my new friend. I wasn't at the point where I wanted to, or even felt able to, explain what had happened.

With an effort, I focused my mind on the present.

We changed for the party, Kinslee wearing black booty shorts and a tight red top that made her boobs look amazing, and as for me—I had no fucking clue, so I let Kinslee choose my outfit, ending up in a tight electric-blue minidress which somehow highlighted and emphasised my minimal curves and long legs. She straightened my dark hair and gave me a smoky eye that made my blue eyes pop. Arranging her tawny corkscrew curls around her shoulders, she blew her reflection a kiss and proclaimed us ready.

"Party time! Let's go." She threw open the door and we headed out of the apartment to the waiting Uber, and what seemed like no time later, we were pulling up in front of a house, music and light spilling out from the open door and windows.

"House" was barely an adequate description for this monstrous residence. A sprawling, two-storey modern brick building, it was all sharp angles and huge black-framed glass doors and windows, the glass-fronted doorway extending the full height of the house, showing a glimpse of the upstairs area and a huge skull-shaped pendant light suspended from the upper-floor ceiling, descending all the way down to the entrance hallway. I sucked in a nervous breath. *You're strong. You can do this.* Squaring my shoulders, I linked my arm through Kinslee's, and we strutted up the pathway and in through the open door like we owned the place.

Kinslee led us through the wide tiled hallway, past a large curving staircase, into a kitchen teeming with people that was easily twice the size of Kinslee's entire apartment. "Drinks first?" She turned to me with a grin.

I nodded, returning her smile, and she made a beeline for the paddling pool in the corner of the room, effortlessly weaving through the clusters of people in her way.

"Paddling pool?" I murmured to myself. Stepping closer, I saw it had been filled to the brim with ice and bottles of beer, cider, and cans of premixed cocktails. Genius idea. Kinslee reached in and grabbed us two cans of premixed mojitos, and pushing through the crowds, she led me into a cavernous room, where the sound system was set up and playing thumping dance music. I let her pull me into the area where the dancing was concentrated, and I lost myself in the music.

Until I felt the weight of four sets of eyes, trained on me.

As I subtly turned my head to look, tingles of awareness spread through my entire body, and I gasped. Carefully, I leaned closer to Kinslee, knowing the answer before I even asked the question.

"Kins, don't be obvious about it, but who the fuck are those guys? The four on the sofas?"

Kinslee peered around me, her eyes widening and her whole body stiffening.

"They're the Four. They own this place. They pretty much run the campus."

They own this place? "The Four?" I echoed. "What lame kind of name is that?"

Kinslee shrugged. "I don't know, it's just what people call them. From left to right you have Cassius, Weston, Zayde, and Caiden. They're all sexy as fuck, and they know it. Spoiled rich boys who think they're above everyone else. Cassius, Zayde, and Caiden are all in the same year at uni as us—they're either nineteen or twenty. And Weston is Caiden's younger brother—he just turned eighteen, and this will be his first year at Alstone."

Of course, I recognised two of them from their photos, but I needed to hear it confirmed aloud. "Caiden and Weston Cavendish?"

Kinslee stared at me suspiciously. "Yes. Why? Do you know them?"

I swallowed hard, my throat suddenly dry. "They're... well, my stepbrothers, I guess?"

"*What*? You've been living with me for a week now, and you never once thought of mentioning that you were involved with the *Cavendish* family?"

"I'm *not* involved with them." I thought for a moment, then added, "Yet." Leaning closer, I lowered my voice. "You know how I told you one of the reasons I moved here was to reconnect with my mother? Well, she remarried a couple of years ago. Anyway, I haven't met her new husband yet, or his sons. I...I didn't attend the wedding. But I guess I'll be getting my chance to meet them soon enough."

"You didn't attend your mother's wedding? Girl, you need to give me all the details. Don't hold out on me."

Chewing my lip, I stared at her for a moment, then sighed. It wasn't like I could keep my connection to the Cavendish family a secret, and as my housemate and new friend, she was owed an explanation. "I will. Let's enjoy the party, and I'll catch you up with everything tomorrow, yeah?"

Kinslee nodded, a sympathetic smile crossing her face as she noticed my hesitation. "You don't have to tell me anything you don't feel comfortable talking about."

"Thanks, Kins." I squeezed her hand gratefully. I wanted to talk to her, to share my fears and worries, but I wouldn't be giving her *all* the details. Not by a long shot. I couldn't.

I surreptitiously studied the Four, but when it became clear they knew I was watching them, I gave up trying to be subtle and stared at them openly, boldly. Kinslee was right. They were the sexiest men I'd ever seen in person. Cassius was all blond, boyish good looks. A girl sat on his lap, and I noticed his hand was inside her skirt. *Classy.* Even with the girl wriggling around on him, he was watching me intently, interest flickering in his eyes. Weston looked the friendliest of the group, his blue gaze open and warm, his lips tipped up at the corners as he glanced in my direction. Zayde looked...dangerous. That was really the only way I could describe him adequately. Thick, deep brown hair, a small sneer on his perfect, full lips, his eyes flickering over me disdainfully before he turned away, dismissing me.

And then there was *him.*

Caiden.

Angular jaw, eyes like stormy seas, rich, raven hair cut short around the sides and longer on the top. He was *gorgeous.*

The way he looked at me, though...

He looked like he *hated* me.

I reeled back, trying to suck air into my lungs, stunned by the contempt pouring off him in waves, thickening the surrounding air, suffocating me.

"What did you do to piss off Caiden Cavendish?" Kinslee's urgent hiss sounded in my ear.

"I have no idea. I've never seen him in person before in my life."

"Winter, this isn't good. You do *not* want to get on his bad side, trust me."

"Looks like it's too late."

Caiden Cavendish. Fucking rich, sexy asshole. I'd never felt such hostility from anyone before, and honestly? I was at a complete loss. It was obvious he was aware of who I was, recognition clear in his eyes. I had no idea why he would hate me on sight, though, unless he was pissed off that I hadn't attended my mother and his father's wedding—not that my mother had asked me to be there.

Unfortunately for me, his visible hatred didn't stop my heart beating faster or my thighs clenching together, desperate for his touch. I'd never had such a visceral reaction to someone before and I. Did. Not. Like. It.

I needed to get laid.

And fast.

Caiden was off limits. That much was obvious. As I shot another covert glance in his direction, I groaned under my breath. How could one person look like a fucking Greek god?

Beside the point.

He was banished from my mind, as of now. For whatever reason, he'd decided he didn't like me, so that was that.

I grabbed Kinslee's arm and turned us so I couldn't see the Four (still hated their stupid nickname), and I let the music carry me away, the beat filling me, flowing through my body. We danced provocatively, attracting the attention of a number of guys in our immediate radius, and the far more hostile attention of the girls clustered around the Four.

Ignoring the glares and disdainful looks, I lost myself in the music, until I caught the eye of a guy leaning against the wall, watching me. Every time I glanced up, he was still looking at me, and I danced closer to Kinslee to ask her if she knew who he was. She informed me that his name was James, and he was also a student at Alstone. He was cute—kind of preppy-looking, light brown hair falling into his blue eyes, lean but muscular build, and when he smiled, he had the most gorgeous dimples. The next time I looked at him, I held his gaze, making it clear that I was interested. He interpreted my signals correctly and a moment later was standing in front of me, leaning down to speak in my ear.

"Hey, there. I'm James Granville." His hand rested lightly on my arm as he spoke to me, not invading my personal space, but close enough to make his intent clear.

Our eyes met and his pupils dilated as I took a deliberate step closer, placing my own hand on his arm and sliding it up over his bicep as I reached up to speak into his ear. "I'm Winter Huntington."

"Winter. You are the most gorgeous woman I've seen in a very long time." He spoke into my ear, his voice clear over the pounding beat of the music. "My evening is certainly looking up, now that I've had the pleasure of meeting you." He spun me around. "Dance with me?"

We alternated between dancing and small talk, Kinslee never straying far from my side, which I really appreciated. Although, in actuality, we barely knew each other, I'd confided in her about how out of depth I felt, starting over in a completely new place and being the new girl when everyone else knew each other. She'd promised to look out for me, and with her by my side, I felt less alone. She seemed to be in her element, flirting and laughing with James' friends, dancing up a storm, her curvy body swaying to the music.

All the while, I could feel the stares of the Four burning into me, and although I tried my hardest to ignore it, I grew increasingly uncomfortable. James noticed, his sharp gaze flicking from me to the sofa, and he leaned closer, pulling my body into his. "You wanna get out of here?"

Did I? I wasn't in the habit of one-night stands, but...fuck, yes.

"What do you propose?" I stared at him, one eyebrow raised.

"My apartment is just around the corner. Why don't you come with me?"

I glanced towards Kinslee, and she mouthed *go* to me. Her okay gave me the reassurance I needed, and I smiled up at him.

"Okay."

"Good. Meet me outside the front door."

He nodded and was slipping away through the crowds before I had a chance to say anything else. After confirming with Kinslee that James was trustworthy and where I was going, and receiving an enthusiastic response of "he's hot and popular, go and fuck his brains out," I headed in the opposite direction to find the bathroom before I left.

I needed someone, and James wanted me. I needed to feel something for one night, to fill the void inside me that had been there ever since the accident had happened. My dad was gone, I was in a new place, completely out of my depth, and I wanted to have fun and just forget. Pretend I was a normal university student, with a normal life.

Mind made up, I exited the bathroom, only to bump into a hard body.

Awareness trickled up my spine.

Goosebumps broke out all over me.

I suddenly found it hard to breathe.

Caiden.

Was.

Here.

Have you ever been so aware of someone that your whole being reacts to them? Like you can't even control it?

His presence surrounded me as his body pressed against mine. "What are you doing..." I whispered, or I might have only thought the words, because he didn't respond. He roughly grasped my chin in his hand, and his touch sent shock waves ricocheting through me.

"You shouldn't be here."

His voice.

Angry, raspy, and oh-so-sexy.

My body arched towards his, unknowing, uncaring that he was basically telling me to leave. Helpless, I let out a small whimper as his thumb caressed my chin, the touch at odds with his hostile posture.

"Fuck," he gritted out, and I felt his lips hover over mine, his hot breath skating over my skin, before he tore himself away, gone, as if he'd never been there.

Dazed, I staggered back against the hallway wall, my legs weak, my breath coming in shuddering gasps. What was that? And why did I have such an extreme reaction to someone I'd never met before? Someone who hated me on sight?

Concentrating on breathing slowly in and out, I willed my racing heart to slow. What could I have done to offend him? And how could I have offended someone I'd never laid eyes on in person, before tonight?

So many questions, and no answers.

Straightening up, I hardened my resolve. Fuck him, whoever he thought he was. Nothing was going to detract me from my reason for being here. If I made a few enemies along the way, it would be worth the price. I needed answers, and I wasn't about to let anyone get in the way of that.

I strode through the house and out of the door before I could change my mind. James was there, leaning against the wall, his dimples popping out as he caught sight of me and smiled.

"Ready?"

I nodded. "Let's go."

He took my hand, and we began walking across the grass and out onto the quiet street. As we walked, he peppered me with questions.

"I haven't seen you around here before. Are you a first year?"

"No. I just transferred here; I'm going into my second year."

He grinned, steering me down a pathway towards a large mansion house, Regency style with white columns and large windows. "Same as me. What's your degree in? I'm doing Accounting and Business Management."

"Business and Marketing Management."

"We'll probably have some lectures together. If you need a study partner, I'm your man." He gave me another huge grin, and I couldn't help smiling back.

"Somehow I don't think there would be much studying involved."

"True." He laughed, leading me up the mansion steps

and inserting a key into the lock. "This way. I'm on the next floor. Where are you living?"

I trailed behind him up the wide staircase to a landing area, where he stopped in front of a door and inserted another key. "I'm in the apartments next to the campus. Hardwicke House?"

"Oh, yeah. Great location. I was in Hawling House last year. Decent apartments, if a bit small."

We entered his apartment, all high ceilings and classic, clearly expensive furnishings. Kinslee had been right. This college really was exclusive—from everything I'd seen so far, the whole place practically dripped money.

I tugged my hand out of James' grip and reached down to slip my shoes off. When I straightened up, he was staring at me hungrily.

He leaned forwards and pressed his lips to mine. I wound my arms around his neck, kissing him back. His kisses didn't set me alight, but it felt good. Good to be wrapped in someone's arms, forgetting everything, filling the emptiness inside me.

He broke the kiss but kept hold of me, walking us backwards into his bedroom. "Is this okay for you?"

"Yes." I shut off my brain, allowing myself only to think about now, this moment, and how good it felt. I'd become an expert in compartmentalising my thoughts and feelings since my dad had passed away, and I locked everything away to be dealt with another time.

We fell onto the bed, losing our clothes along the way. He kissed me with more urgency, until we were both breathless and he was rolling a condom over his hardness, then thrusting inside me.

All too soon, it was over.

"Was that good for you?" He rolled off me, panting.

"Yeah." I wasn't lying—well...not really. I hadn't orgasmed, but that didn't mean I hadn't had fun.

"Stay as long as you like, babe." He swung himself out of the bed and disappeared out of the door.

Thanks, but no thanks. I'd slept with him, it had filled the void for a short time, but I had no interest in taking things any further. I climbed out of the bed and gathered up my discarded clothes, pulling them back on as quickly as I could.

He re-entered the room, bare-chested, a pair of pyjama bottoms slung low on his hips. "Leaving already?"

"Uh, yeah. I don't sleep well in new places."

He nodded. "Okay, let me call you a cab." Before I could say anything else, he'd swiped his phone from the table next to his bed and was dialling. He spoke in a low voice, then ended the call and turned to me. "They'll be about five minutes. There's a cab on its way to drop someone off here, so it'll pick you up at the same time."

"Thank you," I murmured. "I'll go and wait downstairs." I stared at him a little awkwardly, unsure of what to do.

He gave me an understanding look. "Tonight was fun. If you ever want a repeat, I'm your man. If not, no big deal. I think we're going to become friends, Winter Huntington." Crossing the room to stand in front of me, he placed a soft kiss on my lips. "Let me throw on a T-shirt and I'll walk you downstairs."

At the front door, the taxi pulled up and the driver waved at me. "There's my ride. Thanks for earlier. See you around, James." We briefly hugged each other, and then I headed over to the taxi. He waited until I was seated in the cab, before he turned around and went back inside.

My mind churning, I closed my eyes, leaning against the window as the cab moved through the darkened roads towards my apartment. But it wasn't James who occupied my thoughts.

It was the man with hair as black as onyx and stormy ocean eyes.

My stepbrother.

TWO

Winter

"This is it." Talking aloud to myself, I slowed down my car, pulling up to the gated entrance. I noticed a camera focusing on me, and the gates smoothly swung open. I continued up the long gravel driveway and came to a halt in front of a large Georgian house, standing tall and imposing on the headland that stretched into the distance on either side. Other equally large houses were visible on the horizon, but none near enough to make out their features.

I parked my car to the left of the house, unsure where to leave it, and sat for a moment, trying to compose myself.

This would be the first time I'd seen my mother in person for years, and the first time I'd ever met her new husband. I was crossing my fingers that his sons wouldn't be there. It was going to be difficult enough as it was, playing nice with the woman that had shown no interest in my life until I made contact after my dad had passed away, without them around, making me uncomfortable.

Clasping the bottle of vintage wine I'd splurged on, I

made my way up the steps, bisected by tall columns, to the front door and knocked.

It swung open almost immediately.

"Good evening, Miss Huntington. We've been expecting you. May I take your coat?" A short, stooping man stood in the doorway, one arm outstretched towards me.

"Uh, sure." I shrugged off my coat and handed it to him, along with the wine. "Thank you. And who are you? I mean, how do I address you?" I could feel my cheeks grow warm. My dad hadn't been poor, but we certainly hadn't been on the level of having staff.

"I'm Mr. Allan, Mr. Cavendish's butler. You may call me Allan, miss."

I gave him a hesitant smile. "Um. Okay. Thank you, Allan."

He inclined his head towards me. "Follow me. Mistress Cavendish is expecting you."

We walked through a grand foyer, down a long corridor, and entered a large room full of plants, with glass walls on three sides and an absolutely breathtaking view of the ocean.

"Wow." My jaw dropped. The sun was setting, bathing the sea in a sparkling golden glow. From up this high on the clifftops, we had an almost panoramic view of the headland and the sea, stretching for miles.

"Beautiful, isn't it?" A pair of stilettos clicked across the stone floor, and someone came to a stop next to me.

I took a deep breath, turning to face the woman I hadn't seen in person since I was five years old. The woman who'd so easily cut me from her life. "Christine. I mean, Mother."

"Hello, Winter." Christine Clifford had barely aged a day — of course, I'd seen photos of her, but in person I could see how untouched she was by the years. If it was Botox, it was very subtle. She wore an elegant sky-blue dress and skyscraper heels, her dark hair twisted into a knot at the nape of her neck.

She studied me, her cool, appraising gaze taking me in, and then a pleased expression crossed her face. "You've grown into a beautiful woman. Of course, it's only to be expected, with me as your mother." She preened. "I look forward to reconnecting with you, adult to adult."

"Me too." I was shocked to find that I meant the words. I suddenly felt my lip tremble, and my eyes filled with tears. Despite everything, despite my suspicions, she was my mother. The only person connected to me by blood that was left alive.

She must have read something in my expression, because she added, "Now that your good-for-nothing father is gone, I'm all you have."

And just like that, my impending tears were gone, replaced by anger. She watched me with a knowing look in her eyes. I wouldn't give her the satisfaction of seeing that she'd hurt me. With an effort, I swallowed my rage and fixed a smile on my face. Game face on.

"Great. Why don't we start with you catching me up with your life?" If there was one thing my dad had mentioned about my mother, over and over again, it was that she was incredibly self-absorbed and loved to talk about herself.

Her lips curved into a pleased smile. *Good choice, Winter.* "Let's sit, and we can catch up."

I followed her to a set of wicker chairs that faced the glass wall. She glanced at the phone she'd been holding and tapped the screen a few times. "There. Refreshments will be here shortly. Arlo's son, Weston—he has two sons, you know —is a bit of a technological genius. He devised this app that does all sorts, including sending orders to the staff. Very useful."

I mentally filed away that morsel of information about Weston for future reference and sat back in the chair, turning to my mother.

"At the moment, as I'm sure you are aware, we're in the orangery. I suppose *you* would be more likely to call it a conservatory." She sniffed, then waved her hand around to encompass the large space. "Arlo loves his plants, as you can see. This house has been in the Cavendish family for generations. Arlo and I live here alone for the most part, along with the staff, but Caiden and Weston still have their old rooms here."

At the mention of Caiden's name, a shiver ran through me. My mother looked at me strangely but continued speaking. "I took the liberty of having one of the spare rooms cleared for you, should you wish to stay over at any time."

"Thank you. I appreciate it."

"Well, I can't have *those boys* having more than my own daughter, can I?" Her mouth twisted, and the way she'd spat "those boys" told me a lot. There was clearly no love lost between them, although she'd seemed impressed with Weston's technological prowess only moments ago. I had a sudden horrible feeling that my mother's distaste had something to do with Caiden being so hostile towards me. I hoped I wouldn't get caught up in the middle of some game of one-upmanship, because I had zero desire to be involved in any of that.

"I'm on the board of directors of Alstone Holdings. We practically run this town."

I nodded—this wasn't new information to me, but I needed to get every bit of information I could from her. We were practically strangers, after being estranged for so long, but from the information I *did* have on her, I knew that she was a hard woman who didn't appreciate idle conversation. "How many people are on the board, and what do you do?"

She looked pleased at my question. "It's nice to have someone take an interest. Those boys have no desire to learn more about the company they will one day inherit shares in. Not to mention, they'll become board members once they turn twenty-one and graduate from university." She tutted disapprovingly. "Alstone Holdings owns most of the land in this town. In addition, they construct properties all over the country. There are three families that own the company—by marriage I am now part of those three. The Cavendish family, the Drummond family, and the Lowry family."

I listened intently, filing away every piece of information she gave me. What had happened to my dad on the night of his death? There *had* to be a connection here, and every single instinct within me screamed that my mother was the key to solving this puzzle.

At the moment, though, I had questions and no answers.

I leaned forwards, opening my mouth to ask another question, when her phone buzzed.

"Oh. We're being summoned, I'm afraid. No time for drinks now. Dinner is served."

Walking back down the long corridor, we entered a large, dimly lit wood-panelled room, with a long, mahogany dining table in the centre.

"Darling. There you are." A tall, imposing man stood and walked across to where I'd stopped, hovering in the doorway. I barely noticed him, though. Sitting at the table, turned around to face me with a small smile on his lips, was Weston. And opposite Weston, hostility pouring off him just as it had done the first time I'd seen him, was Caiden.

With an effort, I dragged my focus away from Caiden and looked up at the man who was now standing in front of me, radiating disinterest.

"Arlo. And you must be Winter." He shook my hand briefly, then, dismissing me, kissed my mother's cheek and headed back to his chair.

My mother directed me to a seat opposite her.

Next to Caiden.

Fucking great.

Sliding into my seat, I was all too aware of the way he held himself, his posture tense, his eyes glittering dangerously. Every sense I possessed was on high alert, but despite his reaction, despite the fact that he clearly despised me, I couldn't stop the shiver that went through my entire body at his proximity.

"Have you met my sons yet?" Arlo's loud boom made me jump, and I heard Weston snigger.

Assholes. The words came out before I could censor them. "Yeah, we met. I wasn't impressed."

Arlo's eyebrows shot up.

"Winter Huntington!" My mother's scandalised hiss cut through the sudden silence.

Shit.

My mouth was so dry. I needed a drink.

"Not impressed?" Caiden's voice, deceptively calm, came from next to me. "Is that why you decided to hook up with the campus manwhore?"

Everyone's head turned to face his, mine included. He kept his gaze on his father, not even bothering to spare me a glance.

"Miss Huntington here attended a gathering at our house two nights ago. She left with James Granville." He sneered the words.

I gritted my teeth. Was it illegal to stab your stepbrother with a fork?

"Oh, Winter." My mother shook her head disapprovingly. "Even I know of that boy's reputation. Like father, like son," she said, almost to herself.

"The apple doesn't fall far from the tree, dear," Arlo murmured, glancing over at her.

The metallic tang of blood filled my mouth as I bit my lip, hard, to stop myself responding. *Remember why you're here.* The only thing that mattered was finding answers for my dad.

"I hope you used a condom. You'll be wanting to make an appointment at the STD clinic, otherwise." Caiden's focus turned to me, curling his perfect lips at me, his disdain obvious.

"Caiden. That's enough," Arlo admonished.

"Yes, Dad." He dismissed me with his gaze, turning his attention to his phone.

Silence fell, then Arlo clapped his hands loudly, making me jump again.

This time Weston laughed aloud. "Jumpy, aren't you?"

I raised my eyes to his and saw humour there. Okay, my first impressions had been correct. Weston, at least, didn't hate me. Not as much as his brother, anyway.

Next to me, I felt Caiden glare in Weston's direction, and Weston's gaze dropped to his plate. Allan and a woman appeared, gliding into the room almost silently, filling wine glasses and putting dishes in front of us. I waited until the others started eating, then followed suit, hardly able to concentrate on the food thanks to the presence of the man next to me.

Arlo's phone suddenly chimed, cutting through the uncomfortable silence. He glanced at the screen, then stood, his chair scraping back, and headed out of the room without a backwards glance. No one had any reaction to this, so I was guessing this was normal behaviour.

As soon as he'd gone, my mother turned to Caiden, her nose wrinkled in distaste. "When you come for dinner, I expect you to dress appropriately. Your standard of dress is unacceptable."

"Excuse me?" Out of the corner of my eye, I saw Caiden recoil, his hostility redirected from me to my mother.

"It's unacceptable," she repeated. "Even your brother was capable of dressing accordingly." She waved an elegant hand towards Weston, who wisely kept his mouth shut. I glanced between the two of them. Weston had on a smart pale blue polo shirt, his hair neatly styled, while Caiden wore a faded grey T-shirt, his raven hair a dishevelled mess. My stomach flipped as I looked at him, and I groaned internally. When was my body going to get the memo that he was a complete asshole?

"Sorry, Christine. You don't get a say in what I wear or what I do." He stared at her, brows raised challengingly.

She slammed her hand down on the table. My mouth flew open at the sudden display of temper, but Caiden didn't even flinch.

"I am your stepmother. And while you're under my roof, you obey my rules. Is that clear?"

He laughed mockingly. "Nice try, Christine. Never gonna happen."

Arlo returned to the room just as my mother was leaning across the table, preparing to launch another tirade at Caiden. She glanced up at Arlo, and a calculating expression appeared on her face.

"Arlo, darling." She touched his arm, purring her words.

"Don't you agree that Caiden should dress more appropriately for family meals?"

Arlo glanced over at Caiden. He shrugged. "Whatever you say, my love. You're the lady of the house and mother to my sons. If you believe he should, then I'll back you." Lifting her hand, he pressed a kiss to her knuckle, and she smiled triumphantly at Caiden.

Weston's head shot up at Arlo's words, and identical expressions of dismay crossed both his and Caiden's faces.

"She's *not* my mother," Caiden ground out, so quietly that I wasn't sure if anyone but me heard him, gripping his knife so tightly his knuckles turned white. Across the table, Weston scrubbed a hand over his face, before sighing and turning to his phone, his lips curved downwards, misery clear in his eyes.

Silence fell. Again.

I picked at my food, pushing it around on my plate, my appetite non-existent.

"Why are you here?" Caiden's low hiss came as Arlo was engaged in a discussion with my mother, and Weston was ignoring everyone, typing on his phone with one hand while he shovelled food into his mouth with the other.

"I'm here to get to know my mother. Why, do you have a problem with that?" I glared at him.

"Yes, I do." He lowered his voice even further. "I fucking *hate* your whore of a mother, and I know you're just like that evil bitch."

I gasped, my mouth falling open. "You don't even know anything about me. How *dare* you make assumptions?"

"I know enough," he said darkly. "And I promise you, right here, right now, that I'm going to do everything I can to make your life miserable. I don't trust you. I don't want you here. *We* don't want you here. Leave, or you will regret it."

The threat hung heavy in the air between us as I tried to wrap my head around his words.

"Leave? You think you can scare me off?"

"I know I can." His words were stated as fact, and I felt rage building. I welcomed it, using it to bolster me.

"Do your worst. Because I. Am. Not. Going. Anywhere." I clenched my fists, shaking with anger and staring into his eyes, which had darkened to the colour of the ocean at night, black and fathomless.

"Watch your back, Winter. You're out of your depth, and you don't know how to swim in these waters."

"Big words coming from someone who relies on Daddy's money to get by."

"You know nothing," he spat.

He slammed his fork down on the table and rose to his feet. "Dad, I've lost my appetite. I'll call you in the week."

His father rolled his eyes. "At least you managed to last through fifteen minutes of the meal this time. That's an improvement."

"Whatever. Weston, you coming." It wasn't a question.

Weston sighed and rose to his feet. "See you soon, Dad." Both of them ignored my mother, but Weston sent me a half-smile as he turned to leave. I attempted to smile back.

This family clearly had problems, and I'd somehow ended up in the middle of them. Investigating my dad's death was going to involve some very careful planning.

We finished the meal in silence, and then Arlo announced he was going to his study to work. My mother turned to me. "You'd better be getting back now, hadn't you? Don't your classes begin tomorrow?"

Guess it was time for me to leave. I nodded, keeping my endgame in mind. I needed to stay on my mother's good side. "Yes, I probably should. Shall we arrange to get together next weekend?"

My mother pursed her lips. "No, next weekend won't do. I'll get Arlo to talk to the boys and coordinate our schedules." She stood, crossing to the doorway, and stared at me expectantly.

"Allan will see you out. It was...nice to catch up." She swept out of the room, and Allan peered around the door frame. "Miss Huntington? I have your coat."

"Thank you." I smiled at him, and he gave me a genuine, beaming smile, the first proper one I'd received all evening.

The smile was wiped from my face when I walked around to the driver's side of my car. Under the soft outside lights, I could clearly see the words that had been scratched into my door in deep, angry gouges.

Whore.

THREE

Winter

K inslee led me over to the large grey stone building that housed several lecture halls and classrooms. "There. Do you want to meet at the Student Union building for lunch?" She pointed across the campus, where beyond a grassy square, a long building with huge glass walls, stood.

"Sure. Twelve? If you get there first, save me a seat. I'll do the same if I'm there first."

"Sounds good to me."

I smiled. "Brilliant. See you at lunch." She turned in the opposite direction, and I headed into the building in front of me to find my lecture hall. I peered at my schedule, trying to work out where I was going.

"Lost?" The low drawl came from my right, and I spun around to see Cassius, one of the Four, leaning against the white painted wall, staring at me.

"Uh... I have to find the Brunswick lecture hall."

"You're in luck. I'm headed that way." He grasped my arm firmly, tugging me along with him.

"Stop manhandling me," I hissed.

"No can do. I'm under orders from King Caiden." He laughed mockingly. Guess his boyish good looks hid a sadistic bastard. Great.

"You really call him King Caiden?"

"Nah. Just messing with you. But Caiden has decided you're not to be trusted, and until he decides what to do, one of the Four will be keeping an eye on you as often as we're able to."

"You cannot be serious." I stopped dead, yanking my arm away from him. My mind was racing. None of this made any sense. What possible reason could they have for watching me? I hadn't done anything to warrant their attention—I'd only just moved to Alstone.

"What exactly is it you think I'm going to do? And why are you listening to him, anyway? Don't you have your own mind?" The last thing I needed was someone shadowing my every move. I needed to stay as inconspicuous as possible—to find answers for my dad without attracting unwanted attention.

Meeting his gaze, I stepped closer, gritting my teeth in irritation. "Listen to me. You can tell King Caiden that I don't want, or need, a stalker. In fact, I'm pretty sure stalking is illegal. Not to mention, creepy as fuck."

His eyes narrowed at me. "You're new here, so I'll let your comments slide. This time. But you need to get one thing through your pretty little head. At Alstone, our word is law. Do not attempt to defy us, or you will regret the day you ever set foot on this campus."

I stared at him, my mouth opening and closing. What a sanctimonious prick! These boys had a serious case of self-entitlement.

"I don't think it matters. Caiden already threatened me last night."

The contempt in his gaze lessened as he frowned at me. "What?"

"Oh, didn't Caiden tell you? We had a *lovely* dinner with his brother and our parents." I spat the words out. "And I had an even lovelier surprise when I left and found what he'd left on my car."

"What?" Cassius' frown deepened.

"He'd scratched the word 'whore' into my door. Nice and deep, too, so I can't get it buffed out, or whatever the hell they do to remove scratches in the paintwork."

"For fuck's sake," he murmured, almost to himself. "I wasn't totally on board with his plan to begin—" He clamped his mouth shut, shaking his head.

Hmm. Interesting. Was he about to say something he shouldn't have—something I could use to my advantage? Maybe the Four weren't as close as my initial impressions had led me to believe.

"Come on. Let's get to the lecture. We don't want to be late." He gripped my arm, more gently than before, and I sighed.

"I'm coming. There's no need to hold on to me, you know. I'm quite capable of walking on my own."

"Okay." He dropped my arm, and I rubbed it.

"You do realise that'll leave a bruise? You really need to be more careful."

He stared at my arm, and, to my surprise, a remorseful expression crossed his face. "Sorry," he muttered, leading me down a long corridor and pushing open a large door. "After you."

We entered the lecture hall, which had tiered seating, the seats around two-thirds full. I climbed the stairs to the top, preferring to sit near the back. I slumped down into an empty seat, and Cassius swung his large body into the chair next to mine. The seats were close together, and he was huge. Our legs were touching, and I won't lie, I kind of liked it. I mean, yeah, he was Caiden's friend, and Caiden had decided to make me public enemy number one, but he was sexy. As were his asshole friends.

An idea hit me, and I chewed my lip, deep in thought. Maybe Caiden's orders to keep an eye on me, despite being completely ridiculous, could work in my favour. Since it was clear that the Four were the kings of campus, it made sense that they would be the most likely to have information out of anyone at the university. And if they were insisting on shadowing me, maybe I could use that to my advantage. If I could get one of them to drop their guard, they might have answers for me. Something, anything, no matter how small, that could help me put the pieces of the puzzle together, to find out what had happened to my dad.

Mind made up, I studied Cassius, noting the way his shirt stretched across his muscles as he leaned back in his seat, raking his hand through his hair. Getting closer to him wouldn't be a chore, at all.

"See something you like?" he smirked, noticing me checking him out.

"Maybe."

"You're easy on the eyes, too, sweetheart. Shame Caiden has decreed you off limits."

What the fuck?

Oh, I said that aloud.

"Yeah. None of us are allowed to touch you." He sighed sadly. "Such a waste."

"But why?"

He shrugged. "You'll have to speak to him about that."

Like that would happen. "Right. I know he hates my

mother, but I can't work out why or what that has to do with me."

"I know why he hates your mother, and I can understand why he hates you." He thought for a moment, then added, "Kind of, anyway. It's not my place to say. And if he wants me to stop being friendly around you, I'm afraid that I'll have to comply. My boys come first, always."

"Stop being friendly? I must have missed the part where you *started* being friendly with me."

"I just complimented your looks, didn't I?"

I huffed and turned away from him, busying myself with getting my laptop from my bag in preparation to take notes. I was already in a bad mood, and the morning had barely begun.

Cassius didn't speak to me for the rest of the lecture, and I was glad of that. Somehow, I managed to concentrate on what the lecturer was saying. As soon as it was over, I shoved my laptop into my large messenger bag and stepped over Cassius' legs, ready to hightail it out of there.

"Not so fast." Rising out of his seat, he grabbed my arm and pulled me back against him. He held me in place, bending his head to speak into my ear. "Walk with me." I shivered involuntarily at his proximity. It was nothing like the way my body had reacted to the asshole Caiden, but it still reacted. And he noticed.

"You smell good enough to eat." He leaned even closer, trailing his nose down my cheek, and my breath hitched.

He suddenly released me without warning, scrubbing a hand over his face. "Caiden would kill me if I did anything with you."

I stayed silent, my head spinning. What had I ended up being involved in? I hadn't anticipated anything like this at all when I'd made my plans to come here to investigate my dad's unexplained death.

The best thing to do was to keep my head down and stay focused on my goals. I only had two: find out what had happened to my dad, and get my degree. Then I was getting as far away from Alstone as I could.

Mind made up, I walked slowly down the steps, Cassius a silent presence next to me. Several girls tried to get his attention, waving and calling his name, but other than giving a few of them blinding smiles and others salacious winks, he shook the attention off and didn't pause in his stride.

We crossed the large square of grass to the Student Union building, and he left me at the door.

"I'll see you around."

"I thought you needed to keep an eye on me?"

"You can't get into any trouble here. I'll see you soon." He raised his hand in a wave and jogged away from me.

Shaking my head, I went to walk into the SU but realised I was almost an hour early to meet Kinslee. I glanced around me. Ah. The library. I headed over to the tall modern structure, which somehow fit in with the old stone buildings, even though it was completely different in design. The doors swooshed open gently as I neared the entrance, students hurrying past me in both directions. I entered the large, cool foyer and swiped my student ID card to get into the library itself.

Once inside, I found myself immediately relaxing. There was something about a library that always made me feel so at home. Maybe it was because I'd spent countless hours in libraries with my dad. Being a professor, his entire life had involved being surrounded by books. I had vivid memories of being left in a cosy corner of a library, a pile of books in front of me, while he lost himself in hours of research.

I spent the next half an hour familiarising myself with the layout of the library and decided the top floor was my favourite. It was so quiet up here—most students seemed to be staying on the busier lower levels, and I could see over the entire campus all the way to my apartment building from the floor-to-ceiling windows that spanned one wall.

When it neared twelve o'clock, I made my way into the SU, stopping for a moment to check the sign-up lists for the university clubs and societies. As Alstone was a small specialist business school, there wasn't a huge range of choices, but I noticed a couple that caught my eye, and I snapped some photos with my phone camera so I could look at them in more detail once I was back at the apartment.

Making my way into the large cafeteria, I scanned the room for Kinslee but couldn't see her anywhere. I grabbed a tray and loaded it up with a plate of lasagne, salad, and a bottle of water. I spied an empty table in front of the windows and quickly walked over to it before someone else could get there first.

"Is this seat taken?" I glanced up from my plate to see Cassius and Zayde drop into a chair either side of me.

"Be my guest," I muttered sullenly. "More orders from His Highness?"

Cassius snorted in amusement. "I dare you to say that to his face."

"Maybe I will."

Zayde stared at me silently, his sharp gaze unnerving me. Fuck, he freaked me out. There was something about him...something unhinged, almost. As if there was a monster lurking behind his eyes, just waiting to be unleashed. Cassius, I could handle. Zayde, on the other hand, I did not want to cross.

I felt hot, jealous stares boring into me as girls seated around us took in the fact that I, the new girl, was sitting with two of the Four. Like I'd had a say in the matter.

"Is Caiden going to grace us with his presence?"

"Miss me already, babe?" The mocking voice came from right behind me, and I jumped, placing my hand on my heart.

"Told you she was jumpy." I turned to see Weston grinning at me, and Caiden, standing next to him, staring at me with icy disdain. How could they be related? Their personalities were as different as night and day.

They slung themselves into chairs opposite me, placing their trays down, and just like that, the table was full.

"Hey. My friend needs somewhere to sit."

"She can sit right here." Cassius pointed to his lap.

"What if my friend's a man?"

"Hey, I don't discriminate." He winked at me, and I rolled my eyes, noticing Kinslee standing in line to pay for her lunch.

"Look, she's here now. Can someone *please* find a chair? I'm going to have to sit somewhere else, otherwise." I could feel my blood pressure rising. Why couldn't I have a simple lunch with my friend, in peace?

Everyone looked towards Caiden. "Calm down, Snowflake." His voice was dangerously soft. "Cass, get her friend a chair, will ya."

"Snowflake?" I looked at him across the table, puzzled.

"Yeah. You know. Winter. Snowflake." He gave me another disdainful look, as if I should be able to read his mind so he didn't have to waste time explaining.

"Original," I commented with yet another eye roll. At

this rate, I was going to be needing an appointment with an optician to check my eyes weren't being permanently damaged with all the eye rolling going on around these boys.

"Appropriate nickname." Zayde's low drawl came from my right, and I turned to stare at him, raising a brow. "This university is full of snowflakes, always taking offence at the slightest thing, thinking they're so fucking special and unique. You should fit right in with them."

"Funny. That's what they say about you four." I gave him a huge fake smile, and he curled his lips in a snarl, baring his teeth at me.

Turning away from him, I waved at Kinslee, and she waved back, then frowned when she took in the people that were sitting with me. She quickly shrugged it off and sashayed over to us with her usual confident strut.

"Well, well, well, Winter. You didn't tell me you'd found me some eye candy to look at while I eat my lunch."

"That's because I didn't know they'd be here." I injected my voice with as much sarcasm as I could muster.

Everyone ignored me, talking amongst themselves. Kinslee mouthed *are you okay?* and I nodded. I was fine. Just pissed off. Still, if they thought that by following me around everywhere they'd scare me away, or find information they could use against me, they'd be severely disappointed. Nothing was going to deter me from my search for answers.

A tall, curvy redhead dressed in a skimpy black top and tight jeans approached our table, her eyes flicking over me dismissively, a small sneer on her lips, before her focus turned to Caiden. "Hi, Cade." Her voice was all breathy, and she batted her lashes, pushing her tits into his face.

He smiled up at her, and an irrational stab of jealousy hit me. No, it was hatred. Definitely hatred. She sunk down onto his lap, and he continued to eat his food as if having a gorgeous girl sitting on him during lunch was an everyday occurrence. Maybe it was. I noticed Cassius and Weston exchange knowing glances, and I tried to decipher their expressions.

As the girl wriggled in Caiden's lap and he put his arm around her waist, I found myself growing more and more irritated. I clenched my fork so tightly that the metal dug into my hand.

Cassius slung an arm around the back of my seat, as Weston engaged Kinslee in a discussion about a film club or something. He moved his head closer to whisper in my ear. "Babe, you're either jealous, or you want to stab one of them. You need to chill the fuck out, before Caiden notices."

"Yeah, it's not jealousy."

"Right. You want to kill one of them. If it's Portia, I'm down with it. Fucking psycho bitch," he muttered, so quietly, I didn't think he meant for me to hear him.

My eyes narrowed as I glared at Caiden. At this point the girl, Portia, had her arms clasped around his neck, and she was kissing his cheek as he sat, an amused, slightly mocking expression on his face as he watched me growing angrier and angrier. I tore my eyes away, and I saw salvation.

Or more accurately, I saw James Granville.

Flying out of my chair before any of the Four could react, I made a beeline for his table.

"James."

"Winter." He smiled up at me, a genuine, pleased smile, and I felt like crying. At least there was one man here who was normal, who didn't want to play games with me or make my life miserable.

"Winter? What's wrong?" He stood up and tugged me

into his arms. I wrapped my arms around him, letting his comforting embrace soothe me.

"Nothing. It's just nice to see a friendly face, that's all."

He stepped back, looking down at me with concern. "First-day nerves?"

"Something like that," I muttered.

"It'll get better. You're bound to find it tough coming in a year later than everyone else, when friendships have already been established. Stick it out, though. Things will improve."

"I hope so," I sighed, glancing back over to the table I'd left. The Four were all staring at me, with varying levels of hostility. Kinslee was staring between them and me, her expression helpless. As I watched, Caiden shot me another icy glare, then lowered his head deliberately to the girl on his lap, nuzzling her neck. A tiny, frustrated sigh escaped before I could stop it. Why was I so affected by him?

"Cavendish, huh?" James looked at me with a mix of resentment and sympathy in his expression. "I wouldn't waste your time with him. He'll discard you once he's had his way."

"Caiden doesn't like me. And I don't like him. And you know what? Funnily enough, he said something similar about you."

James laughed. "I bet he did. The difference between me and Cavendish is I treat women with respect. I like to stay friends with anyone I sleep with, and if we're both lucky enough, maybe we'll take things further again." He winked at me, and I laughed.

"I'd better get back. I don't want to leave Kinslee alone for too long."

As I turned to walk away, he called me back. "Winter? I think you're wrong about him not liking you. He looked at me like he wanted to take me down a dark alley and beat the shit out of me when we were talking just now."

I shook my head. "No. It's all part of his game. He has it in for me, and I don't know why. To be honest, you're better off not being friends with me. Apparently, he's declared I'm 'off limits'"—I accompanied my words with another eye roll —"and I don't want to give him a reason to cause trouble with you."

"I'm not worried," he assured me, and I raised a brow at him, unconvinced.

"If you say so. Anyway. Thanks for...being there, I guess. See you around?"

"You can count on it." He smiled, sitting back down, and I made my way back to the table to join the others.

As I reached the table, the Four stood, Caiden unceremoniously dumping Portia from his lap. She squealed in protest, and I couldn't help sniggering under my breath.

"See ya," Cassius said, the others acting like I wasn't even there, and they sauntered out, a wall of sexy, tattooed, muscular testosterone, all eyes on them as they left.

"I get the feeling my life is going to become a lot more interesting with you in it," Kinslee murmured as I flopped into my chair.

"You and me both," I sighed.

FOUR

Winter

The next two weeks continued in the same vein—the Four were my frequent shadows, often accompanied by girls that seemed to resent my presence. As if I'd asked for the attention. Everywhere I turned, one of them was there. If I was especially unlucky, it was Caiden and his hostile glares, with his whispered insults and threats to make me leave. Or even worse, Zayde, with his blank, soulless stare, never saying anything, but tracking my movements with the intent of a predator sizing up its prey. It was starting to feel like I was inside a nightmare with no escape. Every scathing look they threw me chilled the blood in my veins, every hissed taunt and jibe cut me, but I refused to back down. There was no way I'd let them scare me away. I was here for a reason, and I wasn't about to let a bunch of entitled rich pricks stop me, no matter how hard they tried.

Unfortunately, at the moment, I wasn't getting anywhere in my search for answers, and, thanks to the Four's presence, I was starting to feel a little isolated. Guys were staying away from me, other than James, and girls didn't want to know me, thanks to their misplaced jealousy. At least Kinslee didn't seem to be affected—I got the impression that she didn't care about anyone's opinion other than her own, and she'd made up her mind we'd be friends right from the first day we'd met.

It was a dull, windy Thursday afternoon when I headed into the Student Union bar with Kinslee. Despite the exclusive, old-money feel of the university, the bar was surprisingly ordinary—a large, L-shaped room in the basement of the Student Union building, with a long wooden bar down one wall, and tables and chairs and several sofas dotted around the space. There was a dance floor area in one half of the room which was used as an additional seating area during the day.

We made our way to the far corner of the room, where there were two pool tables along with a dartboard. I put a coin into the slot and started setting up the table ready to play while Kinslee got us drinks.

"Is this a private game, or can anyone join in?"

The now-familiar voice set my teeth on edge, and I straightened up, steeling myself for confrontation.

"Let me guess, King Caiden has you on stalker duties again?" Spinning around, I saw Cassius and Weston both eyeing me with amusement. At least Caiden and Zayde were nowhere to be seen.

"Nah, not today. West and I just happened to be passing through and saw you two beautiful ladies all alone, so we thought you might enjoy the pleasure of our company." Cassius flashed me a grin, and I rolled my eyes.

Really. As if I'd believe that this wasn't Caiden's doing, that they'd choose to be around me of their own accord. Turning back to the table, I continued setting up the pool balls in the triangle, ready to play.

I felt the weight of their stares on my back and sighed, knowing that I was only delaying the inevitable by ignoring their presence. "I guess you can join us, if you must."

Kinslee strutted over with our drinks, placing them on the high table next to us, and greeted Cassius and Weston as if she'd been expecting to see them. To be fair, she probably was. She'd been curious about the Four's constant presence, and I'd tried to explain what I didn't actually understand myself. Caiden had decided he didn't like or trust me, and as far as I could tell, it stemmed from my mother. When I'd said as much to Kinslee, she'd shrugged and said that I should be glad, because I got to hang out with the four kings of the campus (her words, *not* mine), and she always perked up when they were around—despite me distinctly remembering her calling them "spoiled rich boys who think they're above everyone else."

The initial tension I'd felt when Cassius and Weston had showed up faded as I watched Kinslee interact with them. I laughed under my breath as she fluffed out her hair and sidled up to Weston, trailing her hand up his arm.

"Aren't you a sight for sore eyes," she purred.

A cheeky smirk appeared on Weston's face, his blue eyes sparkling. "You looking to have some fun with a younger man, Kins?"

"Could you handle me?" She raked her eyes up and down his body appreciatively.

"Don't be fooled by his baby face. West probably sees more female action than the rest of us put together. Ain't that right, mate?" Cassius punched Weston's arm playfully.

"I'd say we're pretty even." Weston walked over to the cue rack and pulled down a couple of cues, handing one to Cassius. "Boys versus girls, or mixed teams?"

"I vote we go for mixed teams" was Cassius' immediate reply.

"Mixed teams works for me. I'm with West," Kinslee announced.

"Looks like it's you and me, babe." Cassius handed me the cue. "You break, and I'll stand behind you and enjoy the view."

Ugh. Boys.

I leaned over, and Cassius came up right behind me. I pushed my body backwards, just slightly, and his hands came to my hips. "Your ass is fucking hot." He pressed his hips forwards, his body right up against me.

I rolled my eyes, not that he could see. This boy really needed to learn about personal space and boundaries. Wriggling my ass, which elicited a groan from his lips, I lulled him into a false sense of security, before I lined the cue up with the white ball and drew my elbow back at lightning speed, straight into his stomach.

"What the fuck!" he shouted, and I spun around, laughing helplessly at the pure shock on his face.

"Maybe you shouldn't stand so close to her." I turned to stare at Weston, who was grinning at us both, leaning against the wall.

"Right?" I rounded the pool table, stopping in front of him and Kinslee. I reached over and grabbed my drink, taking a huge gulp.

"I wouldn't want to get on your bad side." He made a point of stepping away from me, and I laughed again.

"You don't need to worry. I think you understand more about personal boundaries than your friend here."

"Although, if you're up for testing personal boundaries, I'm available." Kinslee batted her lashes at him.

As I shot her an amused smile, I was startled to realise

that I was actually having fun with these boys. Maybe things would get better. Of course, would Caiden be happy with me becoming friendly with Cass and Weston...doubtful.

Stepping away from Kinslee and Weston, I headed back to Cassius. "How's the stomach?"

He glared at me, although his expression held no malice. "That was a dirty trick you played on me."

"Lesson learned?" I raised a brow at him.

"Yes. I'll admire you from afar from now on."

"Good boy." I squeezed his arm and blew him a kiss as I headed around the pool table to carry on the game, and he shook his head at me, smiling.

We ended up playing three games, and Cassius sank the winning shot on the third game.

"Celebratory drinks?" Kinslee suggested, leaning into Weston, who had one arm slung around her and the other frowning at his phone.

"Rain check. Cade wants to meet us." He shoved his phone in his pocket and looked down at her. "This isn't over." He brushed one of her corkscrew curls away from her face, and I saw her practically swoon, licking her lips as she stared back at him. He smiled down at her, and I watched, fascinated. It was amazing, the effect these boys had on women. Me included, as much as I would rather not be affected by them. Damn hormones, making life more complicated.

"See you ladies later," Cassius said, and they jogged out of the Student Union, leaving us alone.

I paused as I crested the hill, leaning against the handlebars of the bike I'd "borrowed" from the sheds around the back of my apartment block. So far, no one had claimed it, and I doubted anyone would, but I made it a point to put it back where I'd found it every time I'd used it. It had definitely seen better days—the paint was flaking from the teal frame, rust spots dotting the wheels, the saddle ripped and faded. Still, it was fine for my short explorations of the surrounding areas. After our game of pool with the boys, Kinslee had headed to the library to research an assignment, and not wanting to stay in the apartment, I'd decided to check out a trail leading out of the campus I'd noticed a few days earlier.

I'd followed the signposted track through the fields, and as I took in the vista in front of me, my jaw dropped. I was on the headland, the sea wild and churning beneath me, crashing angrily against the rocks. A small ruined castle stood on the edge of the cliffs, desolate and crumbling, ancient stones scattered amongst the scrubby grass. I climbed off the bike and wheeled it towards the ruins, then left it on the ground. Wrapping my thick cardigan tightly around me, I explored the ruins, trailing my hand along the cool stone walls, some barely standing, a shell of what once must have been a beautiful castle.

I rounded the front of the structure, close to the edge of the cliff, and sank to the ground, my back against the stone, facing the sea. Pulling my knees up and resting my head on my arms, I stared at the horizon as the sun began its descent, mostly hidden behind huge grey clouds.

A faint scratching sound came from my left, and my head whipped round, the hairs on the back of my neck standing on end. My heart beating faster, I stood up, taking a step towards the direction the noise had come from. As quietly as I could, I bent down and picked up a rock from the ground, then inched around the corner of the wall I'd been leaning against.

There was nothing there.

I couldn't shake the sensation that I was being watched, but I couldn't see anything. I stood as still as possible, straining my ears for any further noise, but all I could hear was the sound of the waves crashing against the rocks, far below me, and the gulls in the sky above.

After a few minutes had passed, I concluded that my mind was playing tricks on me. If it was anything, it was probably a mouse, or a rabbit. I dropped the stone and slumped back against the wall, my heart rate eventually returning to normal, the sound of the sea and the tang of the salt in the air soothing me.

My thoughts drifted. Would I ever find out what had happened to my dad? Was I on a wild goose chase, trying to find justification for his death when it had been a horrible accident? Could I get close enough to my mother to investigate her? Would Caiden and his dislike of me ruin my plans? I sighed and closed my eyes, no answers forthcoming, concentrating on the sound of the waves until the sun had disappeared below the horizon and it was time to head home.

FIVE

Winter

"Do you know anything about Caiden and Weston's relationship with my mother?" I leaned closer to Cassius as we sat in the darkened lecture hall, everyone's attention focused on the video playing on the large screen at the front of the room.

Suspicion crossed his face as he turned to look at me. "Why do you ask?"

I shrugged, keeping my voice low. "Just curious, I guess. I don't know anything about them, really, and they are my stepbrothers now, after all. And I picked up on some tension between them and my mother when we all had dinner together, a couple of weeks ago." *That* was an understatement. That dinner had been the most awkward, strained meal of my life. What was going on with this family? Everything so far that had happened since I'd come to Alstone had left me with more questions, and no answers.

He raised a brow, tapping his pen against his notepad. "If you want to know about them, why don't you ask them?"

"You think Caiden would answer my questions?"

"No fucking chance." He laughed softly. "But West might." His face turned serious. "Look, remember what I told you, that first day of classes. It's not my place to say anything—it's up to them if they decide to share anything with you."

"Okay, fine." I sighed, turning back to the video. "Cassius?"

"What, now?"

"Your family's on the board of Alstone Holdings, right?" Keeping my gaze focused on the screen, I held my breath, hoping he'd be more open to talking about this, since discussing the Cavendish family with him clearly wasn't going to happen anytime soon.

"Yeah, why?" He tilted his head towards mine.

"Does my mother have much to do with it all? I know she's on the board, since she married Arlo."

"To do with what?"

I twisted in my seat, turning back towards him. "Decision-making, stuff like that."

His eyes met mine, and he nodded. "She's a shareholder and a board member. So, yeah. She gets a vote, just like the other board members. That's publicly available knowledge."

"And what about—"

He lifted a finger in the air, cutting me off. "I'm sorry, babe. I get that you want to learn more about your new family, but I'm not the person you should be asking. Hasn't your mother told you anything?"

"No. We don't have that kind of relationship." I sat back in my seat with a sigh. "Any kind of relationship, really."

Any reply Cassius was going to make was swallowed by the video ending and the harsh overhead lights flickering on, making me screw up my eyes against the sudden brightness. The room burst into chatter, everyone standing and gathering their things, all wanting to make their escape from the lecture hall as quickly as possible.

Our conversation already forgotten, Cassius was up and out of his chair, lightning fast. "Gotta go. See ya later," he called over his shoulder, and then he was gone, swallowed by the crowd. Not in such a rush to leave, I waited until the room had mostly emptied out, then made my way down the stairs and out into the late-afternoon sun. Although it was sunny, the air chilled me, and I zipped my jacket up to my chin. Swinging my bag over my shoulder, I turned to make my way back to my apartment.

"Winter!" I smiled as I saw James beckoning me over, and started crossing the grass quad towards him.

"Where do you think you're going?" Hot breath fell across my ear, and a shiver ran through me. My heart rate kicked up as I spun around, glaring at my stepbrother.

Seriously? Hadn't Caiden got bored of shadowing me already? And more importantly, where had he appeared from, and why hadn't I noticed him until now?

"Not that it's any of your business, but I'm going to my apartment and saying hi to my friend on the way. Is that okay with you, King Caiden?"

"You need to choose your friends more wisely, Snowflake."

"Lucky for me, but unlucky for you, I don't care for your opinion. Will you stop following me? This is getting tiring."

He stared down at me, his eyes darkening as the silence stretched, tension sparking between us.

"Caiden..." I tried. "Why are you doing this? What have I done to you?"

He took another step closer to me, his eyes never leaving mine. I could feel the heat of his body, even through my thick coat, and for one moment I forgot where we were and that he hated me. Could he feel it, too? This unwanted, magnetic pull between us? I licked my lips, my mouth suddenly dry, and his eyes zeroed in on the motion.

"Winter!" James' insistent voice sounded, much closer than it had been a moment ago. It seemed to break the spell, and Caiden's gaze turned hard.

"We're always watching you, Winter." With one last, scathing look, he backed away and was gone.

"What was all that about?" James raised a brow as he reached me.

"I wish I knew."

"Forget him. He's a dick."

"That's true." A frustrated sigh escaped me. I started walking in the direction of my apartment building, heading towards the car park, and James fell into step beside me, slowing his usual pace to match mine. "What's up, anyway?"

"You looked like you needed rescuing. I saw Cavendish following you." He glanced at me, a small smile on his lips. "I like to think of myself as a knight in shining armour."

I laughed. "Thanks, but I don't need rescuing. I can handle Caiden." We stopped at the entrance to the car park.

"Can you?" He gave me a doubtful look. "Listen, why don't you give me your number? Anytime you want to talk coursework, or need me to rescue you again, I'm here."

"Sure, why not." As I stepped closer to James, pulling my phone from my bag, a chill ran down my spine, and I had a prickling sensation of being watched. I glanced around me, but the car park was deserted.

Shaking my head as I passed my phone to James so he could add his number, I groaned internally. The Four had me so paranoid, I was imagining things.

"You found Alstone Castle, did you?"

"Huh?" I looked up at him.

"Your phone. That's a photo of Alstone Castle." He tapped on the screen.

So that was the name of the castle ruins I'd found. I'd taken the photo when I'd discovered it on my bike ride and set it as my phone wallpaper.

"I didn't know its name. Do you know anything about it?" I asked, curious.

He shook his head. "Not really, no. Not about the history, if that's what you mean. The university use it for events, though. On Guy Fawkes Night, Bonfire Night, whatever you want to call it, they hold a party there. It's one of the biggest events of the year. They have a big bonfire and fireworks—you know, all the usual celebrations. And games."

"What kind of games?" The look in his eye really wasn't filling me with confidence.

"You'll see." He tapped on my phone screen, adding his number, then met my gaze again. I raised a brow in a silent question, and he shook his head again. "It's more fun if you don't know beforehand. Believe me."

"Hmm." I wasn't convinced, but I dropped the subject.

James called his phone from mine so he had my number. We made idle small talk for a bit, and he promised to send me some website links for one of my assignments. Then he hugged me goodbye and headed off in the opposite direction, while I started crossing the car park.

A sudden loud rumble sounded from between two parked cars, and a huge jet-black motorbike came roaring out of the space, heading straight towards me.

I froze in place, my legs unable to move.

Then my instincts kicked in and I screamed, diving to the side just as the bike reached me, collapsing onto the tarmac. The wheels came so close that I felt the whoosh of air as they passed me, the smell of burning rubber filling my nostrils.

What the actual fuck?

The bike skidded to a stop and slowly circled back towards me. I rose to my feet, my legs trembling, shuffling backwards into a small gap between two cars where the bike couldn't reach me.

The rider lifted the visor on his helmet, and a pair of icy, soulless eyes met mine.

"What do you think you're doing? You could have *killed* me, you absolute fucking lunatic!" My whole body was shaking. I'd never been so furious, or scared, in my life. Closing my eyes, I counted to ten, desperately trying not to fall apart in front of Zayde. Threats and being followed, I could handle. But endangering my life? What would have happened if I hadn't jumped out of the way?

"Consider it a warning." His voice was devoid of emotion, as he trapped me with his gaze.

I gaped at him. "What?"

"You should be very careful about who you make friends with."

Almost the same thing Caiden had said to me earlier. "Have you been talking to Caiden?" My voice rose to a hysterical screech. "And I'll ask you again, what do you think you're doing? *Are you trying to kill me?*"

He ignored my questions. "Why are you here?"

"None of your business. I don't owe you an explanation. And that goes for your friends, too."

Curling his lips into a snarl, he spoke, low and threatening. "If you do anything to fuck with any of us, you'll wish I *had* run you down. Your life won't be worth living."

With that, he snapped his visor back down and roared off, leaving me staring after him in shock.

SIX

Caiden

"Seriously, Cade, what is it you expect us to do with this girl?" Cassius paced in front of me, exasperation clear on his face. "I kind of like her."

"So do I," my brother piped up. Little shit. I sent him a glare, and instead of dropping his gaze, he glared right back. "She *is* our sister. Stepsister."

"She's not my fucking sister," I muttered.

"Look." Cassius came to a stop in front of me. "You're my best mate. In this instance I was down for following your directions—until I met her in person. Yeah, you have a problem with her, but I'm not comfortable with being dragged into this shit. I'll still keep an eye her or whatever if you really want me to, but I'm not down for making her life hell. She only lost her dad, what, just over a year ago? Give her a break, yeah?"

"She's her mother's daughter," I bit out angrily, my fists clenched.

"Cade. She's barely stayed in touch with her mother, we all know this. We've been keeping tabs on her mother for the past three years, and I haven't seen anything to concern me when it comes to Winter, other than the fact that she seems too friendly with James Granville." He threw himself on the sofa next to me. "If we need to keep an eye on anyone, it's that slimy fucker."

My jaw tightened at the thought of Granville. Leaning forwards, stretching my fingers towards the ashtray on the table in front of me, I picked up my blunt and took a deep drag, the weed working its magic and mellowing my mood slightly. "Fine. You're out. Anyone else?"

Weston looked at me. "I'm out."

"West. You don't know what...never mind." He was my baby brother and I wanted to protect him. As far as he was concerned, our mother had died of a brain haemorrhage, a horrible accident. I needed to shield him from the truth.

"I'm still in." Zayde watched me intently from the tall leather armchair he reclined in, his sharp gaze taking everything in. "I don't trust her."

"Who said anything about trust? She's only a girl. What damage can one girl do?"

I laughed bitterly at Cassius' words. Women were trouble. Wrapping men around their fingers with their honeyed words and whispered promises, all the while lying through their teeth to serve their own purposes.

"Can I at least ask you to be cautious around her? Don't tell her *anything*. Don't get too friendly with her."

"Deal. I won't back out of our agreement to watch her, either."

I looked at Weston expectantly, and he sighed. "Yeah, same. You know Dad wants us to be friends with her, though, right? Can't have his wife upset." We both pulled identical expressions of distaste.

Christine Clifford...now Christine Cavendish. Even if I

didn't know what she'd done, I'd still hate her. She'd made her dislike for both of us crystal clear the second she'd got her claws into my father, once she had the huge, gaudy pink rock of an engagement ring that sat on her bony finger.

As soon as they'd married, she'd become fucking insufferable. She'd tried to become a mother to me and Weston —not in a loving, motherly way, but in an "I run this house, and you *will* obey me" kind of way. Even worse? My father always took her side, driving a wedge between us that was so big, I doubted we'd ever be able to go back. I shielded West from her barbs as much as I could, but my stepmother was poison, her venom infecting our lives, slowly killing what was left of our family.

Weston thought she was only being friendly to Winter to get to us, but I wasn't so sure. Christine was a snake, and I knew exactly the kind of malice she was capable of. Meaning, I didn't trust Winter. It was just as likely that they'd planned something together, and until I knew for definite what was going on, I was keeping eyes in as many places as possible.

If they were working together, I'd soon find out. I needed Christine Clifford to hurt, and if Winter was the key to getting to Christine, I wasn't about to miss the opportunity to fuck her up.

Winter. *Fuck.* Her pictures hadn't done her justice. She was so fucking beautiful, and she didn't even seem aware of it. Long, silky, deep brown hair, piercing blue eyes framed by dark lashes, smooth, pale skin, minimal curves, but absolutely fucking perfect in every way. My dick stirred as I remembered how her hips had swayed as she'd walked through my house, how her pouty lips had parted, her eyes hazy with desire when I'd been all up in her face.

Fuck. Fuck. Fuck.

My physical reaction made me hate her even more. I could get any woman on campus I wanted with a snap of my fingers, and I fucking *hated* that my mind had fixated on the one person I despised. She looked so much like her mother, it made me sick that I was attracted to her.

"Cass. Women." My voice came out raspy, the effect of thinking about *her*.

"I'll send the message." He grinned and tapped his phone screen a few times, then sunk onto the sofa. "Won't be long."

Less than twenty minutes later, the room was full of women all desperate to get a piece of the Four, and my dick was being sucked by an eager blonde. I tried to focus on her lips round my cock, but my hard-on was more of a semi, until *she* appeared in my mind: her sexy body pressed up against mine, a whimper falling from her lips as I touched her in the hallway.

Fuck. I gripped the blonde's short hair, pushing her head forwards, and she gagged, her eyes watering.

I came, spilling my cum down her throat, and she swallowed hard, trying not to choke.

"Leave," I instructed, doing my jeans up in angry, jerky movements and pointing to the door.

Like the good little minion she was, she clambered up from the floor and meekly left without another word.

Women.

So fucking easy.

So eager to spread their legs or open their mouths.

I glanced to my left, seeing a tangle of bodies writhing on the floor. I spotted the top of Cass' head and rolled my eyes, getting to my feet and leaving him to it.

Still pissed off about Winter invading my mind when I was getting a blow job from another woman, I headed into the kitchen, in severe need of something alcoholic. Weston was there already, pulling a beer out of the fridge. He turned around and saw me.

"Catch." He threw me the beer in his hand and reached into the fridge for another. Popping the top, I raised the bottle in a silent salute, and he did the same, then we both took a swig from our respective drinks. The cool liquid slid down my throat, and I closed my eyes, letting the alcohol soothe me.

"Wanna check the feeds?" Weston offered quietly, seeming to sense my mood. My brother was perceptive. Intelligent and quick, he was a technological genius, and on top of that he seemed to have a knack for reading emotions.

"Let's go."

We made our way to the small room that could only be opened with a retinal scanner, programmed to the four of us only, off limits to everyone else. The computer screens flickered to life as Weston wiggled the mouse, showing the various video feeds we had set up and a number we'd hacked into. I focused on one feed in particular, clicking the mouse so that the video took up the entirety of one of the screens.

"Where are you going, Winter Huntington?" I murmured, watching as she crept out of her apartment building, glancing furtively around her, a hoodie obscuring her face.

She hurried around the side of the building, fading into the shadows, and I lost sight of her.

SEVEN

Winter

Wobbling on the bike, the wheels squeaking as I pushed the pedals, I cursed my drunken self for coming up with this stupid idea. I'd gone for drinks in the Student Union with Kinslee earlier and had been swayed by the 2-for-1 shots offer. When we'd drunkenly stumbled back to our apartment, we'd gone past my car, where I'd seen the word "whore" shining under the car park lights. The whole story had come out when we got back, and Kinslee had encouraged me to retaliate. Back in our apartment she'd handed me a can of fluorescent pink spray paint, with a "don't ask" in reply to my raised eyebrow, and directed me towards the door.

Not that I could blame her for my current situation. No, that was all me.

Bloody tequila slammers.

The house loomed on the horizon, and I clambered off my borrowed bike on shaky legs, turning the lights off and stashing the bike behind a handy hedge. Turning off the maps app on my phone, I crept towards the house, staying on the soft grass that ran alongside the gravel driveway. There were at least seven or eight different cars parked outside, and from the music spilling out of the house, it looked like the Four were having a bit of a party. Good. It meant I could go unnoticed.

I scanned the cars until I spotted Caiden's. Thanks to my observational skills and my social media stalking, it was easy to tell which was his. The low-slung, matte-black Audi R8 Spyder was parked up off to the side of the house, away from the entrance. Perfect.

I inched closer and closer and withdrew the can of spray paint from my hoodie pocket with shaking hands. Clutching the can in my left hand, I reached out with my right and ran it over the smooth paintwork. The cycle here had sobered me up a lot, but not enough to back down. When I thought about how Caiden had acted towards me, I hardened my resolve. I was truly sorry to deface such a beautiful car, but Caiden needed to learn I wouldn't take his shit lying down.

Pulling the lid off, I shook the can in my hand and directed the nozzle at the side of the R8, sending the jet of bright pink paint straight onto the door. Working quickly, I moved the can, spelling out the letters K-I-N-G, then taking a step backwards to admire my handiwork before starting on the second word.

I crashed straight into a body and froze, my heart hammering in my chest.

The can of paint fell from my hand, clattering against the stones that littered the surface of the driveway.

"What the *fuck* do you think you're doing?" a low, furious voice hissed in my ear, and strong arms came around me, pinning my arms down so I was helpless to move away. It would have been pointless to try. He was huge, and I was no match for him physically.

Shit.

"I-I went out for a bike ride."

He laughed darkly. "At least attempt to make your story believable, Snowflake." Pushing me forwards, using his body weight to make me move, he spoke in my ear again, his proximity and hostile tone sending my body into high alert. "You're coming with me."

We walked the short distance to the house—or more accurately, I stumbled along unwillingly, Caiden moving me where he wanted me to go. Inside, he spoke in a clipped tone.

"Upstairs. First room on the right."

My legs carried me up the stairs, and I hesitated at the top.

"Go." He pushed me, and I fell forwards through the open door, catching myself before I could tumble to the ground and turning around to glare at him.

"Stop throwing your weight around, you fucking asshole."

"What did you call me?" He was suddenly all up in my face, his nostrils flaring and his eyes darkening as our angry breaths mingled.

"Fucking. Ass. Hole." I drew out the words slowly, exaggeratedly, leaning into him, my mouth so close to his that our lips were almost touching.

"You're going to pay for that." His angry tone turned into a whispered promise, low and deadly, as his hands reached around me, holding my arms in place. I struggled against him fruitlessly. He was far too strong.

Time to try another tactic.

I went limp, letting my body sag into his. Unprepared, he

rocked backwards, his grip loosening. I took the chance to bring my knee up, smashing it straight into his groin.

He gasped, dropping me altogether, falling backwards and clutching himself.

"You bitch," he wheezed out. He recovered much more quickly than I anticipated, and I panicked at the murderous intent in his eyes, blindly racing for a door on the other side of the room, my heart hammering out of my chest.

There was no point in running—he was much too fast. He threw himself at my back, sending us both tumbling to the floor, rolling over until I was pinned underneath him, my breath coming in short pants. I bucked my body, trying to throw him off, but he slung his full body weight across me.

"I can't breathe." He was like a dead weight on top of me, his hands holding my arms in place, his legs entwined with mine. My forehead and nose hurt where I'd scraped my face across the carpet in our struggle, the burn making my eyes water.

"Good."

"Caiden." My voice was a hoarse whisper. "Can't. Breathe." I gasped, adrenaline and fear fizzing through my veins as I thrashed, trying to turn my head to the side to get more air into my lungs.

"I despise you, you know." He let go of my arms suddenly and shifted his body, untangling our legs, enabling me to get some precious air into my lungs. I lay back, drained, trying to work out how I'd somehow gone from doing shots with my friend to lying under the person who hated me with a passion. I stared up at him, the expression on his gorgeous face full of loathing as he looked down at me.

My fear melted away as my traitorous body reacted to

his proximity. Fuck. He was insanely sexy. All dark, brooding anger, his lethal body tensed and ready to strike at any moment, his muscular, tattooed arms either side of me, holding him effortlessly in place.

"Why do you hate me so much?" I whispered, finding it hard to catch my breath for a very different reason now.

He stared silently at me; then as if he'd become aware of my thoughts, he drew back, an expression of disgust on his face. "Don't look at me like that again."

"Like what?"

"Like you want me to fuck you."

"Ugh, no thanks." My voice held no conviction, and we both knew it.

He moved into a standing position in one smooth motion. "Get up."

I sat up, and he indicated towards the huge bed to the side of me. "Sit there and do *not* move until I come back." He strode from the room, slamming the door behind him, and I heard a loud click. Rushing to the door, I pulled at the handle, but it wouldn't budge. The bastard had locked me in. Who the fuck has locks on internal doors, anyway? People with something to hide, that's who.

I pounded on the door uselessly, until my knuckles were burning, before I finally admitted defeat. Crawling over to the bed, I pulled myself onto it and collapsed back against the soft dark grey covers. The throbbing from my sore head grew more intense, and I closed my eyes, tears leaking from the corners.

That was the last thing I remembered.

"She vandalised my fucking car!"

"Bitch!"

"You keyed hers."

"Whose side are you on?"

"Why did you bring her in here?"

"What happened to her face?"

The voices fell silent, and I slowly blinked my eyes open to find four pairs of eyes staring down at me. They were all here.

Brilliant.

I moved into a seated position, supporting my back against the wooden headboard behind me. The dull thud of music I'd heard earlier had gone, the house quiet. I licked my dry lips and spoke, directing my question at no one in particular. "What's going on?"

"You're hurt." Cassius sat on the edge of the bed, eyeing me with concern. "What happened to your face?"

"Someone thought it would be a great idea to tackle me to the floor, and I scraped my face along the carpet."

"You shouldn't have kneed me in the balls, should you?" Caiden shot me one of his hostile glares, and I looked away, unable to find the strength to go up against him right now. I was tired, in pain, and my friend tequila was no longer my friend. The throbbing headache it had left me with just added to the pain in my face, and I groaned.

Cassius grasped my chin gently, his fingers skimming over the carpet burns on my nose and head, and I hissed.

"Sorry. I'll get something to help." He stood and walked out of the room, while the other three remained standing, their poses mirroring each other—crossed arms and tense bodies.

"I'm going to check the feeds." At least, I think that was what Weston mumbled before he turned on his heel and left us, throwing me a sad smile, disappointment clear in his eyes.

Cassius returned with his arms full of supplies, setting them on the table next to the bed. "Let's patch you up, babe." He dipped a cotton ball in a bowl of cool water and brought it to my face, dabbing it on my skin.

"Ow. That stings."

"Got to get it clean. It won't hurt for long. Take your mind off your pain by imagining all the ways you could inflict pain on Cade."

Despite myself, I laughed, glancing over at Caiden to see a tiny smile appear on his lips, which disappeared almost instantly. Our eyes met, and we both looked away quickly. Zayde stared between us, his face expressionless, before he turned and left the room, leaving me with Caiden and Cassius.

"We need to have a talk," Cassius announced as he put the lid back on the ointment he'd smeared over my sore skin. He handed me two painkillers and a glass of water, and I swallowed them, willing them to work on my headache. "What's all this about you sneaking over here to graffiti Cade's car?"

"Hang on, why aren't you wearing a shirt?" I'd barely been aware of my surroundings, but now I noticed how Cassius was only wearing a pair of grey sweatpants, his muscles rippling and flexing, tattoos snaking up both arms. I tilted my head, studying the intricate designs.

He gave me a sly grin, leaning back and running a hand through his dirty-blond hair. "I prefer not to when I'm in my own home. Enjoying the view?"

I blushed, turning away from him, catching Caiden's eye. He was glaring. Again. Although this time, it was directed at Cassius.

67

Cassius followed my line of sight, and he sighed heavily. "I'm going to get a T-shirt. Can I trust you two not to kill each other while I'm gone?"

I shrugged. "Bring a towel back with you in case there's a bloodbath."

He snorted and left us alone.

"Plastic sheets." Caiden spoke softly.

"Huh?"

"If we put them down on the floor, it's easier to clean up. No blood staining the carpet."

"Okay, now I'm disturbed. How—no, I don't even want to know."

"You brought up the bloodbath."

"You basically attacked me."

"You graffitied my car. You don't want to start a war with me, Snowflake. You won't win."

"A war? Look, I'm sorry I defaced such a pretty car, but you had it coming."

"Such a girl. My car is not 'pretty.' And I did *not* have it coming. That paint better wash off, or I'll be sending you the bill." His words were hissed through gritted teeth.

"It is. And you did. And, please, like you can't afford to have it cleaned off. May I remind you, you started this whole thing by keying *my* car."

"That thing is a heap of junk. I improved it, if anything."

"How is writing the word 'whore' improving it?" My voice rose in frustration. "It's a horrible, asshole-ish thing to do."

He ignored my comments. "Why are you driving that piece of crap around, anyway? Can't mother dearest buy you a better one?"

"I'll never take any money from her," I bit out. "It's bad enough that I had to use her name—*your* name—just to get into this bloody university. I don't want to owe her anything."

He stared at me, his stormy eyes clouding over. "I don't understand."

"What exactly don't you understand?"

Cassius chose that moment to walk back into the room, a black T-shirt covering his impressive torso. "Look at that. No blood. You *can* play nicely together."

Caiden took a step back, his face smoothing into an impassive mask. "I'm out of here. Get her out of my sight."

And there he was, back to being an asshole again. Just when we were having our first civil-ish interaction. Or argument. Whatever. I rolled my eyes as he left the room.

"Right, if we're done here, I'm going home. I've got a tequila hangover already and a ten-o'clock lecture, and it's—what time is it?"

"Two fifteen."

"Great."

"Probably wasn't the best idea to drink tequila on a school night, was it?" Cassius raised a brow at me.

"Ugh. Don't remind me." I stood, gripping my head as the headache returned with a vengeance.

"You're not riding that bike back home," he stated.

"How did you know I rode a bike here?"

"Security cameras. West saw you on the feeds."

Oh.

"Can you drive me?"

"Sorry, babe. I've had a few beers; I'm over the limit. I don't think any of us are under. I'll call you a cab. Or..." A mischievous expression crossed his face. "You can crash here if you want?"

Here? Bad, bad idea.

"What? Here? Are you serious? Won't His Highness go mad?"

"I really want to be there when you call him that to his face," he smirked. "Yeah, stay here. Cade needs a bit of payback for keying your car, and seeing your pretty face tomorrow morning should annoy him. How are you at cooking?"

Should I stay? It was a terrible idea, but I found myself agreeing. Partly because I was feeling the effects of the tequila and I really, really needed to sleep, but if I was honest with myself, it was mostly for the fact that it would piss Caiden off. I touched my head gingerly, wincing as my fingers came into contact with the carpet burn. It would take more than me staying over to pay him back for what he'd done to me, but it was a way to get under his skin, so I'd take it. "I really don't think seeing my face is punishment enough for him keying my car. But whatever, I'll stay. And yes, I'll cook breakfast, if that's what you're trying to ask me."

"Good. You can sleep in my bed if you want?"

"I thought you said I was off limits?"

He sighed. "Yeah, better not. Stay in here, then. It's our spare bedroom. You've got a bathroom through there, and you can lock the door from the inside if you want to."

"Thanks. You're really not so bad."

"I'm fucking awesome. You're not so bad, yourself. I'll get you something to wear."

He disappeared out of the room and returned a few minutes later with a soft black T-shirt that he threw onto the bed.

"There you go. Sweet dreams, Winter."

"Night."

Finally, I was left alone. I took the key from the outside lock, shut the door firmly, and locked the door from the inside, then sent a quick message to Kinslee, although she'd been dead to the world by the time I'd left her, sleeping off the effects of the tequila. Pulling on the T-shirt, I slipped under the covers. How had I ended up sleeping here, of all places?

Overcome with exhaustion, I closed my eyes and drifted into a deep, dreamless sleep.

EIGHT

Winter

Have you ever woken up and stumbled downstairs all disorientated, to be confronted with the hottest guys you've ever seen?

I have.

I thought I was dreaming for a moment, but when I closed my eyes and reopened them, they were still there. "They" being Cassius, Weston, and Zayde. Caiden hadn't appeared as I stood, bleary-eyed, my hair a tangled mess, wearing the T-shirt Cass had thrown at me, chopping mushrooms and tomatoes ready to go in the omelettes. Weston stood next to me at the huge black marble kitchen island, grating cheese.

Did I mention they were all shirtless?

I wasn't the type to mindlessly drool over men's torsos, but anyone with eyes would appreciate this view. Weston's lean, toned body close to mine, and Cassius' golden skin and his tattooed arms leaning on the island across from me, and Zayde. I let my eyes trail across his pecs, his abs, his arms...every single inch of ripped, exposed skin was covered in tattoos, and it was hot. *So* hot.

"Babe, when you've finished eye fucking us, I think the mushrooms are ready." Cassius' amused voice snapped me out of my reverie, and I shook my head, focusing on breakfast.

"Yeah, sorry. I wasn't eye fucking any of you, by the way. I was just...thinking about stuff."

"Course you were."

"Hang on, do you have matching tattoos?" I noticed an IV tattoo on Cassius' left pec, just over his heart, and the same one on West's ribs.

"Sure do, babe. We're the Four. Hence the tattoo." Cassius shrugged.

Right. "Where's Zayde's?" I mumbled under my breath, stealing a look at his inked body again. He gave me a cold, blank stare, and I turned to the range cooker, my face flushed.

As I tipped the eggs into the frying pan, the boys were forgotten and my mind turned to my mother, against my will. I needed to get closer to her, to find out as much as I could. She—

Every thought I'd had flew out of my head as I turned around to grab the mushrooms, right at the same moment Caiden sauntered into the kitchen.

Oh.

My.

Fucking.

Days.

Maybe my stupid hormones were taking over, because my heart rate shot up and my mouth went dry as I drank him in. Faded, ripped jeans, the top of an IV tattoo just showing above the waistband, tantalising me, acres of tanned, tattooed skin, and muscles all over the place. As my eyes trailed up to his face, I saw an angular jaw, a fucking perfect nose, grey-blue eyes shadowed by ebony lashes, and just-rolled-out-of-bed messy black hair. Yep. Caiden was insanely gorgeous. How could anyone be that good-looking?

Hang on a minute.

I did a double take, noting the marks on his jeans, and the way his hands were stained a bright pink. I had to bite my lip to stop myself from laughing.

Anger filled Caiden's face as he noticed me standing by the oven.

"What the fuck? Why is she here, and why is she wearing my fucking clothes?" He practically snarled his question at the other three, and I noticed Weston slinking around the island to put as much distance as possible between us.

"What's the matter, mate? She was tired, and she crashed here, and needed something to wear to bed. I just grabbed what I could. So she ended up in your T-shirt. No big deal." Cassius shrugged, clearly struggling not to laugh. Right. He'd done this on purpose.

"I'll take it off, shall I?" I raised a brow, placing my hands on the hem of the very plain, generic black cotton tee—no idea how Caiden knew it was his.

"Leave it on," Caiden barked out. "No one needs to be put off their breakfast before they've even eaten."

Wow. Could he make it any clearer that he despised me?

Before I knew what I was doing, I'd thrown the mushrooms into the pan and was stepping right up to him, so close that I could feel the heat from his body as he glared down at me. "You might want to wash your hands. They're looking a little pink, King Caiden."

He stepped even closer, his body pressing into mine, and

I suddenly found it difficult to breathe. "King Caiden, huh? If I'm the king, then get on your knees and worship me."

A shudder ran through me at his low, harsh rasp. I met his dark gaze, seeing the barely restrained fury clear in his eyes, and I steeled myself, welcoming the anger that surged within me, smothering the lust. "Fuck you," I spat through clenched teeth. "If you're insinuating that I can suck your dick, I'd rather choke to death on my own vomit than have that anywhere near my mouth."

"Get out of my sight," he hissed, to the sound of muffled laughter behind us, his chest rising and falling rapidly as he struggled to remain under control.

"Sorry, can't. I'm in the middle of making breakfast." I shrugged. He growled and pushed past me, stalking over to the sink and turning the tap on. Thrusting his hands under the jet of water, he scrubbed at them, scowling.

"Did you get all the paint off your car?" There was amusement but also concern in Cassius' voice.

"Yes." Caiden glanced in my direction, a sneer on his lips. "Nice try, Winter, but your spray paint was washable."

"I'll remember to buy the stuff that doesn't wash off next time, then," I snapped, turning back to the cooker, my eyes stinging with frustrated tears. I was so fucking fed up with the constant hostility coming from him, and after the events of last night, I was rapidly reaching the end of my tether.

He'd learn not to mess with me.

I silently made the omelette and slid the large pan onto the centre of the island. "There. I'll make another if that's not enough, but you get a quarter each."

"Don't you want any?"

I gave Weston a forced smile. "No, I'm not hungry. I'm just going to go and change into my clothes, then get going." Watching Caiden out of the corner of my eye, I waited for a moment, then took my chance. I rounded the island, "accidentally" bumping his arm as he raised it, full glass of orange juice in hand, ready to drink, and rushed out of the room to the sound of his angry roar.

Caiden

"What the fuck!" Ice-cold, sticky orange juice dripped down my torso, running onto the floor underneath my chair.

"You're such an asshole sometimes, you know." Weston glared at me, throwing me the roll of paper towels. "You deserved that, and more."

"What have I done?" I wiped as much of the orange juice away as I could, then climbed off my chair to mop the worst of it from the floor. Good thing the cleaner was due today.

Ignoring the smirk Z was giving me, and the fact I was still covered in juice, I bit into my omelette and groaned in appreciation. I may loathe the girl, even more so after that stunt she'd just pulled, but this omelette was the best I'd ever eaten.

"Didn't you see her face when you insulted her? I couldn't decide if she wanted to punch you or cry!" West wouldn't let it drop.

"Yeah, and did you notice the marks on her face look worse today? The marks *you* inflicted on her?" Cassius interjected.

An unwelcome sensation of guilt settled in my stomach, but I chose to ignore it. The room fell silent as we finished eating, tension in the air.

Weston stood, carrying his plate to the dishwasher. "At least offer to give her a lift back to uni."

Cassius nodded, speaking around a mouthful of food. "I agree. I'll take her bike in my car."

"Can I get a lift, Cass?" Weston closed the dishwasher with a loud bang.

"Yeah, mate. Go on, then, Cade, ask her. She's not coming in my car, so you'll have to take her if you want to make sure she's gone. Unless you want her hanging around the house..."

I slammed my fork down and looked between them all, Cass and West staring at me expectantly and Zayde's eyes flicking between us, amusement clear on his face.

"For fuck's sake." I left them to it and headed up to shower the juice off me, before I threw on clean jeans and a T-shirt and made my way to the guest room where Winter had been sleeping. Not bothering to knock, I walked in, and my eyes went straight to the bed where Winter was sitting against the headboard, her head in her arms.

What the fuck was I meant to do? I stopped just inside the doorway, jaw clenched. Why did she have to come here and fuck everything up? My brother and Cassius were already half on her side. As for Z? Who knew what the fuck he thought.

I cleared my throat, and her head shot up, her eyes flying to mine. "Get out of here," she hissed.

"No can do, Snowflake. I'm here to tell you to get your ass showered and ready in the next five minutes, and you're riding to uni in my car."

"No."

"Yes."

"No."

"Yes."

"No!"

"Stop being so fucking stubborn. Look, I don't want you in my car, but the boys insist, and I want you out of my house. If none of them are prepared to take you, I'm going to make sure you're gone."

Her mouth twisted miserably as she stared at me, and then her face brightened, as if something had occurred to her. "Your car. As in, the pretty R8?"

"For the last fucking time, my car is not *pretty*." I gritted my teeth. "Get your ass in the shower, now, or I will put you in there myself. You're not making me late for my classes."

"You wouldn't dare." Her eyes narrowed at me.

"Try me." I took a threatening step towards her, and she squealed, jumping off the bed and rushing straight into the bathroom, slamming the door behind her. I waited until I heard the shower go on, then made my way to my own room to get ready.

Sixteen minutes later we were finally outside the house, after Winter had taken her sweet time getting out of the front door. By the time she'd finished saying goodbye and stashing the piece-of-shit bike in Cassius' SUV, my patience had run out. I stood by the open door of my car, my jaw clenched as I watched her fucking around wasting time.

"Winter, get in my fucking car, *now*. You're going to make me late."

"I'm saying goodbye," she shouted back, then threw up her middle finger at me and wrapped her arms around Cassius. He smirked at me over her shoulder and put his arms around her waist, leaning down to kiss the top of her head.

That. Was. It.

I pushed away from the car and strode over to her, ripping her away from Cassius and hauling her over my shoulder.

"Put me down, right now," she screeched, her hands flailing ineffectually on my back. I heard Cassius' howling laughter behind me. Asshole.

I opened the door with one hand and deposited her inside the car, slamming the door shut, then quickly got into my side and started the engine before she could do something stupid like try to get out.

"What the fuck are you playing at?" I stared at her, my teeth bared in a snarl.

She looked back at me, completely fucking unrepentant. "I told you. I was saying goodbye." Our eyes remained locked, tension filling the space between us. "I don't appreciate you throwing your weight around. I already told you that yesterday. Look at what you did to my face."

My eyes scanned her head and her nose, that same uncomfortable feeling of guilt rising in me as I took in the red, scraped skin. *Fuck.*

"Sorry."

We were both shocked by the words that fell from my lips.

She sighed heavily and collapsed back against the seat, and I put the car into gear, moving smoothly down the driveway and onto the road.

"I'm not sorry for what I did to your car. Or spilling orange juice on you, just so you know."

I snorted and rolled my eyes at her words, not bothering to answer, instead turning on the stereo and setting the volume high enough to get it through her head that there was no more talking. The sooner she was away from me, the better. I broke every speed limit to get us to university and her out of my space as soon as possible.

The second we reached the campus car park, she got out without another word, storming away towards her apartment building. As soon as she'd gone, I felt like I could fucking breathe again.

Until the text arrived from my dad.

The three of you are expected at a party next Saturday that Christine and I are hosting. Formal wear. 7pm. Don't be late and don't do anything to show us up.

Fucking brilliant.

NINE

Winter

"Miss Huntington." Allan smiled as I stepped into the foyer of the Cavendish house, the taxi pulling away behind me with a loud screech. "I'll show you to your room."

I trailed him up the wide, curving staircase, down a long corridor, the walls hung with portraits, to an ornate gilt door. He opened it with a flourish and indicated I should enter the room first.

"This is your bedroom."

The room was huge, with a mahogany four-poster bed taking up the centre, plush carpets, and heavy curtains either side of a large window that had a stunning view of the sea. Dropping my bag on the floor next to the bed, I crossed to the window.

"The bathroom is through those doors." I turned around to Allan as he pointed to my left. "I'll leave you to get settled in. Mistress Cavendish is expecting you downstairs at seven o'clock."

I nodded, and he left, closing the door behind him.

When I'd received the text from Arlo Cavendish, requesting my attendance at a party, I'd begun planning. It was the perfect opportunity to investigate, and I'd managed to wangle an overnight stay—an easy task, as it turned out Caiden and Weston were also staying over. My mother had actually called me herself to discuss the importance of "putting on a united front," as apparently people were curious about me and desperate to sniff out any hint of tension between us. Since I needed to stay on her good side, in order to get to the point in our relationship where I felt comfortable questioning her about my dad, I was prepared to play nice.

So. Here I was. Dressed and ready for the party. My long, dark hair was perfectly curled, falling down my back, and my dress was...not quite the formal wear my mother had insisted on. More an approximation. Black, super short, and silky, with a flared skirt and a deep V-neck that ended underneath my breasts, it made my legs look miles long especially when I paired it with my sky-high Louboutins—a brand of shoes I'd never owned until my mother had couriered me a note written on heavy vellum paper, ordering me to visit a particular boutique in Alstone. I'd turned up to find the shop assistants prepared for my arrival, and I'd spent almost an hour trying on clothes and shoes. While I hated the thought of owing my mother anything, she'd been the one who had planned this party, and if she wanted me to dress in designer wear, I certainly wasn't going to use any of the small amount of money I had remaining on clothing I'd probably never wear again.

I peered into the mirror one last time to make sure that the remaining bit of redness from my carpet burns were covered by foundation and slicked on some lipstick —"Scarlet Witch"—before fastening a delicate gold chain around my neck.

I was ready.

Heading downstairs, I skated around the red velvet rope that marked the upstairs as out of bounds and followed the sounds of talking. I was about to enter the room where the noise was coming from when my arm was yanked back. Wobbling on my heels, I lost my balance and flailed, trying to stop myself from falling.

I was caught by a solid body at my back and large hands at my waist, steadying me.

"Wait." The low hiss was right by my ear, his face so close that his stubble was brushing the side of my jaw.

Caiden. I shivered at his proximity, and then the pain radiating up my arm registered. And just like that, my lust or whatever hormonal reaction I was having to him disappeared as I stiffened in his hold.

"How many fucking times have I told you not to manhandle me?"

He kept hold of me. "Actually, it wasn't me that grabbed you. That was Zayde. I stopped you from falling." His lips were so close to my ear. Too close.

I didn't want to move.

Despite knowing it was a bad idea, I relaxed against him, feeling the heat of his body warming my back.

"What exactly do you think you're doing, Snowflake?" His words were hissed in my ear, vaguely threatening, but his tone was more curious than annoyed.

Interesting.

"Leaning on you," I answered nonchalantly.

I had no idea what I was doing.

He stepped back, dropping his hands from my waist, moving one to my back to make sure I was balanced before he let go.

I whirled around. "Cai—" My words died away as I took in the four of them. Weston, Zayde, Cassius, and Caiden. All dressed in formal suits.

So. Fucking. Hot.

Cassius and Weston were smiling at me, as usual, Zayde gave me a blank look, and Caiden stared at me, his stormy eyes darkening as his gaze raked over my body.

"Fucking hot," Cassius stated, licking his lips.

"I was just thinking the same about you. All of you." It was easy to see why they were so popular on campus.

I shifted on my heels, suddenly uncomfortable with being the object of their focus. "Why'd you stop me, anyway?" My question was to Zayde, but he ignored me. It was Weston who spoke up.

"We need to display a united front. No sign of tension, act politely, mingle, basically act like we're all friends. Oh, and like we just *love* being around our parents."

A united front. I guess they'd been given the same talk I had. Of course—that was why Caiden had stopped me from falling. Keeping up appearances. No doubt he would have let me drop to the floor in a heap if we hadn't been in our parents' house.

"Why do you want to do this? You're all adults. Why do you even have to be here, if you don't want to?"

"Trust fund. We don't get it until we've graduated from university, so until that point, Dad likes to remind us that he has control over what we do. If we don't play nice when he wants us to, we don't get the money." Weston shrugged, and Caiden glared at him. Guess he didn't want Weston sharing that piece of information with me.

"Right." I rolled my eyes. Money was more trouble than it was worth. I mean, yeah, it was great to have it, but I'd rather not be indebted to anyone. Then again, I'd never been rich. Maybe my view would be different if I was.

Of course, I didn't have to worry about the trust fund issue since I doubted my mother would have made provisions for me. I had no idea what her financial situation was, either. All I knew was that she was on the board of Alstone Holdings, which probably meant she had money of her own, but it could well be tied to Arlo Cavendish. If he had any sense, he'd have made her sign an ironclad prenup before they got married.

I sidled up to Weston, tucking my arm through his. "Come on, bro. Let's do this."

"The feelings I'm having about you right now in that dress aren't very brotherly," he told me, pulling me closer to him.

"That's okay, we're not properly related. I'm fine with you ogling me."

"I don't think Cade shares your opinion."

Swinging my gaze from Weston's to Caiden's, I noticed the tense set of his jaw and the way his fists clenched at his sides.

"I'll escort her in," he bit out. "I'm the older brother. It should be me."

"You're pulling the older brother card. Really?" Weston snorted in amusement.

"Woah, boys. No need to argue. I don't need escorting anywhere." I stepped back from Weston, towards Cassius.

"You can walk with me, babe." He bent down to murmur in my ear, and I smiled up at him.

"Why can't Caiden be as nice to me as you?" I didn't mean to speak as loudly as I did.

I noticed Cassius smirking over the top of my head. "His social skills aren't as good as mine. It's sad, really." He raised his voice. "You want some pointers on how to treat a woman, Cade?"

"Fuck. Off."

I turned to look at Caiden, his eyes flashing with anger, an irritated frown on his face. Despite his general behaviour towards me, I didn't actually want to cause a scene at this party. I needed things to go smoothly, so I guessed it was up to me to pacify him.

I sighed heavily, addressing Cassius. "I'm going in with Caiden. If he kills me, you can have my car."

"Thanks, but no thanks. I'll have your laptop, though."

"Deal."

Before Caiden could say anything else, I was by his side. "Shall we?" I held out my hand, silently pleading with him to accept. He stared at me, his mouth set in a flat line.

"What's that tattoo?" he said suddenly, pointing at my upturned arm.

"You've seen it before, haven't you?" I raised a brow at him.

"I haven't really taken any notice of it before," he admitted, finally taking my outstretched hand and pulling me closer.

Why did my hand feel so good in his?

"Quadrantids," I managed to stutter.

"The fuck are you saying? Is that English?"

"The tattoo."

He dropped my hand and lifted my arm to inspect it, trailing a finger across the meteor shooting across the sky—well, across my arm. What was he doing? I shivered, again. For fuck's sake.

Swallowing hard, I tried to concentrate on what he was asking me.

The meteor itself was tattooed near my wrist, and the trail extended almost all the way to my inner elbow, sparks flying all along it. I had a few tattoos, but this was by far my favourite. It held a special meaning to me.

"It's a shooting star?"

"Yeah. Well, a meteor, really. The Quadrantids are a meteor shower that happens every January. My dad is—*was* an astrophysics professor, and he liked to tell me this story of how I was born. And it reminds me of him, so I had the tattoo."

"What's the story?" I looked up to see Weston, his head cocked at me, and Cassius and Zayde eyeing my tattoo. They were standing much closer than they had been a moment ago. My attention had been so focused on Caiden's hand on my arm, I'd completely tuned out my surroundings.

Caiden's head shot up, too, and he blinked several times, as if he'd been as surprised as I was. He dropped my arm, looking away from me.

"You really want to hear the story now? Right before we're about to go into the party?"

"No."

Right. I rolled my eyes at Caiden. "I'll save it for another time. We can compare tattoos and bond with each other. You can tell me *all* about the matching tattoos you four have."

Cassius' lips curved up in amusement at my sarcastic tone. "The more time I spend around you, the more I like you."

"I'm very likeable."

"Enough of this. Let's just get inside and get this shit-show over with," Zayde commanded, striding towards the doors. I quickly tucked my arm into Caiden's before he could say anything. He stiffened but didn't protest.

Zayde opened the doors.

Showtime.

TEN

Winter

I t was amazing, the change that came over the Four. Their faces became blank masks, their postures straightened, and they strode into the room like they owned the place. Heads turned, women openly admiring them, the men ranging from admiration, to envy, to something akin to hatred.

As their attention turned to me, I saw curiosity and disdain, and from some of the men...looks that I *really* didn't want them to be giving me, making my skin crawl. Maybe this dress had been a bad idea. I stumbled once but recovered and adopted my own blank expression to match the boys, trying to channel their confident stance. Even though I'd felt confident earlier, being the focus of all this attention now...I won't lie, it shook me. Still, fake it till you make it, right? I wouldn't let anyone see that I was freaking out inside.

"You're okay," Caiden murmured in my ear, proving that I wasn't so good at faking the confidence, after all. Then he added, "Stop digging your fucking fingers into my arm."

Oh yeah. I did have a bit of a death grip going on. I loosened my fingers as Caiden, Weston, and I headed over to where our parents were standing, while Cassius and Zayde worked the room, turning on the charm in a way I'd never seen before.

"Winter, darling." A huge, fake smile spread across my mother's face as she pulled me away from Caiden and into a hug, kissing my cheek. I stood stiffly, surprised, but at Weston's throat clearing, I reciprocated the hug, pasting an equally fake smile on my face as she held me at arm's length to look me over critically. "Couldn't you have chosen a longer dress?" she tutted, frowning in displeasure.

"You didn't specify. I've never been to one of these parties before, so I didn't know," I shrugged, playing innocent.

Her face smoothed. "Of course. John was never one for parties. I'm surprised you've turned out so well mannered, all things considered."

I tried so, so hard to keep my control, speaking through gritted teeth while I dug my nails into the palms of my hands to take my mind off the sting of her insulting words towards my dad.

"Please don't talk about him that way."

She gave a light, tinkling laugh. "It's the truth, dear. That man was completely hopeless."

That was it. I couldn't stop myself. I opened my mouth, but before I could speak, Caiden slid his arm around my waist and turned me away from my mother.

"Keep it together," he hissed in my ear. I looked up at him in shock. He stared down at me, his stormy eyes swirling with a mix of frustration and—was that sympathy? No, I must be mistaken.

I took a deep breath, blinking back the angry tears that

had formed, and forced myself to focus on Arlo Cavendish, who stood in front of us. Caiden kept his arm around me, and whatever his reasons were for doing so, I was glad of his presence.

"I'm glad to see you and my son are getting on better, now." Arlo smiled at me. His smile actually seemed genuine, which was unexpected but not entirely unwelcome.

Some of the tension left me, and I unclenched my fists, wincing slightly at the sting left from digging my nails so tightly into my palms. "Oh, we're great friends now. Aren't we, Cade?" I smirked at him, and he rolled his eyes.

"The best of friends," he drawled.

"Me too," Weston interjected.

I grinned at him, my body easing as the remaining tension drained out of me. "We are most definitely friends. I wouldn't let just anyone beat me at pool."

"I was taking it easy on you last time we played. Just you wait till we have a rematch."

"I hate to interrupt this fascinating conversation, but you remember what you're here to do?" My mother spoke, and Caiden's arm tightened around my waist in warning as he answered her.

"Yes. We're here to show everyone what a happy little family we are, and how we just *love* spending time with each other, blah fucking blah."

Weston snorted as my mother's eyes shot icy daggers at Caiden. "Enough of the rudeness. Go and mingle, and don't do anything to show us up."

Clearly not trusting himself, or any of us, not to say anything insulting, Caiden steered me away from them, keeping his hold on me, Weston at my side. "I need a strong fucking drink for this shit," he muttered as we headed to the bar that had been set up in the corner of the room. He moved away from me once we reached it, and as we stood, waiting for a drink, I took the opportunity to look around the room.

You could feel the power and influence radiating from all angles. And the money. Women and men of all ages worked the room, expensively dressed, looking down their noses at one another, their sense of entitlement obvious. It was no wonder the Four acted the way they did on campus, growing up around these people. And now I had to play nice with them, too. I groaned internally. I had to keep my end goal in mind. Stay focused, stay on my mother's good side, and remember I was doing this for my dad.

"You want a drink?"

I turned to Weston. "Just water, please, or a Coke if they have it." My plan was to stick to non-alcoholic drinks so I could do some investigating later once everyone was either too drunk to notice, or failing that, asleep.

"Are you sure?"

"Positive."

He nodded and placed my order with the bartender. He waved off my offer of paying, laughing, telling me that it was a free bar and we never paid for drinks at parties. It kind of seemed obvious when I thought about it.

Another sign I had no clue what I was doing here.

Picking up my Coke, I thanked the bartender, then took a long sip. Perfectly chilled. Mmm.

"Hello, beautiful."

I spun around, seeing James standing there with a blonde girl in a short black dress, fishnet stockings, a fuckton of eyeliner, and a sullen expression on her face. She looked to be about sixteen or seventeen.

"James!" I threw my arms around him, happy to see him. He hugged me back, leaning down to kiss my cheek.

His expression darkened as he released me from the hug, taking in the two men that had come to stand either side of me.

"Granville." Caiden's tone was hostile.

"Cavendish." James matched his tone, taking a step forwards. They stood for a moment, glaring at each other, neither backing down.

For fuck's sake.

"Lena? What're you doing with Granville?" Weston stared at the girl who had been standing with James, and she rolled her eyes.

"He gave me a lift. Get over it. I'm here—that has to count for something." Dismissing us, she strolled off and disappeared into the crowds.

"Who was that?"

"Lena Drummond. Cassius' sister. She's seventeen and... mad at the world? Or something? I don't know. She's moody."

"Right. Thanks for your insightful comments, West."

"Pleasure." He grinned and picked up his pint, downing half in one go before he placed it back down on the bar.

I glanced to my left to see James and Caiden *still* glaring at each other.

"What the fuck is your problem?" I directed my question at Caiden, since he'd given me the same look on more than one occasion. Almost every occasion, actually.

He finally looked away from James, his eyes meeting mine. "None of your business." He pushed away from the bar and brushed past me, heading away without another word.

"Sorry. Old family rivalry," James said by way of explanation.

"Ah, I see," I said, as if I understood, when in actual fact I had no fucking clue. I decided that was a conversation best saved for another time and linked my arm through Weston's. "Shall we go and mingle?"

He groaned. "We'd better. Come on."

"See you later." I smiled at James, and he nodded, raising his hand in a goodbye wave as he leaned on the bar to order a drink, and Weston steered me towards a group of women.

Hours passed. Long, dull hours. The evening was a blur of introductions and watching and waiting for everyone to get drunker and drunker, interspersed with periods of dancing and making polite (and not-so-polite) conversation. I'd wanted to discreetly keep an eye on my mother, but she'd disappeared around an hour into the party, and I hadn't seen her since.

When she finally re-entered the room, making a beeline for a tall, blonde woman standing by the windows who was waving to get her attention, I turned to Weston. "I want to talk to my mother quickly. I'll come and find you later?"

"Are you sure you want me to leave you with her?" Weston eyed me doubtfully.

"I'm sure."

"Okay." He scanned the room, his gaze passing over Caiden lounging at the bar, talking to an older man. "Cass and Z have both disappeared. I'm gonna look for them. Come and find us when you're ready?"

I nodded, and he headed towards the doors, leaving me to face my mother. Taking a deep breath, I made my way to where she stood, glass of champagne in hand.

"Mother." I pasted a smile on my face, and she returned my smile, equally as false. Guess we had something in common, after all. She introduced me to the woman she was standing with, who I promptly forgot the name of, and we made polite small talk, discussing such scintillating topics as the weather and a couture dress my mother was having flown in from Paris. My mother's friend excused herself partway through the dress conversation, and my mother turned to me.

"I trust you've settled in at university?" Even as she asked the question, her gaze flitted over my head, her attention already elsewhere.

"Yes, thank you. Maybe you'd like to come and visit the campus, sometime?" I suggested tentatively.

"No, thank you. I'll talk to Arlo, and maybe we can arrange a get-together soon." Taking a step back, she placed her now-empty champagne flute on the windowsill. "Excuse me. I must catch up with Estella before she leaves." Before I could say anything else, she was gone, leaving me alone.

I guess that was as good as I was going to get. While I hadn't spoken to her for long, I was confident that I was gaining some headway with her. Part of my rough plan for the evening was complete; now, all that remained to do was try and explore some of the rest of the house, preferably without attracting any attention. I wasn't exactly sure what I was looking for, but if I could find anything that would connect my mother to my dad, then it *had* to be here.

Before I could make a move, an arm slid around my waist, and I looked up to see James grinning down at me. "You finally managed to shake your shadows, then?"

Meeting his gaze, I returned his grin with a wry smile. "Not quite. Caiden's over there." I stared over at the bar where he still stood, now with Portia hanging off him. Ugh. I took a step closer to James, placing my hand on his arm. "Anyway, enough about them. Are you having a good night?"

"I am, now." He winked at me, and I rolled my eyes.

"James. Please."

"Sorry. You are the most beautiful woman in the room, though."

"Uh, sure, if you say so," I laughed. "Thanks for those links you sent me, by the way. I'm feeling pretty confident about my essay grade now."

"You're welcome. It helps that I have connections in the faculty, and I'm always happy to hook you up." We chatted about our university coursework for a while longer. Eventually, the gathering thinned out a little, the remaining guests well on their way to being wasted, and I was able to slip out of the room, away from James, on the pretence of using the loos.

Where to explore first? I turned left and headed down a long corridor, past another velvet rope marking the area as out of bounds. There was a suit of armour standing next to a door. An actual suit of armour. I idly wondered if it was my mother or Arlo who had purchased it. It was a little creepy, to be perfectly honest.

I peered around the suit of armour to look through the door that was slightly ajar and wished I hadn't.

I sucked in a shocked breath.

What. The. Fuck.

ELEVEN

Caiden

I *hated* these parties. Even worse? Winter. Strutting around in that dress, fucking clueless that men old enough to be her dad were drooling over her. Not to mention that fucker, Granville, who hadn't taken his eyes from her since he turned up. Asshole.

Downing the rest of my whiskey, I leaned back on the bar, nodding my head at the bartender to pour me another.

"Hey, Cade."

Portia.

My occasional fuck buddy. Never anything more than that, as much as she liked to pretend otherwise. Tall, curvy, amazing tits—shame her body didn't make up for her irritating as fuck personality. Even if her personality had matched her looks, I wouldn't have been interested. Women were great for fucking, but nothing more, as far as I was concerned. I'd had first-hand experience of what our world did to relationships. Putting trust in someone? Hoping they stay faithful to you? Fuck that. Not in our world.

"Hi." Out of the corner of my eye, I saw Granville

making a beeline for Winter, curling his arm around her waist and leaning down to speak in her ear. She beamed up at him, her whole face lighting up, and I clenched my fists.

"Caiden!"

"Huh?" I turned to see Portia frowning at me, her lips pursed in disapproval.

"I was talking to you, but you were too busy watching *her*," she hissed. "Why are you interested in Granville's sloppy seconds, anyway? She's nothing. A trashy whore with no class. You even wrote as much on her car, remember?" Her lips curved into a sneer. "Look at how she's dressed, for goodness' sake! She doesn't even come from money, so why are you wasting your time lusting over her?"

I bristled at her words, for some reason. "Babe, jealousy doesn't suit you. But believe me when I say, Winter Huntington means *nothing* to me."

"Prove it." She arched a challenging eyebrow, and I pulled her closer, letting her run her hands all over me, while I picked up my replenished drink and tipped it back, feeling the smooth whiskey slide down my throat. As Portia kissed up my neck, I watched Winter over her shoulder. Our eyes met, and hers narrowed.

I smirked. Snowflake didn't like seeing me with other women. It was fucking obvious that she liked me, staring at me with those horny eyes every time I was around her. When she wasn't trying to fight with me, that is.

She slid her hand up Granville's arm, and he tucked a piece of hair behind her ear. She tore her gaze away from me and returned his smile.

I'd had enough. I downed my drink and turned to Portia. Yeah, I'd been planning to keep an eye on Winter for the rest of the evening, but I couldn't stomach watching her with Granville anymore. "Want to get out of here, babe?"

"I thought you'd never ask," Portia purred.

We headed out of the main party room without another backwards look, Portia well on her way to being drunk already, prancing along next to me, hanging off my arm.

Nah. Away from the crowds and the sight of Winter with Granville, I remembered this was a bad idea. Bad. Portia was more trouble than she was worth. Abruptly I stopped in the corridor, and she stumbled into me.

"I changed my mind. Go find another cock to suck." I shook her arm off and strode away, ignoring her outraged whine behind me. She'd get over it. Opening the door to the study, where we normally ended up at these parties, I found Zayde, Cass, and West there already, Cass rolling a joint with a girl on his lap, a huge bottle of vodka in front of him, and West and Zayde playing darts, of all things. I raised a brow.

"You boys having fun?"

My brother spun around, his face splitting into a grin when he saw me.

"Want to join us, bro? We're playing for money. So far Z owes me three grand."

"Two."

"Sorry, mate, it's three."

"Whatever," Zayde muttered, taking aim at the board. I shook my head and left them to it, helping myself to Cass' vodka and rolling my own joint.

"Winter looked hot tonight, don't you think?" Cassius gave me a sly smile.

"Not as hot as me, though, right?" the girl on his lap piped up, turning her head towards his and pretending to pout.

"Don't make me pick. You know you're fucking sexy, babe," he murmured, kissing up her neck and sliding his hand between her legs as she moaned in pleasure, her eyes falling shut.

Rolling my eyes, I pulled out my phone, taking a long drag of my joint. Might as well check the security feeds since the boys were all occupied. Tech genius that my little brother was, he'd set up an app where we could check the cameras from our phones. I idly scrolled through the feeds; nothing out of the ordinary. It reminded me, though... "Hey, West?"

"Yeah?" My brother took aim at the dartboard, the dart rebounding off the side and falling to the floor with a clatter. "Shit," he muttered. "You made me lose my concentration."

I ignored his comment. Glancing over at the girl with Cassius to make sure she was occupied, I beckoned him over. "Can you install your tracking app on Winter's phone? We can check her messages on that."

He frowned. "Yeah, I can, but you can't check the contents of the messages. Just who she's sending to and receiving from. It's a bit of an invasion of privacy, though, isn't it?"

"Do you trust her? When she's been hanging around Granville, not to mention I watched her looking very friendly with her mother earlier. Don't be fooled by her, bro."

"Whatever. I'll see if I can get hold of her phone." He shook his head at me and returned to his game.

Grabbing Cassius' vodka again, ignoring his frown, I tipped it to my lips, the burning liquid sliding down my throat.

Someone started banging loudly on the door, and my head shot up.

"Who's that?" Weston called.

"How the fuck would I know?" Since everyone else was

occupied, I got up with a sigh, heading over to the door and throwing it open.

Cassius' younger sister, Lena, burst into the room, her usual sulky pout in place, but I barely noticed her. My attention was caught by a familiar figure, way down the corridor. Winter, looking shifty, glancing around her furtively. Staying back so she didn't notice me, I watched as she slipped past the roped-off area that marked this corridor as out of bounds to most guests, other than those who were in my dad's inner circle.

Every one of my senses was on high alert.

What are you up to, Snowflake?

She shuffled down the corridor and suddenly stopped in front of a door, peering in. *Bad, bad idea, Winter.* I shook my head at her stupidity. Didn't she know that curiosity killed the cat? She needed to be more careful, otherwise it wouldn't just be the cat that ended up dead.

I turned away, crossing back to the sofa and sinking back down. It was so frustrating, not being able to hack into my dad's security system. West had tried so many times, with no success. I needed to know where else Winter had been tonight, since I'd left her. Clearly, she was up to something. I shouldn't have left her alone.

Too late, now. She'd wandered somewhere she shouldn't, and now she was going to wish she'd never gone exploring.

Out of the corner of my eye, I watched Lena as she threw her phone down with a huff. "Can someone take me home?"

"You're a fucking mess, sis." Cass looked up from the girl and frowned at her. "Your eye...make-up stuff is all over your face, and your hair looks like you've been dragged through a bush. What have you been doing?"

"Who have I been doing, you mean." Her pout disappeared for a moment, replaced with an evil grin.

"Don't. Whoever it is, I'm going to kill them. No one touches my sister."

"Fuck off, Cass. I'm old enough to take care of myself."

"But you still need someone to take you home," he said dryly.

"Ugh. Can you stop playing the annoying big brother and just take me home?" She stamped her foot, and both Cassius and I snorted.

"Really mature. How did you get here, anyway?"

"James kindly brought me." She smiled, a dreamy look coming into her eyes.

What the fuck was everyone's obsession with Granville at the moment? The guy was an asshole. And a *Granville*.

She continued speaking. "He can't take me home since he's had a drink. Mum and Dad left ages ago, and I just tried to get an Uber, but they can't come for another forty-five minutes."

"I'll take you," my brother called, walking over to her.

"No, I'll take her." Zayde came to stand next to him.

Weston turned to him. "I already offered."

"I'm taking her," Zayde stated flatly.

I watched their exchange with interest as I swiped the vodka and took another large swig. They both stared at each other, neither willing to back down. I actually admired my brother for even having this stare-off with Zayde—he was a scary fucker.

"Sorry, West, but Z has a bike. And I need to feel the power between my legs, if you know what I'm saying."

Cassius groaned while the side of Zayde's mouth tipped up slightly. "Come on."

"Look after my sister, and don't touch her!" Cassius

shouted after him as he followed Lena out of the room, the door swinging shut behind him.

"What was all that about, West?"

"Nothing," he muttered. He walked back over to the dartboard and picked up a handful of darts, throwing them at the board with no care or finesse, clearly angry, but it was obvious I wasn't going to get anything out of him.

"You never answered my question." Cassius leaned back against the sofa, the girl now perched on the arm, scrolling through her phone.

"What. Question."

"Do you think Winter looked hot tonight?"

"Fuck off, mate. I'm not in the mood." I grabbed the vodka and took another quick swig before he could swipe it.

"I knew you did," he said smugly, eyeing me.

"Fuck off."

"Give me my vodka back." I pushed it across the coffee table towards his sofa, and he picked it up. "Get your own drink. I need this."

"I'm out of here." Weston, still frowning angrily, threw the last dart as he was turning away from the board, sending it rebounding off the wooden cabinet surround and clattering to the floor.

I scrubbed my hand across my face and took another drag of my joint. What a great fucking evening this was turning out to be.

TWELVE

Winter

My hands were shaking with rage.

Deep breaths.

Okay, maybe I was overreacting, but it was my mother's house. I wasn't expecting to see anything out of the ordinary, as far as the party went. I assumed it would be a bunch of rich people, standing around drinking or whatever.

Peering through the small opening, I could make out a huge darkened room, heavy curtains covering the windows. A few dim lamps were scattered around, providing the only sources of light. In the near corner to my right stood a large roulette table, people surrounding it, laughing, watching as the wheel decided their fortune. Well, probably not their fortune, going by the wealth that practically oozed from their pores, but it decided whether they were lucky or not.

Straight ahead, off to my left, there was a giant TV screen, with another smaller screen next to it that looked like some kind of betting scoreboard with lists of names and odds next to each name. A large group of people—mostly men—gathered around the screens, shouting and cheering.

It was what was on the larger screen that made my blood boil, my heart pounding, fury and nausea filling me. I could see two dogs fighting in some kind of pit, snarling and snapping at each other, foaming at the mouths. I watched as one of the dogs grabbed the throat of the other and began to shake it in its jaws, red blossoming on the fur. The other dog desperately tried to get away, scrabbling on the dirt floor, but it was no use. It let out a horrible high-pitched whimpering screech that was abruptly cut off. Its struggles died away, until... I couldn't watch anymore. Bile rose in my throat, and I stood for a moment, clenching my jaw, struggling to contain my emotions.

Anything to do with animals fighting, animal cruelty, basically any kind of animals struggling, and I was raging. The jeers and laughter from the spectators in the room only fuelled my anger.

A memory flashed through my mind, long buried, repressed and forgotten until that moment. My father, buying me a puppy for my fourth birthday. My mother, screaming at him for being irresponsible, that dogs were a waste of space, the argument raging on and on. My poor puppy quivering in fear, until I'd scooped her up, and we'd both hidden in the laundry room, huddled in a corner against the dryer. The next morning, coming downstairs to find the front door wide open and no sign of my puppy. Running outside and seeing the small, limp bundle of fur under the back wheel of my mother's car. Her insisting it was an accident. My inconsolable cries.

Fuck. I swallowed hard, pushing the memory away and coming back to the present, to the people taking joy in the torment of these animals.

I had to do something. Anything.

Reaching out my hand, I hesitated, then took a step

forwards, ready to throw open the door.

"I wouldn't, if I were you."

I whirled around to find the speaker leaning casually against the wall, one eyebrow raised. He looked so much like an older version of Zayde, I immediately guessed who he was. I temporarily forgot what I was so angry about as I took him in.

"Zayde's dad?"

"Michael Lowry, at your service." He bowed exaggeratedly, his dark eyes twinkling at me, and I laughed, surprised. How different could he be from his son?

"Winter Huntington. Lovely to meet you."

"Enchanté." He took my hand and kissed it, a smile on his handsome face, his eyes crinkling at the corners. As he lowered it, he stepped a little closer, dropping his voice.

"Whatever you were thinking, don't."

"I-I just...I," I stammered.

"Let me guess. The dogs?" He sighed heavily, a sympathetic twist to his mouth.

I nodded, my fists clenching.

"Listen. There are some things in this world you need to turn a blind eye to. Believe me, you don't want to be meddling with those people. It could get you into serious trouble."

"But—"

"There's nothing that can be done. Those dogs were bred for violence. Besides that, they're at a protected location, so you wouldn't be able to do anything about it, other than cause a scene. Should it be happening? No, but it is what it is. Do not, under any circumstances, do anything to put yourself on the radar of the people here. You don't want to get on their bad side. Trust me."

The warning in both his tone and his eyes gave me

pause. What could I do, really? He was right—I'd just be causing a scene if I said anything, and it would all be for nothing.

"I guess you're right," I whispered, defeated.

"Chin up. Why don't you go and find your friends? Last I saw of them, they were in the study." He pointed down the hallway to another door off to the left.

"Okay. Thanks." I gave him a small smile, and he winked at me, then walked around me into the room I'd been peering into and closed the door behind him.

I headed down the corridor, still upset and angry. Fuck staying sober for the night. I needed a drink.

Bursting through the door that Zayde's dad had indicated, I came to a sudden stop, almost running into Weston, who gave me a muttered "hi" before he slipped out of the room.

"What's the matter with him?" I asked myself, making a beeline for the crystal decanter standing on a polished walnut sideboard straight in front of me. Yanking out the stopper, I poured a generous measure into one of the glasses on the silver tray next to the decanter. I threw the drink down my throat, gasping at the burn and shuddering at the taste. Whiskey. Ugh.

I poured another. And downed it.

As the fire warmed me from within, I turned around to survey my surroundings. Through a haze of smoke, I saw Cassius reclining on a brown leather chesterfield sofa, a bottle of clear liquid dangling from his hand. He watched me with a mixture of amusement and concern. A beautiful brunette sat on the arm of the sofa next to him, and his hand lazily trailed up and down her thigh. Directly opposite him on an identical sofa was Caiden, glaring at me. A-fuck-ing-gain.

My blood was boiling, I was all riled up from the dog fighting, and the alcohol was kicking in. I wanted to pick a fight.

I stormed over to Caiden, ripping the joint from his mouth and taking a deep drag, then throwing it into the ashtray on the side table next to the sofa. "What exactly is your fucking problem?" I stood right in front of him, hands on my hips, glaring right back at him.

He blinked slowly. "What the fuck? Did you just take my joint?"

Ignoring his question, I stepped closer, leaning down and prodding a finger into his hard chest, so angry I wasn't thinking straight.

I was sick of this. Sick of his hostility towards me; the way he treated me 90 percent of the time; the way he clearly thought I was beneath him.

I directed all of my wrath at him as our eyes met, and his darkened, his brows pulling together. "What. Is. Your. Pro—"

His arms shot out, and he yanked me onto his lap. Before I could process what the actual fuck was happening, I was straddling him, he had one arm tightly around my back, the other gripping the back of my head, and his lips were on mine, hard and furious.

It was like fireworks.

Explosions of sensation that I felt all over my body as his mouth attacked mine. I kissed him back just as savagely, channelling all my rage into the kiss, biting his bottom lip, hard. I tasted blood and my tongue darted out to swipe at his lip.

He growled low in his throat, pulling me closer.

I never wanted this kiss to end.

His tongue swiped at mine, and I opened my mouth for

him, the kiss turning from savage and punishing, to more... *Fuck*. I couldn't even describe it. I shifted against him, freeing my arms from where they'd been trapped between us when he pulled me onto him, winding them around his strong shoulders, stroking my hands over the short hairs at the back of his neck.

He shivered and bit my lower lip, more gently than I'd bitten his, and I moaned, moving my hands up to thread my fingers through his hair. He responded by sliding his tongue into my mouth, sending shock waves of pleasure through me, and I lost myself in his kiss.

"About fucking time." The amused voice came from behind me, and Caiden and I broke apart, dazed, the mixture of lust and confusion whirling through me reflected in his eyes. What the fuck had just happened?

I brought a trembling hand to my lips, staring at him, wide-eyed. His eyes were heavy-lidded, his lashes sweeping down to hide his expression from me as I studied him. My mind was scrambled, I was buzzed from the alcohol and the weed, and now, after that mind-blowing kiss, I was horny as fuck. For *him*.

Choosing to ignore Cassius, I rolled my hips, moving against Caiden. Fuck, he was hard.

This felt so good. I needed more. I rolled my hips again, and he groaned, moving his hands to cup my waist, his head falling back against the sofa.

"Get a room."

This time round, Cassius' voice seemed to snap Caiden out of the lust-induced bubble we'd been in. "No." He shook his head. "No," he repeated, lifting me off him and depositing me on the sofa. He staggered to his feet and stormed out of the door, slightly unsteady.

"What just happened? And why did you have to ruin it?"

I looked over at Cassius, who, in the time I'd been...occupied...with Caiden, had managed to lose the girl he'd been sitting with, and he was reclining against the sofa, every now and then lifting the bottle to his lips and taking a swig.

"C'mere, babe." He patted the sofa next to him. Obediently I stumbled over to him and collapsed onto the seat, scrubbing my hand over my face.

"What's going on, Cass?"

"Drink." He handed me the bottle, and I took a large swig, coughing and spluttering as the vodka went down my throat. The next swig went down more smoothly, and I sighed, leaning into his arm.

"Smoke?"

I took the joint from his outstretched fingers.

We sat there for a while, passing the bottle and the joint between us until I was pleasantly numb, my big plan to investigate my mother completely foiled by vodka and weed.

"Here's the thing, babe," Cassius finally said, his words slurred from the effects of the drink. "It's obvious Cade thinks you're sexy as fuck, yeah? But he kind of hates you, y'know. Seeing you looking like that tonight—" He waved a hand lazily in my direction. "—and with the drinks, and the weed, and his jealous thing with Granville...think he just gave in to his urges. He'll be kicking himself tomorrow."

Through my drunken haze, I tried to make sense of what he was saying. "I don't get why he hates me."

He lowered his voice. "You look like your mother. He hates her. You remind him of her." Swallowing hard, he mumbled, "And he doesn't trust you, does he. Thinks you might be working with her."

"Huh?" I tried to get my addled brain in order. "Working with her? What do you mean?"

"She's up to something. Bad. We've been keeping tabs on her. And you."

He stared down at me, dawning horror in his eyes as he realised what he'd said. "Fuck, shouldn't have told you that. I'm too wasted for this. Don't ask me anything else."

This was a conversation I needed to have with all the boys, and sober. I had to get one thing straight, though. Maybe the alcohol and weed had lowered my inhibitions or whatever, but I felt like I could trust Cassius.

"Cass." I waited until he looked at me, his eyes glazing over. "Cass."

He blinked a few times. "What?"

I carefully climbed onto my knees on the sofa, using Cassius' arm to steady myself, and leaned in so I could whisper in his ear. Somehow, I managed to get the garbled words out. "I came to Alstone to investigate my mother. I think she may have had a hand in my father's death."

"What?" His stunned inhalation echoed loudly in the room.

"Yeah. Talk about it tomorrow, hmm?"

Shock at my words warred with the drunken stupor he was falling into. "Yeah. Tomorrow." He yawned widely and slid down, arranging himself so he was lying lengthways, his head propped up on a cushion which leaned on the arm of the sofa. He tugged me down so I was lying with my back against his front and draped his arm over me.

"Closing my eyes for a few." He yawned again.

"Don't get any ideas," I warned him as he smoothed down my hair so it wasn't in his face.

"Cade would kill me."

Then he was asleep, and seconds later, my eyes drifted shut, and I was lost to my dreams.

THIRTEEN

"Something you want to tell me?"

I slowly peeled my eyes open at the disapproving voice, wincing as I did so. Everything hurt, and my mouth tasted disgusting, as dry and arid as the desert. I licked my cracked lips and swallowed, my parched throat begging for some liquid.

"Need. Water," I groaned, my voice hoarse. I tried to sit up, but I was weighed down by a muscular, tattooed arm.

Oh, yeah.

Last night came back to me. That epic kiss with Caiden, and getting wasted and high with Cassius afterwards, then falling asleep with him. I blinked rapidly, trying to get my eyes to focus.

"What time is it?"

"Nine." Cassius spoke in my ear, his own voice husky from sleep. He tightened his arm around me. "Need more sleep."

"Again, something you want to tell me?" This time I forced my eyes to stay open, and I managed to focus on

Caiden, eyeing me and Cassius with a mixture of disapproval and what I think might have been a tiny bit of jealousy, but was probably just as likely to have been my hazy vision playing tricks on me.

"We fell asleep. Nothing happened." I didn't know why I was bothering to explain—Caiden had been the one to storm out and leave me with Cassius last night.

"Yeah, mate. Nothing happened," Cassius mumbled lazily, moving his arm off me. I gingerly raised myself into a seated position, groaning again as my head swam. My eyelids fluttered as I swayed to the side, and the next minute Caiden was crouching right in front of me, peering into my face.

"You look like shit," he stated. "How much did you have to drink?"

"Uh...we finished all the vodka and shared a joint. Maybe two. I think." My stomach rolled. "I feel sick."

"For fuck's sake. Are you going to be sick?"

"I don't know. I feel horrible." I felt too ill to spar with him, or to do anything. "I need to lie down." I went to lie back down next to Cassius, but Caiden stopped me.

"Oh no you don't. Come here."

He scooped me into his arms and carefully climbed to his feet. I laid my head on his chest and closed my eyes again. "Where are you taking me?"

"To bed," he said shortly. I curled my body into his, the nausea twice as bad now we were moving. As good as his arms felt cradling me, I really hoped I didn't throw up on him. That wouldn't go down well. I tried to concentrate on breathing slowly, in and out, my head spinning, as I felt him carry me up the stairs.

He nudged open a door with his foot—I heard it creak as it opened—and a few moments later he'd deposited me on a soft bed. I groaned in relief as the pillows cradled my sore head, and attempted to open my eyes.

"I'll be back."

I gave up on trying to open my eyes and curled into a ball on my side, my stomach churning. What was probably a few minutes later I heard a clattering sound and managed to peel my eyelids open to look at Caiden. "Water, and a bowl in case you're sick. Try to sleep it off."

"Thanks, Cade." I reached out my hand and fumbled for his, giving it a squeeze. "I mean it."

He grunted, roughly tugging his hand free from my grip. "Sleep."

I managed a few sips of water as I heard the door close behind him, and then I passed out.

The next time I woke, it was to Weston's face as he gently shook my shoulders.

"Stop it," I moaned, burrowing into the covers. "I need sleep."

"No." He prodded my cheek. "Get up. You're coming with us. Did you bring a change of clothes?"

I tried to focus on his words. "Blue bag."

"Okay. I'm gonna turn on the shower for you. Fuck, Winter, how much did you and Cass drink last night? He's been throwing up for the last hour."

"Please don't mention being sick."

He sighed and pulled the covers off me. "Come on. Stop feeling sorry for yourself. If you were gonna be sick, you would've been already. I reckon Cass drank way more than you—he was already drunk by the time you started." He helped me up, and I used him as a convenient crutch to walk to the bathroom, where I sat on the side of the bath with my pounding head in my hands while he started the shower and brought my bag in.

"I'll wait in the bedroom. Be quick."

"Do I have to?" I whined.

"Fucking hell, if this is what having a sister is like, I'm not sure I want one, after all," he muttered.

"Hey!"

"Just kidding. Get your ass in the shower. Everyone's waiting."

"Fine."

He walked out of the door, and I peeled my clothes off, trying not to move too much. I happened to glance at my face in the mirror over the sink as I was changing and immediately wished I hadn't. My make-up was smeared all over my face, and I mean *all* over. My hair was matted and tangled, and the dark circles under my eyes just added to my overall unkempt look. Lovely.

Somehow, I managed to stumble into the shower, and by the time I was done, my head wasn't hurting quite so much. I cleaned my teeth, washed the remaining traces of my make-up off, and dressed in the jeans and tank top I'd brought with me. I pulled a thin cardigan on top and wound my wet hair into a messy bun. That would have to do. I re-entered the bedroom to find Weston reclining on the bed, scrolling through—wait, was that *my* phone?

"West! That better not be my phone!"

He held up a hand. "One second...okay, done." He threw the phone down on the bed. "You should be thanking me. You didn't even have a password on there. I installed my app on it—it'll give you all sorts of security options now." His smile dimmed, his voice turning serious. "You can never be too careful around here."

I narrowed my eyes at him, still not sure if I could trust him or not, but deciding to give him the benefit of the doubt. "Um. I see. Thanks, then."

"I put all our numbers into your contacts list, too. You can message me whenever you want." He gave me a cheeky wink, and I couldn't help smiling.

"Maybe I will." I grabbed my phone from the bed, and he jumped up, taking my bag. Together, we made our way downstairs through the silent house and out the front door, where Cassius' SUV was waiting, Caiden in the front passenger seat, sunglasses on, so I couldn't make out the expression on his face.

"Where is everyone, anyway?"

Weston turned to me. "Think your mum and my dad must still be asleep. Dad gives the staff the morning off after parties so they don't accidentally disturb anyone. Z didn't come back after he dropped Lena off, so I guess he's at home." He shrugged, brushing it off, but I noticed the tense set of his jaw.

"Oh. Okay." I stepped closer and threw my arms around his neck, overcome with a sudden feeling of protectiveness and gratitude for him. Taken by surprise he stumbled but then steadied himself and hugged me back tightly, burying his face in my neck.

"Thanks, West," I mumbled into his hair. "As far as step-brothers go, you're really not that bad."

He laughed, then squeezed me and kissed my cheek. "I'll take that as a compliment. Now get in the car so we can get breakfast. I'm starving and I need a bacon sandwich."

"Bacon? Mmm, me too." I climbed into the back of the SUV next to Cassius, who was leaning against the window, groaning, and Weston hopped in the front and started the engine.

The car rolled away from the house, and I closed my eyes, letting Post Malone's lazy, laconic vocals wash over me as "Goodbyes" played softly through the speakers. Caiden and Weston talked in low tones, while Cassius slipped into sleep.

Eventually I felt the car slow to a stop, and the engine turned off. I trailed the boys into their house, noticing Zayde's black bike next to Caiden's R8, a shiny red helmet propped on the seat. The combination of fresh air and the shower had me feeling slightly more human, and I sat at the dining table watching as Weston and Zayde, who had appeared as soon as we turned up, fried eggs and grilled bacon for everyone. Cassius sat across from me, leaning his head on his arms, and Caiden sat at the island, talking to the boys, every now and then stifling a yawn. The memory of his lips on mine played on my mind, and I shifted in my seat. I'd never been kissed like that before. Fuck, I wanted to kiss him again, despite the small matter of him being an entitled asshole who hated me. One problem, though—he'd been drunk last night. I wondered what had happened to him after he'd left me and Cass. He didn't seem that hungover, only tired, but who knew.

Weston slid a plate under my nose, temporarily distracting me from Caiden. Oh. Yes. The smell of the bacon, the perfectly cooked egg, HP sauce oozing out the sides, all sitting snugly between two slices of thick, soft bread—perfection in a sandwich. I took a huge bite and moaned in appreciation, blissful flavours exploding on my tongue.

We all ate silently, the food accompanied by huge mugs of tea and coffee courtesy of Zayde. He might not say much, but he was bloody good in the kitchen.

Unfortunately, his cooking skills came with a downside.

I tried to avoid his icy stare as I ate. If looks could kill, I'd be dead and buried by now. And actually... I eyed my almost empty mug of coffee with suspicion... I wouldn't put it past him to try and fuck with my brunch in some way. I sighed. Well, if he'd poisoned me or something, it was too late now.

As we finished up the food and Weston loaded the dishwasher, I glanced at Cassius, who was looking less green. "Feeling better, Cass?"

"Yeah." He smiled at me and stood, his chair scraping across the tiled floor. "I'm having a shower, then we all need to discuss things." He gave me a pointed glance, and our conversation from last night came back to me. My mother. The investigation.

Time to get to the bottom of what was going on with the Four.

FOURTEEN

Winter

Caiden, Zayde, and I assembled in the huge lounge area to wait for Cassius, Weston heading off to check in with some online contact he had while we were waiting. I settled on the huge, squashy sofa, at the opposite end to Caiden, facing the biggest TV screen I'd ever seen in someone's house, and Zayde flopped into a reclining armchair to the side of us, picking up a game controller and turning on the TV. He threw another to Caiden, and soon they were engrossed in some kind of shooting game.

"We need some fresh air in here." Zayde paused the game, screwing up his nose, and walked over to the window, opening it. I shivered and pulled my thin cardigan tighter around me as a cool breeze blew in, a chill coming over me.

"Cold?" Caiden murmured, close to my ear. My head whipped around, and he was *right there*. How and when did he get so close?

"A bit," I managed to whisper, staring at his lips as the kiss filled my mind for the hundredth time.

"Here." He pulled off his thick black hoodie and handed

it to me, leaving him in a tight slate-grey T-shirt that stretched across his muscles in the best way.

My heart rate picked up, and my mouth went dry. Somehow, I managed to mumble "thanks" and pulled the hoodie over my head, snuggling into it. It was still warm from his body heat, with a faint ocean scent, and I sighed in appreciation.

"Why are you being nice to me?" I leaned closer as Zayde resumed the game.

He gave a heavy sigh, his eyes flicking between me and the TV screen. "Z, I'm out," he announced, pressing some buttons on his controller, and the split-screen view on the TV was replaced with a single screen. Turning to face me fully, he stared at me, frowning and biting his lip uncertainly. "Fuck," he muttered, taking a deep breath. "Look. I don't like or trust you as far as I could throw you. That should be fucking obvious, even to someone like *you*. But I'm not a complete asshole."

I arched a brow at him, and he gave me a small wry smile. "Most of the time, anyway. You were cold, so I gave you something to keep warm. Don't read anything into it." His face turned serious. "I mean that. Don't."

I debated whether to say what was on my mind, but in the end, I knew I had to ask. Leaning closer to him, I pulled my legs up onto the sofa, curling them under me, our eyes staying locked the entire time.

"What about the kiss?"

He was so close that I could feel his breath on my lips.

"Snowflake..." His voice was low and steely. "That kiss should *never* have fucking happened."

"Shouldn't it?" I moved even closer, and his eyes darkened, his lips parting.

"No. It. Was. A. Fucking. Mistake." He tilted his head

down so there was a millimetre of space between our mouths.

"A mistake. Really," I breathed. "Cade—"

"Stop. You're the last person I—"

"I fucking *knew* it!" Cassius' triumphant shout cut straight through the atmosphere between us, and I jumped, scrambling away from Caiden, confused, and to be honest, pissed off.

"Whatever you think you saw, you're wrong." Caiden sat up straight, his voice flat and unemotional as he looked at Cassius, daring him to disagree.

"Right." Cassius rolled his eyes. He sauntered over to the sofa and sank down in between us, throwing his arm around me. "Nice hoodie, babe. Sure I've seen Cade with one just like it."

Zayde continued mashing the Xbox controller, oblivious to the rest of us, while Caiden gave Cassius an irritated look. "Fuck off. I'm getting West." He disappeared out of the room, and I curled my legs under me more tightly, turning to look at Cassius.

"Why do you wind him up like that all the time?"

He shrugged. "It's what we do. It's fun."

"If you say so."

"Being serious for a minute, are you ready to talk about what we told each other last night?"

I tried to recall our conversation, remembering something about him saying they were keeping tabs on me and my mum. And I'd told him I'd come to Alstone to investigate my dad's death. I absently rubbed my fingers across my meteor tattoo, thinking of my dad. If his death hadn't been an accident, the people responsible were going to be brought to justice, no matter what.

"I'm ready."

"Good girl." Cassius grabbed my hand and squeezed it as Caiden walked back into the room with Weston in tow, and they both took a seat. "Time to get some answers."

I looked around at the Four, each one of them giving me their full attention. Zayde had turned off the Xbox, and the room was silent. Cassius kept hold of my hand, his touch bolstering me. I took a deep breath and began, stumbling over the words, racing to get them out.

"Okay. Quick rundown of my life. My mother got pregnant when she was young, and she didn't want me, she left us, then me and my dad moved away, we didn't stay in touch—"

"Slow down," Cassius interrupted me. "And start at the point where *you* think she had something to do with your dad's death."

There were three sharp intakes of breath, Cassius smiling smugly since he was already privy to this information.

"Why and how?" Zayde leaned forwards in his armchair, his intense gaze boring into me.

"It all sounds weird, but there was something that didn't seem right. It could all be a coincidence, of course—"

"Get to the fucking point, will you?"

I leaned around Cassius to glare at Caiden. "No need to be rude." I added, "Asshole," quietly under my breath, and Cassius snorted as Caiden glared back at me.

"*Anyway*, before I was so rudely interrupted—knowing what I do now, I suppose it all started around five months before my dad passed away." My voice cracked, and my eyes filled with tears as I spoke about my dad.

Weston moved from his position on the floor to sit on the arm of the sofa next to me, running a soothing hand up and down my arm, and Cassius tightened his grip on my hand. I gave them both a brief, tremulous smile, and continued. "I don't know if you guys were aware, but he kept in touch with my mother sporadically. I think he felt sorry for her, and he wanted her to be involved in my life. Neither of us were particularly interested to be honest, but he used to send her updates on me, and whatever."

My voice cracked again, and I coughed to clear my throat. "Sorry, I need a drink."

"I'll get you one." Cassius jumped up. We sat in silence until he returned with a bottle of water, which he handed to me.

"Thanks." I unscrewed the cap and took a large swig. "Okay. Back to it. I'd been accepted to university, and my dad was so excited for me. It was always his dream for me—to get a good education. My mother wasn't answering his calls, so he drove here to talk to her in person. He was desperate for us to reconcile, and he wanted her to share in his excitement. I don't know if she ever loved him, but he never stopped loving her. He never looked at another woman, as far as I'm aware."

I stared down at the floor, not really seeing it, lost in my memories. "He must have arrived back home late at night, after I'd gone to bed. The next morning, I went downstairs, and he was acting weird—all jumpy and shifty. I asked him what was wrong, and he brushed me off. He shut himself in his office for most of that day, and I couldn't get anything out of him."

I looked up, to find the Four watching me with rapt attention.

"What happened next?" Weston breathed.

I sighed, my mouth twisting. "He drove up to Alstone a few more times, even staying overnight once or twice, and he spent ages shut in his study or staying late at work in his office there. I didn't connect any of it until afterwards."

"Did he ever tell you anything?" The question came from Zayde, who was staring at me, the usual blank, unreadable expression on his face.

"No, and to be honest, I stopped pushing him. I could *feel* that something was off, but I rationalised it in my head, telling myself that he was researching stuff for work or whatever." The tears were starting to come in earnest now, and I choked back a sob. If only I'd pushed harder. Maybe I could have changed something. Maybe he'd still be alive.

"Um...sorry. I need a minute."

"Winter." Weston slid down off the arm of the sofa, squashing up next to me, and pulled me into his arms. I curled into him, and he stroked my hair, Cass gripping my hand.

I breathed deeply, gathering myself, wiping the tears away with the sleeve of Caiden's hoodie. "Okay. Let me get the rest of this out. It was the day I left for university. Dad drove me there and I'd waved him off, and I guess he decided to take a detour to Alstone on his way home. He... he sent me a text, when I was just falling asleep. It was the last time I heard from him."

I swallowed hard, fumbling in my pocket for my phone and handing it to Weston with a shaking hand. The tears obscured my vision, and I buried my face in his chest as he read out the text.

"Winter. Just left your mother. I have something important I need to speak to you about. I'll call you tomorrow morning and update you. Hope you're settling in well. Love you."

"The next day I got a visit from a police officer," I sobbed, "and-and she said there had been an accident." The memory that I'd managed to keep buried for the past few months tore through my mind, and I curled myself up into a tight ball, huddling into Weston as I broke apart all over again.

I sat, numb, as the police officer told me that there had been a "catastrophic gas leak," which had caused my entire home to explode, with my dad inside. The fire service was going to investigate, but it was thought to be a freak accident. I couldn't care less about the fact the house was gone. Never mind that it had been my home for the past thirteen years and everything from my childhood was blown to smithereens. My dad was gone.

"Miss Huntington? Are you okay? Is there anyone I can call?" The female detective placed a gentle hand on my arm, her soft brown eyes full of concern.

I swallowed hard, darting my tongue out to moisten my dry lips. "N-no. Thank you."

She remained unconvinced but let out a heavy sigh and rose to her feet. "Here's my card. Please don't hesitate to call me if you need anything at all." She flicked her eyes to the male officer with her, and he gave a tiny nod. As one, they headed towards the door. She paused, turning back to me. "I mean that. Anything at all. We're here to help."

"Thanks." My voice came out as a hoarse whisper.

Then they were gone, and I was alone. I felt the bile rise in my throat, and I stumbled over to my wastepaper basket, retching until my throat was so raw from stomach acid that I was coughing up blood and tears were streaming down my face.

Curling into a ball on my bed, I succumbed to the sorrow that was pulling me under, sobbing until there were no tears left to cry, and the darkness swallowed me whole.

. . .

"A few weeks later, after they'd officially ruled that his death was an accident, I received a box, addressed to me. The return address was the university my dad worked at. I opened it to find a note on the top from one of my dad's colleagues, saying he'd packed up the stuff from his work office, and all his personal effects were in the box. He thought I might like to have them." My voice broke again as fresh tears streaked down my face, remembering opening the items, carefully packaged in bubble wrap. The first thing I'd unwrapped had been a framed photo of the two of us, taken one summer when I was around ten years old, sitting on the beach eating ice cream. It was his favourite photo of us. There had been other things that had sentimental value to him—his crystal ball with a 3D model of the solar system suspended inside, that I'd given him for Christmas, his favourite heat changing mug, and a bunch of star charts and diagrams of constellations he'd had on his walls.

I cleared my throat, swiping the tears away. "Sorry. Um... underneath the other stuff, there was a manila file, that just said 'Personal' on the front. I opened it up, and there was a load of scribbled notes, most of which don't make any sense to me, some printouts about Alstone Holdings, and a photo of my mother."

"Do you have the file?" Cassius interrupted before I could continue.

"Not here. It's in a safe place."

"What do the notes say?"

"They're mostly just words or really short sentences and dates. I realised that the first dated note corresponded with that first day my dad went to Alstone and started acting all weird, and all the dates match with the times he went to Alstone. I'll get the file to show you when I can, but it set off alarm bells, and from what I can make out, he thinks my mother is...planning something that's quite possibly illegal, and dangerous, and worth a lot of money. And somehow Alstone Holdings is mixed up in it, maybe even behind it."

"Babe, you need to get that file to us. With our knowledge, we might be able to work it out." Cassius stared at me, his gaze serious.

"I know, and I will. Thanks, Cass. I've been feeling so alone," I whimpered, my voice hoarse and my throat raw from crying. "I want to get justice for my dad, but I didn't even know where to start. And then last night I find out that you think I've been working with my mother, the person who I believe might have had something to do with his death..."

"No, Winter." Zayde's voice, firm and steady, had my head shooting up. I'd never heard that tone from him before, not directed at me, anyway. He held my gaze, a flicker of remorse in his eyes. "We were wrong." He nodded at Cassius, who continued.

"Yeah. Look. We had our suspicions about your mother, and your dad, for that matter, because we knew she'd had contact with him. And then there was you... Anyway, now isn't the time or place to go into details, but we'd heard about your dad, and it seemed suspicious that you'd left home the same day it happened, and then West found out you'd been in contact with your mother."

"That's because I needed to get closer to her so I could come here to investigate!"

"We know that now. As soon as you told me last night why you were here, I was sure of it. You know, West and I have believed you're most likely innocent for a while now, but it took these two dicks a while to catch up." He jabbed a finger at Zayde and Caiden, who, while I was talking, had left the sofa and was crouched on the floor next to Zayde's chair, facing me, his expression shuttered.

"There's no way you were putting on an act just now. No one can act that convincingly," Cassius continued.

"You're not alone anymore." Weston kissed the top of my head. "You have me. I'm appointing myself as your official brother now."

"And me. Not the brother part, but we're now officially friends. Maybe even fuck buddies." Cassius nudged me, and I laughed, feeling like a weight had been lifted.

"I don't think you could handle me, Cass. But thanks. And thanks, West. I'd really like that."

"I could handle you. I'm very good with my hands. And did I mention the size of my di—"

"Shut the fuck up." Caiden finally spoke. "No one wants to hear about your dick."

"Rude," Cassius muttered, but he was grinning.

"We'll help you, and in return, you help us," Zayde told me, and I nodded.

"Sounds fair."

"Cade?"

Everyone looked at him as he got to his feet, crossing his arms across his impressive chest and staring down at me. "One thing straight, Snowflake. This doesn't mean I like you. I don't. Don't expect us to be friends. But the Four will have your back, and we expect you to have ours. Understood?"

"Yes, Your Highness."

"Sorry, what the fuck did you just say?" His eyes narrowed.

"I said. Yes. Your. Highness." I enunciated each word clearly. Out of the corner of my eye, I saw Cassius collapse back on the sofa, laughing.

"I'm so glad I was here when you said that. His face!" He

succumbed to hysterics again, and Caiden shot a look of pure ice at us both.

I shook my head at Cassius. "I really don't know what was so funny about that, but as long as I've amused you, I guess."

Finally, he managed to calm himself and lumbered to his feet, pulling me up with him. "Now you're one of us, let's forget all the heavy stuff for now. I'm gonna cheer you up by showing you around our house properly."

I followed him out the door as he mumbled something about a hot tub, leaving Caiden standing there, his arms still folded and his brows pulled together in a frown, staring after me.

FIFTEEN

"Afternoon! You're back later than I thought you'd be." Kinslee looked up from her laptop screen. She'd covered our kitchen table with books, papers, and her laptop.

"Busy? Want a cuppa?" She nodded, turning back to her screen, and I dumped my bag in my room, then filled the kettle with water and set it to boil. "In answer to your comment, I had brunch with the Four before I came here."

Pulling out two mugs from the cupboard, I waited for Kinslee's brain to catch up with my words. I heard a sharp intake of breath, then a loud screech, and I turned around, grinning at the shock on her face.

"You *what*? You had brunch with the Four? How did that happen? What's going on? Are you friends with them now? Wait, are you fucking one of them? Or all of them?"

"Slow down," I laughed. "Let me finish making our tea and I'll tell you all about it."

Sitting at the kitchen table, my hands wrapped around a steaming mug of tea, I gave her a rundown of the situation, minus the parts about my dad and my suspicions about my mother. Her eyes grew round and her mouth dropped open, and she peppered my story with her interruptions.

"The Four in suits, with those tattoos underneath? I would have come on the spot!"

"Dog fighting? That's barbaric!"

"You kissed *Caiden Cavendish*?"

"You're so lucky. If I'd slept with Cassius, I would've made the most of it."

"I want to be dickmatized by that boy."

"Zayde. Cooked. You. Brunch. Zayde, possibly the sexiest, but definitely the scariest man I've ever seen in my life. He can cook? Fuck me sideways."

"So you're all best mates now?"

I finished recounting what had happened with a shake of my head. "Not exactly. Caiden explicitly stated that we weren't friends and he didn't like me. The others? I'm not completely sure, to be honest. I still get the feeling that they're just waiting to catch me doing something bad. But I think they're thawing out. I hope so, anyway. And because the others have said they've accepted me now or whatever, whether they mean it or not, Caiden's going along with them."

"You need to have hate sex with him. So hot." She fanned herself dramatically.

"No thanks. Yeah, he's sexy, and from what I could feel of his dick when I was grinding all over him last night, it's biii-iig. But that doesn't excuse the fact that, one, he's not interested, and, two, he's an asshole, and he proved that again to me this morning with his comments to me. If the Four are the kings of Alstone College, he's King Asshole."

"True. But I still think you should. Have you even slept with anyone since James?"

I shook my head. "I—"

"Whose hoodie is that?" Kinslee interrupted me, jabbing an accusing finger at me.

"Uh. It's Caiden's." I could feel my cheeks heating as she raised an eyebrow at me.

"Oh, I see. And how, pray tell, did you end up wearing it?"

"I was cold, so he let me borrow it."

"Uh-huh. Right." She gave me a knowing look over the top of her mug. "Let me guess. Was he wearing it at the time?"

"Maybe. Anyway, can we *please* stop talking about him now?"

Kinslee huffed but relented. "Come on. Help me brainstorm for my assignment. It's enough to take anyone's mind off their problems."

"Go on, then."

The next day I struggled through my university lectures, not really able to concentrate. The weekend's events kept playing on my mind. After my lectures ended, I headed to the library, knowing I needed to at least attempt to work on the assignment that was due at the end of the week.

There were a few students around, but most had left campus for the day now that classes were over. I reached the back row of the stacks and stopped, taking a moment to look out of the window. From my vantage point on the top floor, I could see lights flicker on all over the campus, as the sky began to darken with the setting sun.

As I added another book to the teetering pile on the

table I'd commandeered, I turned around to see a small group enter through the electronic sliding doors.

Ocean eyes arrowed straight to mine. Caiden looked almost angry to see me. Shocker. I squared my shoulders and approached the table where he was now lounging with Cassius and a couple of girls.

Cassius' face broke into an easy grin when he saw me standing there. "Hey, babe. I was just talking about you. You up for a party at our place on Friday? Just a small gathering. You can bring Kinslee if you want—tell her to wear something short and tight."

"Ugh." I rolled my eyes. "Yes to the party, and I'll ask Kinslee, but it's a hard no for asking her to wear something short and tight." I thought for a moment. "Although knowing her, there's a good chance she'll be wearing something along those lines anyway."

"Why are you inviting *her*? That's scraping the barrel, Cassius."

Bitch. I took a good look at the blonde girl who was sulkily pouting at Cassius like a petulant child.

I made my voice syrupy sweet. "Aww, sorry, hon, didn't you hear? Cass is my BFF. And maybe more—who knows what might happen." I smiled widely and slid onto his lap, both to piss her off and to see what Caiden's reaction would be. I knew Cass would play along, shit stirrer that he was.

Cassius chuckled in my ear and put his arms around me. "She's right. Winter here is not only a very good friend of mine, but I'm working on us becoming very, *very* good friends, if you catch my drift." The blonde girl looked genuinely shocked, her mouth falling open, and I laughed to myself, stealing a glance at Caiden. He was acting like I wasn't even there, his attention on the other girl, but I could see a muscle ticking in his jaw, and his posture was tense and rigid. In some small way, I managed to affect him, as much as he clearly disliked it.

"Anyway, it's been a pleasure, but I have work to do. Call me later, babe." I jumped up from Cassius, and he blew me a kiss as I walked off, grinning.

I looked up from my laptop about an hour later and noticed it was fully dark outside. Cassius and the girls had long gone, but Caiden was still sitting at the same table, staring at his laptop and every now and then running a hand agitatedly through his dark, messy hair. I saw him let out a breath and rub his hand tiredly over his face, before he shut his laptop lid with a bang and stood up to leave. I should do the same.

Gathering up my pile of books, I headed for the stacks to place them back where they belonged. I spun around the corner and collided with a solid body, books raining down onto the floor, and all the air was knocked out of me.

Flustered and winded, I raised my head to see Caiden standing there. He still had that same dark stormy look on his face. *Fuck.*

I licked my lips, suddenly feeling parched.

His eyes flashed, and he bent his head towards mine. Grabbing the back of my neck roughly, he slanted his lips on to mine in a hard, angry kiss. My arms reached up of their own accord, tugging on his hair and drawing him closer. Pressing his chest into mine, he pushed me into the stacks, and I distantly heard books crashing to the floor, but I was too caught up in him to care. He set me on fire, and I was burning up.

He moved his hand from the back of my neck to lightly grip my throat, biting at my bottom lip. I moaned and scraped my nails down his back, making him shiver.

Abruptly, he wrenched away from me. Breathing hard,

we stared at one another, the mixture of confusion and lust that he seemed to spark in me making my head spin.

"Caiden, what the fuck is going on? Is this a game to you or something?"

"That shouldn't have happened." He turned on his heel.

"You don't just get to walk away from me like that!" I grabbed his arm, spinning him back round to face me, seriously pissed off.

"Leave me alone," he gritted out. "I want you to stay the fuck away from me." He shook my hand off his arm as if I'd branded him.

"Fuck you, Cade. You're the one who keeps instigating the kisses!" He. Was. So. Infuriating. How dare he act like that? He was the one who had kissed me first, both times. And yet he claimed to hate me. "Do you know what I just realised?" I got all up in his face, practically breathing fire. "I. Don't. Like. You. At all. I want *you* to stay the fuck away from *me*."

"Good. Fine."

"Fine!" I stormed off, uncaring that I'd left books scattered all over the floor. King Asshole could pick them up.

Men.

SIXTEEN

Winter

Tuesday, Cassius leaned over during a long, tedious economics lecture and asked if I could bring the file with me to their party and stay over so we could go through it at the weekend.

Wednesday, I skipped my afternoon classes and drove to the locker I rented at an out-of-town storage unit around ninety minutes' drive away from Alstone and retrieved the file.

Thursday, I was feeling overwhelmed with everything, and I rode my borrowed bike to the castle ruins, where I spent a couple of hours trying to untangle my thoughts. Something about the fact the ruins had been standing there for hundreds of years, plus the sound of the sea against the cliffs, soothed me like nothing else.

Friday was the party...

———

Strolling up the pathway arm in arm with Kinslee, my

overnight bag slung across my shoulder, I had a strong sense of déjà vu. We'd turned up slightly early so I could get settled in and talk to the boys without the others being there.

So, here we were. I'd parked my car next to Caiden's, the contrast between the two ridiculous: my tiny car with the word "whore" in huge letters, next to his perfectly buffed and polished R8. I wondered if he'd notice if I swapped our car keys...I laughed to myself, thinking about him squashed into the driver's seat of my car. "Compact" was a generous description.

Kinslee lifted her hand to the huge metal door knocker, painted matte black and shaped like a skull, and rapped it against the door. The door swung open, and we entered the house, and I noted the security camera facing us. Knowing what I knew now, it was laughable that I'd even attempted to key Caiden's car when it was parked right outside, but at the time I couldn't have imagined the surveillance they had going on. It wasn't like I had any experience in that—my old university apartment block had an intercom buzzer, and that was the height of technology.

"Where's..." Kinslee's words trailed off on a breathy sigh as we entered the foyer and looked up the curving staircase to the landing.

The Four stood, staring down at us. They hadn't bothered dressing up—not yet, anyway. All I saw as my eyes greedily licked over them were bare torsos, muscles, and tattoos. I wondered, not for the first time, how exactly I'd ended up involved with them.

"Come on up," Weston called, and that shook me out of my trance. I smiled up at him and led the way up the stairs, Kinslee following behind me. As I reached the landing, my entire focus turned to Caiden, helplessly.

Shorts. A sheen of sweat on his golden, tattooed skin, muscles rippling as he stretched his arms above his head. His raven hair was all tousled like he'd been running his fingers through it, a pair of headphones around his neck.

Fuck. Me.

He stared at me blankly, then turned away. "Shower," he grunted, striding into his room and closing the door firmly behind him.

"You want a bucket of ice to cool off?" Weston smirked at me.

"What?"

"I think we all noticed the way you were looking at my brother like he was your last meal."

"No, I wasn't," I said weakly. Just because the asshole was the hottest man I'd ever seen, didn't change the fact I disliked him intensely. Then, because I had no pride: "Why was he all like that?"

"If by 'that' you mean a sweaty mess that badly needed a shower, he's been in the basement. In our gym." Cassius stepped forwards, swinging me up into a hug and planting a huge kiss on my cheek. He released me and did the same with Kinslee, grinning at her exaggerated squeal and spinning around with her in his arms.

"Have I mentioned how much I love being your friend?" Kinslee smiled and winked at me as Cassius put her down.

"Ha ha. You're welcome." I headed towards the guest room, assuming that was where I would be sleeping. No one stopped me or mentioned otherwise, so I opened the door and threw my bag onto the bed. The file was safely tucked away amongst my clothes, and I knew it would be safe here. I closed the door behind me and followed everyone down the stairs, into the kitchen.

"So, how many are you expecting tonight?" I directed my

question to Weston, as Cassius and Zayde got beers out of the fridge and, after popping the tops, slid two across the large island towards me and Kinslee.

"Not many. We're keeping this one small. Intimate."

"Intimate, hmmm?" Kinslee purred, raking her eyes over him and licking her lips.

"Did you bring a bikini, Kins?" His voice dropped an octave.

"Maybe. Why?"

"Wanna go in the hot tub?"

"Mmm, yes. I'll be right back." She slipped off her stool, beer in hand, and headed off towards the stairs.

"West, don't go fucking with her," I warned.

"I'm not going to be fucking *with* her, I'm going to be *fucking her*." He smirked at me.

"Right. I gathered that."

"Don't worry, sis. We both know it's just a bit of fun."

"Okay. Just making sure."

He walked around the island to me and pulled me into his arms, dropping a kiss on my head, and I hugged him back. "I wish Cade was more like you," I mumbled into his bare chest.

"No, you don't. You and me—we're brother and sister. You and Cade—you're...fire. A blazing inferno, burning everything in your path."

I drew back to look at him, raising a brow. "Uh. I'm not really sure what to say to that. It was quite poetic, actually, especially coming from you. And not true."

"Isn't it?" He held my gaze.

I had to look away. Grabbing my bottle, I took a large swig. The doorbell rang, saving me from any more awkward conversation, and Zayde disappeared, presumably to let whoever it was into the house. Kinslee returned to the kitchen, and both Cassius and Weston drooled at her tiny blue bikini that showcased her curves perfectly.

"Kinslee, babe. You look good enough to eat. You want me to join you in the tub?" Cassius trailed a hand down her arm, and she shivered, looking torn, her eyes flicking between him and Weston.

"Cass. Come with me?" I questioned to save her the decision, and she gave me a quick smile, slipping her arm into Weston's and heading out of the sliding doors to the hot tub that was on the back deck.

Cassius followed me into the lounge area with the huge TV screen, where Zayde had made himself comfortable in his reclining chair, a T-shirt now covering his torso, blunt in hand, and a girl perched on him, kissing his neck while he glanced over at us, expressionless.

There were another three girls standing around in front of the fireplace, chatting and giggling, flicking their hair and stealing glances at Cassius and the other guys in the room, who I vaguely recognised from seeing them around campus but not spoken to.

As Cassius led me to the sofa and pulled me down next to him, I saw Caiden enter the room. He glanced at me and immediately dismissed me as if I wasn't worthy of his attention and moved to the fireplace where the three girls stood. One of them, an absolutely gorgeous brunette with poker-straight hair down to her waist, huge pouty lips, and a tiny dress, threw her arms around him. She ran her hands up and down the bare skin of his back, because *of course* he hadn't bothered to put a shirt on, and he hugged her back, glaring at me over her shoulder.

"Oh, it's like that, is it?" Cass leaned closer and murmured in my ear, his gaze following mine. "Watch what he does, and be ready to act." He lit a blunt and passed it to me, keeping his eyes on Caiden and the girl.

"Who is that?" I asked in a low tone, inhaling, then passing the blunt back.

"Jessa. She's alright. Maybe not to you." We both watched as Caiden spun her around to face us, sliding his arms around her waist, and she gave me a triumphant smile.

"She sucks cock like a fucking porn star." Cassius continued to twist the knife, and a mixture of blinding rage, hatred, and jealously filled me as Caiden leaned down to kiss her neck, and she turned her head, running her hand up the side of his face and kissing him. He kissed her back, moving his hands up to stroke the underside of her barely covered tits.

"Fuck him," I seethed, downing the rest of my beer and slamming the bottle down on the table in front of us.

"That's the spirit, babe. Let's give him a taste of his own medicine, yeah?"

"Yes."

Cassius took one last drag of the blunt and carefully placed it in the ashtray, then pulled me onto his lap, his arms coming around my waist. "Tell me if you want me to stop, at any point, okay?"

I nodded and closed my eyes as he trailed his lips down my neck, his mouth hot against my skin. "Sometimes I wish you weren't Caiden's," he murmured, kissing the top of my shoulder.

"I'm not Caiden's."

"You are," he sighed. "But since he's in denial and playing dirty, I get to play with you." He ran his hands over my bare thighs in slow, caressing strokes, then reached forwards to grab his beer, gulping down the rest.

146

My unwilling attention was drawn back to Caiden. His eyes were almost black, furious, as he stared at us, palming Jessa's tits as she ground her ass into him. I gasped, and Cassius grabbed me around the waist, spinning me around so I was straddling him, our faces close together. He pressed his soft lips against mine, and I kissed him back, winding my arms around his neck.

His lips felt wrong. I kissed him harder, trying to feel something. He was an amazing kisser, but there was no passion, no spark, no fire.

Without any warning I was suddenly yanked off him and half dragged, half carried out of the room.

"What the fuck! Let go of me, right now, you asshole!" I screamed in Caiden's face, flailing against him. He ignored me and dragged me up the stairs onto the landing, where he let go of me and I stumbled, falling forwards and catching myself on the wall.

I spun myself around to face him, raging, my hand swinging out to slap him.

He caught it with lightning reflexes and gripping tightly onto my wrists, crowded me up against the wall so I was trapped by his body.

I could feel the heat and fury pouring off him in waves, as he stared at me, breathing heavily, his teeth bared in a snarl, his eyes completely black. His chest was bare, his perfectly ripped torso pressed against me. His grey sweatpants, low on his hips, did nothing to hide the outline of his hard cock.

As if of its own accord, my body arched towards his so I could feel his hardness pressing into me, and I whimpered, hating myself for my reaction to him.

He growled low in his throat. "We're not doing this."

"No, we're not," I agreed, leaning against the wall for

support and curling my leg around the back of his to nudge him closer.

"You were grinding all over Cassius downstairs. Did you think I wouldn't notice?" He viciously nipped at my collarbone, then licked over the stinging bite mark.

"Yeah, like you had your hands all over Jessa's tits?" I leaned closer, biting his neck. "Is your dick hard for her or for me?"

"Fuuuuck," he groaned, letting go of my wrists and slipping his hand between us, under my short dress. "You're so wet. Are you wet for him or for me?"

"I hate you."

He ground the heel of his hand into me and I moaned, my hand reaching down between us to slide along his cock, stroking it through his sweatpants. "We're not doing this," he repeated, his voice hoarse and desperate, his eyes darkened with arousal.

"I know."

He smashed his lips onto mine.

The fire between us blazed to life as I opened my mouth for him. His arms came around me, and he effortlessly picked me up, carrying me along the landing. The next minute a door was slammed, and he was pushing me up against it, tugging my dress off over my head.

I yanked his sweatpants down and his hard cock sprang free, and I curled my hand around it and squeezed lightly.

"Fuck," he groaned, undoing my bra and ripping my underwear away from my body. He picked me up again, and I hooked my ankles around him as we fell onto a bed, biting at his bottom lip, then savagely raking my nails down his back. I wanted to punish him for what he'd done downstairs.

"Why are you such an asshole?" I asked in between

biting kisses, my words ending on a moan as he dragged his thick cock against my wetness.

"Why are you *always in my fucking head*?" His voice was agonised as he moved his head lower, biting and sucking at my nipples until I had to tug his hair forcefully, to pull him back up to me, unable to bear the torture of pleasure and pain any longer, needing him inside me.

I reached down between us and gripped his cock, gliding my thumb over the precum on the tip. He let out a shaky breath and stilled my hand, raising himself up onto his elbows and reaching into the drawer next to the bed, pulling out a foil packet. Then he rolled it on and was thrusting inside me, filling me completely, before I could even catch my breath. He pounded in and out of me, a punishing rhythm that I matched as I gripped his ass, digging my nails into his skin, pulling him even closer.

He suddenly pulled out and flipped me over, pulling me onto my knees and thrusting back inside me, reaching around to my clit.

"Cade." I moaned his name over and over as he fucked me, hurtling towards my orgasm. I came so hard that I thought I was going to black out, feeling his cock pulsate inside me as he gripped onto me tightly, his whole body shuddering as he found his own release.

I collapsed onto the bed, breathless and panting.

"Snowflake," came the soft whisper, and the barest brush of lips against my spine.

I passed out.

I awoke, disorientated. Where was I? I sat up and glanced around me. I was in a bed, under the covers. Cool charcoal sheets, a dim lamp with a black ceramic skull-shaped base on the bedside table, casting shadows across the room, slate-grey walls with white wood trim, honey-toned floorboards, and a huge rug.

Okay. This wasn't the guest room.

Caiden's room?

If so, I was in his bed.

There was a weight pinning my feet down, and I noticed my bag sitting at the end of the bed. I guess someone must have brought it in, because I'd definitely left it in the guest bedroom. I pulled my phone out of the side pocket, surprised to see that only around an hour and a half had passed since I was downstairs.

Grabbing my bag, I padded out of the room, stopping to pick up my dress and underwear which had been left in a pile on the floor next to the door, and went back into the guest room.

My head was spinning as I walked into the bathroom on autopilot and stood under the shower, letting the warm water cascade over me, carefully avoiding getting my hair wet.

Caiden. How the fuck did we get from hateful glares to the hottest sex of my life, bar none?

No idea.

As I wandered back into the lounge room dressed in pyjama shorts and a navy camisole, barefoot, my hair piled on top of my head, I stopped dead. Oh yeah. I'd somehow managed to forget there were other people here. Next to the girls with their heavy make-up, short dresses, and killer heels, I felt severely lacking. I turned on my heel and walked straight out, instead heading into the kitchen, where I rummaged in the fridge for a drink, pulling out a bottle of Prosecco. Funny. The Four didn't strike me as the types to drink sparkling wine. I shrugged and twisted the bottle until the cork released with a satisfying pop and poured the fizzing alcohol into the closest cup I could find—which happened to be a pint glass.

"Winter!" I turned towards the open sliding doors to see Kinslee waving at me from the hot tub, Weston and Cassius both in there with her. "Get your sexy ass over here and bring that Prosecco," she called.

"I don't have my bikini."

"That's okay." Cassius gave me an exaggerated wink, and I couldn't help laughing. I'd actually been worried about how he'd react to me after what had happened earlier, but at the moment, anyway, he seemed to be acting like his usual self. Although...

I quickly walked out to them before I could change my mind, handing the Prosecco bottle to Kinslee and placing my pint glass on the ledge that ran around the edge of the decking. It was bloody freezing, my breath making clouds in the night air. I took a deep breath and pulled my top over my head so I was in my navy bra and shorts, rolling my eyes as Cassius and Weston both whistled at me. I figured the material was thick enough that it would do instead of a bikini.

The boys eyed me as I sank into the water next to Cassius.

"Cass?" I leaned close to him, relaxing into the bubbling heat of the tub.

"Yeah?" His eyes were glassy, his voice a little slurred.

"Are we okay? After earlier?"

"Babe." He slid his arm around me, pulling me closer. "Course we are. Like I said, you're Cade's. We were helping the situation."

"Um, if you say so." I leaned back against his arm,

closing my eyes. We sat in silence for a while, Cassius reaching over to his blunt every now and then, until he spoke in my ear.

"You fuck him?"

"Yeah."

"Good."

Silence. Then—

"You two gonna kiss?" He prodded my shoulder, his voice louder than before, and my eyes flew open.

"Huh? Who two?"

"You and Kins."

Kinslee and I stared at each other for a second and started laughing at the same time.

"Uh, I have no idea what your thought process was there, but that would be a no. Sorry."

Kinslee smirked and turned to whisper something in Weston's ear while I stood up and leaned over to grab my pint glass, which started steaming up as soon as I held it over the tub. Settling back down next to Cassius, I sipped my drink, idly making swirling patterns in the water with my hand.

"Alright, mate?" Cassius' lazy slur had my head snapping round.

Caiden stood in the doorway, ignoring Cassius, his eyes on me and his expression unreadable.

SEVENTEEN

Caiden

She looked at me uncertainly, biting her bottom lip, her eyes huge. I took in the setting—Kinslee wedged between my brother's legs, swigging straight from a bottle of wine, and Cass sprawled out in the tub like a fucking king, his arm around Winter. My eyes flicked to his, and he smirked at me. The fucker was stoned; his eyes were half-closed, and from experience I knew he'd be passed out soon enough.

"West. Help me out, will ya." I nodded over to Cassius.

"I'm fine," Cassius protested.

"Yeah, I see that. Just...get back in the house, mate."

He gave an exaggerated sigh, his head lolling back.

"Cass."

"Fine." He clambered out of the tub, his movements sluggish, picking up one of the towels draped over the decking railing and pulling it over his shoulders. He disappeared inside and I stood, my mind torn between checking on Cass and the girl that was right in front of me.

My brain caught up, *finally*.

What the hell did I do? Fuck Snowflake. As in, sticking my dick in her.

Self-loathing filled me as I looked at her. Yeah, maybe I'd been wrong about her working with her mother. Maybe. Probably. But it still didn't change the fact that she *looked just like her*, with that long dark hair, those huge eyes, and the way she tilted her head...yeah, that sounded minor, but it was identical to her mother. My stomach lurched. How could I have been so fucking weak? I was no worse than my father, and because of him, because of *her*...the only woman that I'd ever loved, the only woman I'd ever cared about, was dead.

The unwanted, *hated* memory rolled through me, and I pressed my palms to my temples and closed my eyes, trying to block it out, but it was no use.

"Mum?" I banged on the bathroom door. No answer. I banged harder. "Mum!"

No answer.

Dread coiled in my stomach, and I pounded at the door with all my might. She hadn't been the same since she'd found out about dad's affair with that fucking snake. She'd become withdrawn, distant, shutting herself away from us.

"Mum!"

No answer.

Frantic, I hit the door over and over, until my knuckles were throbbing.

No answer.

Shit! What should I do? The only thing I could think of was something stupid I'd seen in movies, but at this point I was ready to try anything. I ran back along our hallway and took a running leap straight into the door, kicking out my foot with all my strength. I guess although the door was made of thick, solid wood, the lock was weak, because it burst open, sending me hurtling into the room.

I fell to my knees.

No.

No.

No.

She was lying on the floor, on her side, one arm outstretched and her bottle of pills spilling out on the floor in front of her. She looked like she was asleep, but her skin had lost all colour, looking like a waxwork version of the living, breathing woman that was the most important person in my life.

I stumbled across the floor, barely aware of what I was doing. I reached out for her hand and clasped it in mine, knowing it was too late as soon as I touched her.

Fuck.

Fuck.

Fuck.

An inhuman scream burst from my lungs, and stabbing pain raced through my body, taking my breath away. I curled into a ball, still clasping her hand, my eyes squeezed shut, my brain going offline.

I wasn't aware of what happened after that.

"Caiden!"

I opened my eyes to find my brother crouched in front of me, dripping wet, worry clear in his eyes. I realised I was sitting on the decking, my head in my hands, my whole fucking body shaking.

Fuck.

"I'm fine. I guess I drank more than I thought. Guess that's my cue to go to bed." I forced a laugh.

Weston eyed me cautiously. "Cade..." His voice trailed off as I shot him a warning look. He could say or do whatever the fuck he wanted, but I was *never* telling him what had happened to our mother. I wanted his memories of her to be pure, untainted.

As far as he was aware, she'd died of a sudden brain haemorrhage, and that was how it was going to stay. It was pretty much the only area where me and my dad were in complete agreement. My dad felt a sense of guilt—not enough to get rid of the bitch, but he at least cared enough about Weston to try and stop him feeling the fucking crushing failure and regret I felt.

Why hadn't I done something sooner?

She'd still be alive.

I launched to my feet, turning towards the house, needing to be inside, and alone.

"Caiden?"

A pair of slim arms encircled my waist, and I saw red.

"Get the fuck away from me, *right now*. We fucked—that doesn't give you the right to touch me. You're the last person I want near me."

She flinched, immediately dropping her arms, and I laughed cruelly, letting the hatred for her mother seep through me, filling me, smothering the pain of losing my mother.

"You're nothing to me. You weren't even a good lay."

She gasped, and I cringed internally, because that was an outright lie. I *hated* admitting it, but fucking her had been the best sex of my life.

My dick needed to get the memo that it was never going to happen again.

I wrenched away from her, and from the guilt and the

pain, and escaped upstairs, slamming my door behind me and flipping the lock before throwing myself on the bed.

Fuck.

My bed smelled like sex and a subtle scent of sugar and spice.

I couldn't sleep there.

I pulled a blanket from my cupboard and slept on the floor.

EIGHTEEN

Winter

Morning. The first thing I'd done when I'd woken in the guest room, head pounding, was to check the door was unlocked. I wouldn't have put it past Caiden to lock me in again. Thankfully, the door opened.

As the memories of last night assaulted me, I cringed. I showered as quickly as possible, and not even bothering to check my appearance, silently slipped out of the room and crept down the stairs, intent on leaving before anyone else made an appearance.

I made it to the front door without incident and reached to open it, but before I could make my escape, arms came around me, pinning me in place.

"Not so fast," a low voice hissed in my ear. "Where do you think you're going?"

A chill went through me at Zayde's threatening tone, but I steeled myself.

"Let go of me. King Caiden made it clear last night that he didn't want me here."

His laugh somehow managed to sound dark and sinister.

"Oh no, sweetheart. You're not getting away that easily. Let's make one thing clear. I believe you're not working with your mother, but I still don't trust you. Trust needs to be earned."

With that comment, he disappeared, just as silently as he'd arrived, and I was left by the door, staring after him.

I sighed. He was right, in a way. If I didn't share this file with the Four, didn't explain my reasoning for suspecting my mother had a hand in my father's death, how could I expect them to just blindly trust me? They needed to see the evidence for themselves and come to their own conclusions. Mind made up, I headed towards the kitchen.

After a silent breakfast, during which only West was present, I entered the spy room, as I was calling it. The one with all the computers and camera feeds. I was in a bad mood, still pissed off about Caiden's behaviour towards me, to be honest. I'd been worried about him last night, and I'd acted on instinct, trying to provide comfort. But as soon as I'd gone to him, he'd made it perfectly clear that sleeping with me had been a mistake.

So, as far as I was concerned, we were back to normal. Normal, meaning I'd have to ignore his hateful glares and asshole behaviour, unless a miracle somehow occurred.

Weston directed me to a large leather office chair, and I amused myself by spinning around in it while I waited for the others to turn up. My whirling trajectory was suddenly halted by Zayde, who silently appeared in the room and stopped me with a hand on the back of the chair.

I pouted at him for ruining my fun, and he gave me an amused smirk.

Taken aback by the contrast in his behaviour from earlier that morning, I gaped at him but recovered quickly. "Why, Zayde, was that an actual smile?" I raised a brow.

"From Z? Never." Cassius strode into the room and took

the other chair next to mine, and Zayde leaned against the desk, his face already back to its usual impassive mask. "Morning, babe. How's your head?"

"Fine. Ish. More importantly, how's yours?"

"All good, thanks. I'm touched by your concern for me."

I laughed. "Always. I'm thinking Kins will have the worst head this morning, out of all of us." After all the shit with Cade, I'd been pissed off and agitated enough that doing shots with Weston and Kinslee had seemed like a great idea. Kinslee had also finished up the Prosecco (which had turned out to belong to a very unimpressed Jessa), and then West had ordered an Uber for her, while I'd stumbled up to the guest bed, my head swimming.

The last I'd heard from Kinslee, before sleep claimed me, was a drunken rambling text saying she was back at home, and she'd had the best night ever, and then waaaay too much information on West's dick. Thanks, Kinslee.

To be completely honest? I'd wanted to leave with her the night before, still upset about the way Caiden had acted towards me, but Weston had convinced me to stay, telling me I'd regret it if I didn't. He'd insisted that if I wanted answers, I needed the help of the Four. In my exhausted state, I hadn't taken much persuading.

This morning, though, I was full of doubts.

The door opened and Caiden walked in, dark circles under his eyes, avoiding my gaze. Cassius stared between the two of us, confusion all over his face, as the tension in the room ratcheted up by about a thousand notches. Of course—he'd disappeared before Cade had insulted me and stormed off.

What the fuck? Cassius mouthed at me. I shook my head at him, trying to convey to him that now wasn't the time or the place. He heaved a heavy sigh and glanced back at Caiden.

"You don't look too good, mate. Here, take my seat." Cass jumped up and moved across to me, pulling me out of my chair. That mischievous glint in his eye...I had a fairly good idea of what was coming next.

"You can sit on me, beautiful." He collapsed into my chair and patted his thigh.

"No." Caiden's voice rang out, startling me.

Every single head turned towards him.

"Where's the fucking popcorn when you need it," I heard Zayde comment under his breath.

"No? Why not, huh?" Cassius stared at Caiden challengingly, and Caiden stared straight back, unblinking.

For fuck's sake.

"Caiden, can I have a quick word with you?" I eyed him cautiously. "Please," I added. I walked to the door and out into the hallway, hoping he'd follow me. Leaning against the hallway wall, I waited.

A few moments later he slipped out of the room and came to a stop in front of me. His expression was shuttered, but I saw the muscle ticking in his jaw, and his clenched fists.

"What was all that about?" I kept my voice soft and quiet, trying not to provoke him. "Do you have an issue with me and Cass?"

"There is no *you and Cass*," he said roughly, planting his arms either side of me so he was all up in my personal space. Again.

"Why not?"

"Because I said so."

"Well, I'm afraid that's not a good enough reason." My body was reacting to his proximity, shivers running down my spine and my heart beating faster, and I closed my eyes briefly, trying to regain control.

I could feel his hot breath on my ear as he leaned even closer. "You're not his."

"I'm not yours, though, right? You made that pretty fucking clear last night." I let some of my anger over his behaviour bleed through into my tone, but my voice still sounded breathy and lustful, even to my own ears.

"No. You're not. How many fucking times do you need to hear it?"

"So you don't want me, but you don't want anyone else to have me, is that it?"

He looked at me silently for a moment, then shrugged, a quick, jerky movement. He lowered his thick lashes, his gaze darting to my mouth as I bit my lip, thinking hard. Should I say it? Fuck it. It's not like I could make things much worse between us.

"You want to know what I think?" I waited until his eyes met mine before I continued. "I think you *do* want me. I think you're lying to yourself." I slid under his arm and stalked away from him, but he grabbed my arm, pulling me back.

"What?" I snapped, my patience finally running out.

"Stay the fuck away from Cassius."

"He's my friend. Unlike you, he can actually admit that he enjoys spending time with me."

He laughed darkly, his grip on my arm tightening. "Don't flatter yourself, Snowflake. He'd drop you in a second if I wanted him to."

"Whatever you say." I sighed. "Look, as low as your opinion is of me, I have no desire to cause trouble between the two of you. But maybe you should look at why you have such a problem with me and him." I shook off his arm, and this time he didn't stop me.

"Great talk. Really productive," I muttered to myself as I re-entered the room, Caiden on my heels.

"Enough fucking time-wasting. Let's get down to business," Zayde commanded, and I nodded. This conversation was over, for now, and we had more important things to worry about.

Sinking into the empty chair at the desk, I picked up the manila folder I'd left there. The Four crowded around me, peering at the contents.

"Right. There's not much to go on, but this is all I have." I spread out the papers in front of me. "There's the Alstone Holdings printouts—all generic information that you could easily find online." I indicated the sheets that I'd placed together with a paperclip.

"Then, we have this photo of my mother. I don't know if it means anything to any of you?" I handed the image to Zayde. It was a grainy, blown-up image in black and white. She was sitting at a table, partially obscured, and I could see a man's hand but hadn't been able to glean anything useful from it.

"Give it here." Zayde handed the picture to Weston, and he wiggled the computer mouse next to me, the screens coming to life. He walked to the corner of the room and opened the lid of a scanner, then started tapping on the computer keyboard.

"Should be ready in a few." I tuned out as he began talking about image processing software, staring blankly at the screen as various boxes and lines of writing flashed up and disappeared as quickly as they'd appeared.

"Done. The software should have enhanced the image for us. I'm hoping it makes it a bit clearer." He clicked the mouse a few times, and the picture appeared on the huge computer monitor directly in front of me, much sharper and clearer than the original.

"Ooh, that's impressive," I told Weston, and he grinned proudly.

"Yep. I'm amazing."

Turning back to study the screen, I noticed more details I'd missed originally.

"West, can you zoom in there?" I pointed, and he nodded. As he zoomed, I gasped. "I completely missed that before. Look."

The hand of the man sitting at the table with my mother was far easier to see now.

The tip of his little finger was missing.

"Littlefinger."

I glanced over at Weston and raised an eyebrow. "Huh?"

"You know, in *Game of Thrones*? That could be his code name. I mean, that's what we can call him."

"Littlefinger wasn't called Littlefinger for that reason. All his fingers were intact," Cassius argued.

"Whatever, still works." Weston shrugged.

"Not really. What about what's-his-name? Theon? He had his dick cut off."

"A dick is not the same as a finger."

"Didn't say it was, did I?"

"Please. Can we just get back to the task?" I begged, drumming my fingers on the table. "Let's agree to call him Littlefinger for now; since West said it, it's kind of stuck in my head."

"Fine. I'm picking the next code name, then," Cassius muttered.

Seriously. I rolled my eyes.

"*Anyway*. If you've finished pretending you're James

Bond or whatever, assigning code names to people. Does anything about this picture mean anything?"

Caiden moved closer to the screen, leaning his arm on the back of my chair. I shivered as it brushed along the back of my neck. "Something about this place rings a bell. What's that symbol there? Zoom in." We watched as the blurry shape on the window at the back of the picture grew bigger, but it was difficult to make it out.

"It almost reminds me of a crown or something," I mused, squinting at it.

"That's it! You genius!" Caiden fist pumped the air, his voice triumphant. I was so shocked by the unexpected compliment I froze, then smiled to myself. Bet he hadn't meant to compliment me.

"The Crown and Anchor?" Zayde spoke.

"Yeah, that's it. The one in Highnam. West?"

"Already on it." The screen next to the one we were looking at lit up, and Weston began typing.

"Highnam?" I murmured to Caiden.

"Yeah." He leaned a little closer to me. "A town about half an hour away. There's not much there, but there's a hotel."

"Oh." I sat, watching as Weston pulled up the website.

"No pictures of the interior, but look. That's the same symbol."

Caiden's finger brushed against the strands of my hair and moved to touch the back of my neck. I hardly dared to breathe.

"Let's start a list," Weston suggested. "First item—check out the hotel."

"We need to be careful not to be spotted. We don't want anyone getting suspicious." Caiden's voice was firm. He drew tiny, slow circles on the back of my neck with his finger.

Goosebumps erupted all down my arms, and my breath hitched.

"I agree. What if I go with James, or Kinslee, like for a drink in the bar or something?" I somehow managed to sound normal.

His finger stilled. "No fucking way. Not Granville. And I don't want you and Kinslee going near there without one of us, not until we know what we're dealing with."

"Yeah. If it was important enough for your dad to take a photo, enlarge it, and include it in this file, then we need to proceed with caution," Cassius added.

Caiden's finger resumed making lazy circles on my neck, and I glanced at him out of the corner of my eye. He was looking straight ahead at the screen, seemingly completely focused, but he continued to draw patterns on my skin as the boys discussed the best way to proceed. As much as I was loving it, I *really* wished he wouldn't blow so hot and cold with me. I was starting to get whiplash.

Not that I'd stop him.

Okay, concentrate. Forget how good Cade's touch feels. Think about why you're here.

A thought occurred to me, and I interrupted the discussion. "West? Do you want to scan the notes as well? It might be easier if they're all up on the screen."

I passed him the folder, and a few minutes later we were looking at the scribbled notes. "See, there's the first date, and that corresponds with his first trip here."

Underneath the date, it said:

CC MTG MAN. ALS HLDS. PLANNING?

There were other words and dates.

TRANSACTION. ILLEGAL???
DEAL WORTH £££££
TRANSACTIONS ONGOING. WHAT??
CC PLANNING. TRANSPORTING MERCH.

The paper had a few water spots, and thanks to my dad's penchant for making all his notes with a fountain pen, a couple of the words were difficult to make out, but the Four came to the same conclusion I had—that the words were Arlo and possibly Davis.

AR(letter missing)O (letter missing)AVIS. TUES NIGHTS.

Underneath the final date, the date he'd sent me the text, there was a woman's name and a sentence that still sent shivers down my spine.

ANDROMEDA. CC KNOWS I KNOW.

"I know it's not much to go on, but putting together the notes with the picture of my mother and the printouts, plus the way he'd been acting, and the text...it seemed too big a coincidence. Maybe I'm just grasping at straws, but I owe it to my dad to get to the bottom of it. He was obviously concerned enough to make a file."

Caiden straightened up, removing his hand from the back of my neck. "I think we have something here. We've had suspicions about your mother for a while. We haven't done much, mostly background checks, watching her where we could on the security feeds, having her followed on occasion." He gave a bitter laugh. "Clearly the wrong occasions since we missed all this shit. Oh, yeah, and we knew about you and your dad, and we kept a basic file on you both."

"A file on us?"

"Standard procedure for any person who becomes involved in Alstone Holdings. They do a background check, investigate their relationships, criminal records check, and so forth. West here has worked out how to bypass their security systems, so he was able to get hold of copies of all their checks."

"So you found something that made you suspicious?"

"Not in the checks, no. It's her shady as fuck behaviour. The way she wormed her way into dad's life, and..." Caiden's voice trailed off as he glanced at Weston. "Just the way she works people. She gets them wrapped around her little finger, and she's managed to go from a disowned school dropout to the wife of one of the most powerful men in the country and a shareholder in Alstone Holdings. None of the four of us trust her, and we won't make the mistake of underestimating her."

"I see. I guess that makes sense." I held his gaze. "The file wasn't the only thing you had on me, was it?"

"No." His eyes flicked between the others, and Zayde gave an almost imperceptible nod. "We've been watching you. On and off."

"Yeah, that was pretty obvious, from the way you shadowed me all the time." I rolled my eyes. "Other times, too, though?"

Caiden nodded. I'd gathered as much, from what Cassius had mentioned before, but I was glad he'd actually admitted it. I decided not to mention that I was more than a little pissed off with their invasion of my privacy. They didn't know me when I'd first arrived, and to be honest, I'd have been suspicious of me if I was in their position.

"Also," West added, leaning forwards in his chair and placing his hand over mine, "we got a code blue notification when your dad died. The day after, if you wanna be precise."

"Code blue? Huh?" I stared at him.

"Yeah." He removed his hand from mine and tapped on the computer screen, indicating a small icon in the bottom corner. "If any kind of serious issue happens relating to anyone either involved in, or related to someone in Alstone Holdings, they have an alert system so the other board members can be notified. Since I can access their systems, I have a connection to that, too, and that got sent out as a code blue alert at the time. Because we knew he'd met with your mother—we didn't know he was investigating her, but we knew he'd been up here—and because you happened to be away at the time it happened, we weren't sure what was going on. Whether you were involved or if it was just an accident."

I was starting to get a clearer picture of the situation, and I was now almost positive that she was somehow involved in my dad's death. At the very least, she was planning or already involved in something shady, and that deserved to be investigated.

"You know what, I bet he had a load of stuff on his computer. Like, proper evidence. Everything was destroyed in the explosion, though."

"What about his work computer?"

"Nothing. Or if there was something, the hard drive was wiped, but I don't think he would have risked storing anything on there. We're lucky that we even have this file."

"Let's go through the other notes and write them out." Weston brought up the document where he'd started making the to-do list.

"Well, CC has to be Christine Clifford, my mother. Since

my dad had the photo, and from what he said in the text to me. So I think the first bit says 'Christine Clifford. Meeting man. Alstone Holdings. Planning?' That's all pretty obvious, right?"

"Yeah." Zayde agreed, and the others nodded.

"The other notes seem fairly self-explanatory, but we need to know who these people are. Davis, if that's what it says, and Andromeda."

"So you think my dad's meeting or somehow connected with a Davis on Tuesday nights?" Weston mused. "I've lost track of his schedule now I don't live there anymore, but there were plenty of evenings I was home alone."

"Davis could be a first name or a surname," Cassius interjected. "It might not even be Davis. Could be Mavis. All we can see is the first bit of the letter."

"Good point. Add it to the document," I said to Weston.

"And then we have Andromeda. No fucking clue who she is. Or what." Weston turned to the others. "Anyone?"

"Sounds like a stripper to me."

"Hey! It's a lovely name, don't be rude." I reached over and smacked Cass' arm playfully.

"Sorry." He grinned, clearly not sorry at all.

We brainstormed for another ten minutes or so while Weston finished making all the notes, and we had the beginnings of a list of things to check.

Leaning back in my chair, I rubbed my hand over my face. "Okay. I think I'm done here for now. This is a lot to take in, and I need more sleep. Can we come back to this once we've had time to process it all and come up with some ideas?"

"Sounds good to me. I need to go back to bed," Cass yawned.

I stood and made a point of looking at each one of them

in turn. "I just wanted to say thanks to you all for helping with this. I know you have your own reasons, but it means a lot to me."

"I told you. You're one of us now." Cassius winked at me, and I smiled.

"Yeah. Right, I'm going to head back to my place. Do you want me to leave the file?"

"Nah, take it and put it in a safe place. I've scanned in everything, anyway, and I've saved it to my secure storage. No one else is getting hold of that info." West handed me the file.

Caiden and Zayde both disappeared without a goodbye while I was talking to Weston, but I shrugged it off. The dynamics of the Four intrigued me, so much. Weston and Cassius, making me feel welcome. Yeah, Cass was probably a little too welcoming...but Caiden and Zayde? Those two were a lot harder to read.

As I drove home, my mind raced with all the new information I'd been given this morning. One thing was for sure: I needed to speak to my mother and subtly ask questions, to see if I could find out anything at all that could be of use, no matter how small.

I groaned aloud. No way was I going through that alone. I guess it was time to set up another family dinner, so Caiden and Weston could be involved, too.

Fingers crossed it would go better than the last one.

NINETEEN

I parked in my usual spot outside my dad's mansion. As West and I got out of my R8, he nodded at Snowflake's car.

"You gonna do something about that?"

I stared at her car for a long moment.

"Yeah."

Pulling out my phone, I checked the time and made a call to my usual garage. "Alright, Joe. It's Cade. Glad I caught you before you left... Can you fit in a car for a complete respray? A rush job if you can... Yeah...it's a burgundy Fiat 500. There's some damage to the driver's door... Matte black... Yeah. Put it on my account. Cheers, mate. Appreciate it." I ended the call and turned to my brother. "Done. Booked in for eight a.m. on Tuesday. It'll be in for at least a week, so you might want to break the news to her. Can you get hold of her keys?"

"Matte black?" He raised an eyebrow.

"Just get the keys, will ya?"

"Alright, alright. No need to bite my head off." He stomped up the front steps and stopped at the top, waiting for me. "You ready?"

"Let's do this."

The game plan we'd agreed with Winter was simple enough. Act nice, no arguments, start some subtle digging. No mentioning the names we'd found written on Winter's dad's notes—it was too dangerous. We probably wouldn't find out much this first visit, which meant we'd have to return. Couldn't fucking wait.

As well as that—Z, Cass, and I were going to be taking a more active interest in Alstone Holdings, and West, to a lesser extent since he was younger. We were due to receive our shares and take our places on the board once we graduated from university and received our trust funds, so we'd use that reason to gather as much information as we could. We were part of Alstone's three founding families, after all, and it was about time we took advantage of that. The trip to the hotel was postponed for now, until we could agree on who should go, and when.

Sauntering into the house, we were greeted by Allan, who led us into the formal living room where my dad stood at the window, a tumbler of amber liquid in his hand. Snowflake stood with her back to us, her hair tied up and some kind of tight knee-length black dress that made her ass look amazing. *Fuck.* Images flashed through my mind— her, kneeling on the bed, ass pushing back onto my cock as I thrust in and out of her tight pussy... I adjusted my dick, trying to act normal, casting around to think of anything to make my hard-on go down. I glanced up—reluctantly—and caught my brother's eye. He frowned at me, nodding his head towards Christine, and just like that, all thoughts of what had happened with Winter disappeared. Her mother was talking to her, a disdainful expression on her face, and I clenched my jaw. Fuck, I hated that woman.

"Evening." I silently moved behind Winter, and she jumped about a mile as I leaned close to her ear, sliding my arm around her waist. "Remember, we have to act like we can tolerate each other," I hissed under my breath.

She turned into me and threw her arms around my neck, catching me off guard. "Cade! I'm so happy you could make it," she announced loudly, then went up on her toes and pulled my head down, whispering into my ear. "Try not to act like an asshole, and we'll have no problems."

She stepped away from me quickly, smirking, and threw her arms around Weston with genuine enthusiasm. "Hi. Did you get your grade back for the assignment yet?"

"Yeah, my lecturer was so impressed, he wants me to present it to the rest of the class." He smiled down at her a little shyly, their arms still round each other. What the fuck was going on?

"That's great! I'm so proud of you, West. If you need to talk through anything else, I'm always here."

"Thanks. Couldn't have done it without you." He kissed her cheek as he released her.

"What's going on?" I struggled to keep my voice even, as Christine stared between the three of us curiously.

They both blinked at me as if they'd just remembered that I was there. "Uh, Winter's been helping me out with some stuff. Remember I told you I have Professor Andrews for one of my modules—he's the *worst* at explaining concepts."

"I see," I bit out through clenched teeth. What the fuck was wrong with me? I had no reason to be angry at my brother.

He flashed me a knowing grin and turned to Christine,

switching on the charm. "Christine. Thank you for hosting us this evening."

She gave a gracious, completely fake smile. "It's a pleasure."

West moved over to greet my dad, and I stared at Christine, swallowing hard, trying to force myself to greet her.

"Cade." Snowflake put her hand on my arm and squeezed lightly, a warning. She kept her hand where it was as I hissed out a greeting to the bitch.

"Christine."

"Caiden." Her tone was as hostile as mine. Fuck. I hated having to play nice with her. I'd managed to ignore her for the most part, these last few years, but ever since Winter had come into the picture I'd been forced to interact with her.

"Cade, show me where the drinks are." Winter's grip tightened on my arm, and she tugged insistently.

"The staff will bri—" I stopped speaking as she signalled at me with her eyes. "Fine. Come on, then—Dad keeps the best ones in his office. Fucking hurry up, will you."

We walked down the hallway, entered my dad's office, and she closed the door behind her, then stood with her arms folded, staring at me, her eyes narrowed. "Look. I know you don't want to be here. I know that my mother is fucking awful, and I know you have a problem with me. But can you please get it together? You're going to ruin this whole evening, otherwise."

"Fuck." I slammed my fist into the nearest object. My dad's solid oak desk. "Fuck!" I shouted again, grabbing my throbbing wrist in my other hand.

"You idiot. What did you do that for?" I glanced at her, and it looked like she was struggling not to smile.

"Are you laughing at me?" My voice turned low, deadly.

A laugh burst out of her, and she clapped a hand over

her mouth, shaking her head. She visibly composed herself and moved closer to me, amusement still dancing in her eyes.

"Let me see." She lifted my hand and examined the knuckles, lightly running her finger over them, before dropping a light kiss on my clenched fist. I bit down on my lip to stop a groan escaping.

"I think you'll live," she announced, letting go of my hand. "Come on, while we're in here, let's see if we can find anything."

"No." I shook my head, moving closer and tilting my head down to whisper in her ear. "We don't know what he has in here. There could be cameras, or bugs, or anything."

She turned to speak into my ear, pulling my head closer. "I didn't think of that. Sorry. Is..." Her voice trailed off as she took a step closer, our bodies flush with one another.

My control snapped.

I stopped fighting myself.

I gripped her chin and twisted her head so our faces were lined up and slanted my lips over hers.

Fire blazed.

She opened up for me, hungry, demanding, tugging my head closer, pulling at my hair. I slid my hand down from her chin to her throat, feeling her pulse kicking wildly under my hand, and she moaned into my mouth. Reaching my other arm around her, I gripped onto her ass and pulled her even closer, grinding my dick into her.

I barely registered that she was shoving me away, until she was collapsed against the desk, breathing hard, her lips swollen and lust still thick in the air between us. "No. *No*. We can't do this. Not here, not now." Her voice came out hoarse and shaky.

Fuck.

"That—"

"—shouldn't have happened? Or were you going to say it was a mistake, again? That you don't want me?" she said bitterly. "Yeah, I know. I know all the lies you tell yourself, that you tell me."

She straightened up, smoothing her dress down and wiping a hand over her lips as if to scrub our kiss away. "I'm in agreement this time, though. This shouldn't have happened. It isn't the time or the place, not just because of the fact we might be being watched right now, but regardless of where we are, I wish it hadn't happened, because you just can't stop lying, to both of us. You're blowing hot and cold *all the fucking time*, Cade. You're messing with my head, and I can't deal with it anymore."

I didn't have anything to say back to her.

She looked at me expectantly, then when the silence between us stretched to breaking point, pushed away from the desk with an angry growl and stalked out of the room.

The rest of the evening went as well as could be expected—i.e. it was awkward as fuck. We ate a strained dinner, Winter avoiding even looking in my direction, West carrying most of the conversation with my dad. I did get my dad to agree to let me start shadowing him in the business, so at least the evening wasn't a total waste. He was very cagey about Tuesday nights, though, so that line of questioning was a dead end.

By the time we'd finished eating, we'd all reached our limits of patience.

Outside, I got into the car without saying goodbye to

Winter but rolled the window down so I could hear her conversation with West.

"You need a new back tyre. Look." He pointed, crouching next to the wheel arch and shining his phone light onto the wheel. "The tread's really worn."

She sighed. "Really? Great, more money to shell out."

Weston climbed to his feet and glanced over at me, then back at her. "Leave it with me, I can sort it for you. I know a place that does them cheap. Part-worn ones."

Because it was Weston, and she trusted him, she didn't even question it. "Thanks, that would be great. Let me know how much I owe you."

"No problem. I'll pick the car up early Tuesday morning, is that okay? You can give me your key on Monday at uni if you don't want to get up early."

"Yeah, perfect. I don't think I'll need to use it that day."

"Sorted." They hugged each other, and then he walked around and opened the R8 passenger door. He paused for a moment, leaning across the car roof. "Hey, Winter? You coming to the big bonfire night party next Saturday for Guy Fawkes?"

"What party?"

"Didn't you hear about it? At Alstone Castle?"

She shrugged unenthusiastically. "Oh, yeah. I don't know. Maybe. I'm not really in a party mood at the moment, but ask me again at the end of the week."

"I will. And you'd better be there."

She gave him a half-smile and got into her car, while Weston slid in next to me.

"Happy now?"

"Not really." I started the engine, and the car purred to life.

"When are you going to admit that you want her?"

"Don't fucking start," I warned, gripping the steering wheel so tightly that my knuckles turned white.

He huffed and slumped back in his seat.

We drove home in silence.

Pulling up outside the house, I couldn't shake the tension running through me. Weston climbed out of the car, slamming the door behind him, but I couldn't bring myself to move. I clenched and unclenched my fists on the steering wheel, my leg bouncing restlessly.

The next minute, Zayde was sliding into the car next to me. "Let's go."

I hit the music system and peeled away from the driveway with a screech, the sounds of Breaking Benjamin reverberating through the surround sound speakers, matching my black mood, and we raced down the country lanes and onto the wide road that ran parallel to the headland. I let the car fly down the mostly empty road at high speeds, adrenaline pumping through my veins.

We reached a smaller built-up area, with rows of red-brick Victorian terraced houses, all identical, and I turned the music down low. I slowed the car and cruised to a stop outside a house with a nondescript faded red door, my mood calmer after the rush of speeding down the empty roads in my R8.

Z punched out a message on his phone, and a couple of minutes later, a dark hooded figure emerged from the house, silently closing the door behind him.

Zayde rolled down his window, and the guy leaned in.

"Z." They bumped fists, and then he nodded to me. "Rich boy."

"Alright, Mack." Zayde handed him a roll of notes, and

Mack slipped a bag out of the sleeve of his hoodie, placing it in Zayde's hand.

"Cheers."

"See ya next time." Mack backed away from the car and jogged back to the house, disappearing inside. I started up the engine, smoothly pulling away and heading back towards Alstone.

The car was silent, moving through the empty streets, the sea on one side and fields on the other. As we reached the outskirts of Alstone, nearing our home, and houses became visible on the horizon, something caught my eye. I spun the steering wheel, screeching to a halt outside a large Regency-style mansion house, and I was up and out of the car before I could think twice, Zayde right there with me.

"Granville!"

James Granville turned around at my shout, annoyance crossing his face. "What do you want?"

In four strides I was in front of him, crowding him against the wall. He glared at me, pushing against my chest. "What the fuck, Cavendish?"

"I'm here with a warning. Stay away from Winter."

He gaped at me. "Are you serious?"

"Deadly. If I even hear a rumour that you've tried anything on with her, you won't like the consequences."

"Yeah? What are you going to do?"

"How does a broken jaw sound?" Zayde's tone was conversational, but his eyes were hard and icy.

"She belongs with us, not assholes like you. Don't fucking forget it." I shoved him, hard, in the chest, and he stumbled to the side, scrambling to get away from me.

"Alright, alright, I get it. She's not worth the hassle."

Bastard. I took a threatening step towards him, and the coward ran up the steps, fumbling in his pocket for his keys.

"Stay away from Lena, too," Zayde shouted after him, as the door slammed shut. He turned to me, shaking his head. "You don't want Winter, huh?"

"No."

"Deluded fool."

TWENTY

Winter

Saturday. Guy Fawkes. The day things took an unexpected turn.

The Four had talked me into going to the celebrations—well, Weston and Cassius had, anyway. All they'd tell me was that I didn't want to miss the fireworks.

"So, what happens at one of these things?" I asked Kinslee, not for the first time. She was standing at the kitchen counter, mixing some kind of cocktail for us both.

She turned around, ice cube tray in hand. "I told you. Fireworks, a bonfire, and games."

"I want to know what the games are. I need to know what I'm getting myself into."

Kinslee shrugged. "I don't want to spoil the fun. Last year was my first time, and it was all the better because I didn't know what was going to happen. You're going to love it, though, I guarantee. I wouldn't be so insistent about you coming, otherwise."

"I guess so."

She handed me a glass brimming with ice. "Drink up. Then we can go."

———

Our group of five girls from our apartment building crested the top of the hill and stopped. The castle stood out in stark relief, spotlights cycling through all the colours of the rainbow, lighting up the stones and casting long shadows across the clifftop. The castle itself and a huge area around it had been fenced off, and there was a gap with a queue of people waiting to enter, with two huge, bulky men dressed all in black scanning the barcode tickets on everyone's phones as they passed. Thumping music vibrated through the air, warring with the sound of the waves far below crashing against the cliff, and generators hummed loudly near the perimeter.

"Wow. This isn't what I was expecting." I sucked in a surprised breath, snuggling deeper into Caiden's hoodie, which I'd conveniently forgotten to give back to him after he'd let me borrow it.

"Welcome to Alstone College. Where if you have the money, you can turn a simple bonfire into a massive event," one of the girls laughed.

As we drew closer, I noticed a huge unlit bonfire, piled high with wood. To the far left was a makeshift bar area and a DJ with giant headphones next to it, just visible behind the huge sound system. Not what I was expecting, at all.

The security guy scanned our tickets and handed us each a strip of fabric as we entered. "What's this for?" I asked Kinslee, bemused.

"You'll need it later. Keep hold of it."

I shrugged, shoving it into my pocket, and tugged the

hood of Caiden's hoodie over my head. It was fucking freezing tonight, everyone's breath coming in clouds. I'd worn thermal leggings and black boots lined with sheepskin —not the most stylish outfit, but I was glad of the warmth.

I spotted a familiar face as we made our way closer to the castle. James leaned against the stone wall with a group of guys, all dressed in black. He normally looked suave and sophisticated, but tonight, dressed down with a hoodie, black jeans, boots, and a beanie hat pulled low on his head, I hardly recognised him.

"Hey." I smiled, hugging him. "How are things? I feel like I haven't seen you for ages."

A frown crossed his face as he released me, glancing around us, and spoke to me in a low voice. "Yeah. Well. I thought I'd keep my distance for now, after Cavendish and Lowry fucking threatened to break my jaw if I made any advances towards you."

"What? Are you joking? When?"

"Last week. The assholes cornered me outside my apartment."

For fuck's sake. "Were they serious?"

"Deadly. Honestly, Winter. I'm not afraid of them, but it's not worth my time to...y'know."

"Yeah." I sighed. "I'm sorry, James. I have no idea what their problem is."

He raised an eyebrow. "I would've thought it was obvious. Cavendish is into you, and he doesn't like to share."

Ha. "Hmm. He's pretty good at denying he's into me. But even so, he doesn't get to dictate who I'm friends with."

"Maybe you should try having a conversation with him. I'm sorry, too. I like you, Winter. You're gorgeous, and sweet, and fun to be around. But I don't want to cross him. His family could make things...difficult for my family."

"I see. Look, I'll speak to him. All I can say, again, is I'm sorry. Sorry you got caught up in all this. Caiden needs to learn that he doesn't get to control everything." My mouth twisted, and I stepped away from James. I needed to give Caiden a piece of my mind.

The group of girls I'd come with had disappeared while I'd been talking to James, so I wandered towards the bar, looking around to see if I could see anyone I recognised. I waved to a girl I vaguely knew from one of my classes and finally spotted Kinslee, at the bar already, drink in hand.

"Drink?"

"Not at the moment, thanks," I told her. "I had a feeling I'd find you here, though."

She laughed, then peered at me more closely, her brows pulling together. "What's wrong?"

"Oh, nothing. Only that I just found out from James that Caiden and Zayde threatened to break his jaw if he dared to flirt with me or anything."

Her brows shot up. "Wow. Caiden must be into you."

"Either that, or he's a possessive asshole."

"Both, probably."

"Th—" My words were cut off by a loud screech of feedback from the DJ's microphone, and his voice boomed around the headland, bouncing off the walls, echoing all around us.

"Ladies and gentlemen, welcome to Alstone College's annual Guy Fawkes celebration. I'm here to give you all a rundown of tonight's events for our newbies, and for those who need to refresh their memories."

He grinned widely. "We'll begin our first game in a few minutes. The captain of our winning team will do the honours of lighting the bonfire, then we'll get the party started. I'll announce a few more games during the evening, then we'll end the celebrations with a fireworks display that I've been promised will be even more extravagant than last year's, although I'm not sure how anyone could top that."

He stopped talking to take a swig of drink, then cleared his throat and continued. "When you arrived, you will have been given a strip of material: red or blue. This is your team colour for the first of tonight's games." He ducked down behind the table, then reappeared, holding up a strip of material in each hand.

"The material must be tied around your waist so that it can be easily seen. The object of the game is simple. Try to tag a member of the other team, without being caught yourself. If you're caught, you're out of the game and must give up your material to the person who tagged you and return to the area here." He pointed and the spotlights swung around to illuminate the large area in front of the DJ, where most of us were already standing.

"The winning team will be the team who has the most members remaining at the end of the game. When you hear this sound—" He pressed something and a loud klaxon sound echoed around us. "—that means the game is over. Everyone clear? Basically, try not to let the opposing team catch you."

I groaned. This sounded like hell. "Tag? Really? Do we have to do this?" I muttered to Kinslee.

"No, but it's fun. Get into the spirit of it."

Okay, I could do this. I wasn't usually one for these kinds of games, but the palpable excitement in the air was contagious, and despite my reservations, I found myself shifting towards the edge of the crowd, ready to run.

"Everyone, tie your material round your waists, and spread out as much as you can. When I sound the klaxon, the game will begin."

There was a rush of movement as people hurried to find a good hiding place. I tried to remember the layout of the ruins from my previous visits and quickly raced through the crumbling archway to the far side of the castle, my heart pounding. There was a gap where the walls were completely missing, then a little corner section where I should be able to hide.

As I reached the corner, I noticed someone else, also with red material tied around their waist, had beaten me to it, so I carried on going, flying across the remains of an open courtyard, weeds and cobbles underfoot. I skidded through another crumbling archway and flattened myself against the wall, trying to slow down my breathing. I distantly heard the klaxon and tugged my hood further over my head, edging around the corner, hugging the wall, to see if I could spot anyone from the opposing team without being seen. It was so dark over here. At least it was a clear night—the moon provided a dim glow, although the shadows were so black it was difficult to see.

I heard what sounded like a pebble being kicked, and I whirled around, but no one was there. I was suddenly grabbed from behind in an iron grip, my arms pinned behind my back. Fuck. Fuck. *Fuck*!

A hand clamped over my jaw, and I instinctively tried to bite at it but couldn't get my mouth open. My assailant was too strong.

Another figure appeared in front of me, hood up, a bandana with a grinning skull mouth covering most of their face other than their eyes, which were shadowed by their hood, so I was unable to make them out.

"What are you doing, hiding out here, all alone?" he whispered, his tone sinister, sending shivers through me. Definitely a man. If we hadn't been here, in the dark, I probably would have laughed this off—well, maybe—but here, I was starting to feel a tiny bit scared.

He raised his hand and the moonlight glinted off a sharp, wicked-looking blade.

I panicked and started to thrash around, my assailant still gripping me tightly. "Stay still and you won't be hurt," a muffled voice whispered in my ear. Something about his voice was familiar, and I stopped my thrashing, my panic receding slightly until the man in front of me stepped nearer.

I watched, helplessly, as he brought the blade closer, whimpering as the cold metal touched my cheek.

"So pretty," he crooned, moving the knife away from my face and trailing the flat of the blade down my body, in between my breasts, and down to my waist. I was frozen to the spot, not daring to move a muscle in case he accidentally cut me.

With a flick of his wrist, he sliced the fabric at my waist and it fluttered to the floor. The blade disappeared and I breathed a sigh of relief, only for my heart rate to kick up again when another hooded figure appeared, again with a skull bandana covering everything but his eyes.

"What do we have here?" He joined the other hooded figure. "What's a beautiful girl like you doing all the way out here, on this side of the castle, with nobody else around?"

My body relaxed at his words, and the person holding me removed his hand from my jaw, placing his arm around my waist instead. "Come closer," I challenged. "Let me see your eyes."

"Let me see yours," the man in front of me countered, stepping right in front of me and lowering my hood. "There you are," he murmured.

"Cass?" I questioned. I was pretty sure now that this was

three of the Four. What the fuck they were playing at, I wasn't sure, but what I *was* sure of was that they wouldn't harm me.

He didn't answer me but leaned forwards and lowered his bandana. He kissed me softly on the lips, then stepped back, sliding the bandana back into place. Definitely Cass.

"My turn," came that same sinister voice. That had to be Zayde. Only he could give off those creepy serial killer type vibes.

Cass moved to the side and Zayde was in front of me, cupping my cheek, then sliding his hand down to grip my throat.

"I could crush you so easily," he mused, pulling down his bandana and pressing his soft, full lips to mine. Despite his disturbing words, he kissed me gently, slowly, taking his time exploring my lips. *Nothing* like I would have imagined from him.

Whether this was some kind of game to fuck with me, I had no idea. This whole moment seemed so surreal, and somehow, I found myself kissing him back, experimentally, opening my mouth as he slid his tongue in. I gasped as smooth metal touched me. He had a tongue piercing? How did I miss that?

"Enough," came a voice, and Zayde released my throat, stepping away from me. I saw his face before he pulled the bandana back into place—he flashed me a quick grin, so unlike him, that I could only gape at him.

"You okay?" the person holding me whispered in my ear, and I nodded, as Cass switched places with Zayde. Again, he pulled his bandana down, and again, he kissed me softly, then pressed kisses along my face and down the side of my neck. "You taste so sweet," he groaned, sliding his hand through my hair.

My brain was scrambled. Was this actually happening, or was I hallucinating?

"What's going on?" My words were barely discernible, breathed rather than spoken, then Cassius was kissing me, and he had both hands tangled in my hair, and I could feel him growing hard against me. He was suddenly gone, and Zayde was back, running his tongue piercing over my lips, then, when I opened my mouth for him, swirling it around my tongue. He pressed his body against mine, one hand gripping onto my throat again, and the other sliding under my hoodie and T-shirt, onto the bare skin of my stomach.

I heard the klaxon sound somewhere in the distance as I moaned involuntarily, my eyes closed, my body reacting with pleasure at the sensations. Another hand joined Zayde's, inching higher. Someone brushed my hair away from my neck and kissed me there, then moved his mouth to my ear, nipping at the soft skin, making me shiver, before dropping his mouth back to my neck.

"Enough." The savagely growled command came from behind Zayde, and my eyes flew open. "I said, *enough!*"

"Are you sure about that?" Zayde turned around, shielding me from view. "Because now I've had a taste, I want more."

"Get. The. Fuck. Away. From. Her. Now." Caiden's tone was low and menacing.

Cassius removed his hand from under my hoodie and moved his mouth from my neck back to my ear. "We thought this might provoke him into action." He raised his voice so Caiden could hear, taunting him with his words. "Did we turn you on, babe? Did we make you wet? Because I'm horny as fuck right now."

"On a scale of one to stupid, this is the worst idea ever," I whispered, dread filling me.

"Don't worry," Weston breathed from behind me, his face close to mine. "He won't hurt you. And if he starts anything with any of us, we can take it."

In what world did it seem like this would be a good idea?

They were fucking *insane*.

I gritted my teeth and prepared for the worst.

TWENTY-ONE

Winter

The boys melted into the shadows, and it was just us.
Tension grew thick in the air as Caiden stared at me. His hood was partially obscuring his face, but his bandana was pulled down, and I could see the tight set of his mouth as he prowled towards me. I took a step back, then another, suddenly afraid. My back hit the cold stone wall, and suddenly there was nowhere else to go.

His hands hit the wall either side of me, and he leaned his body into mine.

"What the *fuck*, Winter?" His whole body was vibrating with anger.

I swallowed hard, trying to stop my voice from shaking. "Do you have any right to be angry?" I whispered.

"Yes, I fucking do," he snarled.

"Why?"

"Because you're not theirs."

Fury replaced my fear at his harshly spoken words. "You sound like a broken record, Caiden. I told you that I couldn't deal with this anymore. Leave me alone, *please*."

I pushed against his chest and ducked under his arm, running blindly, needing to get away from him. I tripped over a loose cobblestone, and I was falling, the ground slamming up to meet me.

Arms caught me, and he spun me around, pulling me to his chest. "Stop fucking running from me. You didn't let me finish," he gritted out through clenched teeth.

Manoeuvring my arms from his grip, I reached up a shaking hand and pushed his hood back, needing to see his face. In the dim moonlight, his eyes were hard, angry, black and fathomless like the ocean below us. "Finish, then."

"You're not theirs," he repeated, glaring at me.

"Yeah, I heard you the first time. Do you have anything else to add?"

He stared silently at me for a long time.

He let go of me.

He let me walk away.

Tears filled my eyes as I reached the castle wall once again, and I slumped against the stone, defeated, hidden by the shadows. He was never going to change. He was too fucking stubborn.

I sniffed, wiping a tear away, furious at myself for crying over him.

"Snowflake." I nearly jumped out of my skin at his voice, right behind me. I let him turn me around to face him, and our eyes met, his face blurry through my tears.

He let out a pained groan and grasped my face in his large hands.

The sob ripped from my throat.

"I'm not my mother. I wish you would see *me* when you look at my face. Not *her. Me.*"

"Winter." He kissed away a tear trailing down my cheek and wiped the tracks with the pads of his thumbs. "I know I'm fucked up."

"I can't do this with you anymore. It hurts too much," I whispered brokenly, shaking my head, attempting to move away from him.

"Don't go."

"Why?"

He was silent for a long moment.

"Because I want you, okay?" His voice was rough, low, and he wouldn't meet my eyes.

My heart stuttered.

"Look me in the eyes and tell me that."

I wasn't sure if he would. My heart was racing, and I could feel his own heart beating wildly against my chest. I kept my arms pinned to my sides, needing him to do this of his own accord.

I held my breath.

His stormy eyes met mine.

He took a deep breath, moving his head closer.

"I. Want. You." He rasped the words against my lips, his grip on my face tightening.

"Cade," I breathed and wrapped my arms around his neck, pulling his face to mine.

I could taste the salt of my tears as he claimed my mouth, taking what he wanted, pressing me into the wall. I moaned into his mouth, his kisses sending need throbbing through me, straight to my core.

He released my lips and buried his face in my neck, raising my hoodie and sliding his hands across my stomach. "You're wearing too many fucking clothes."

I shivered violently, both from his words and the cold

sea air that hit my bare skin as he exposed it. "Take me home. Or somewhere warmer."

I felt his words vibrate low against my throat. "Home's too far. I'll keep you warm." He picked me up, and I wrapped my legs around his waist as he carried me around the front of the castle. Lowering me to my feet, he grabbed my hand. "Come on. Climb over here. Careful." I let him guide me over a teetering pile of rubble, through a small gap, and then we were inside the remains of one of the rounded towers—open to the sky and the sea, but sheltered from the wind. We must have been close to the bonfire—the tower we were in was almost warm, compared to the temperature outside, anyway. I could see an orange glow coming from high above us, through the arrow slits, and hear music and the sound of people on the other side of the thick stone walls.

"You deserve to be punished," Caiden growled, pushing me up against the wall and nipping at my neck, then pulling my hoodie and T-shirt over my head in one go.

"No, you do," I told him, unzipping his hoodie and sliding it off his shoulders.

"You let them kiss you. Touch you." He undid my bra, ripping it from my body and throwing it to the side, then took my breasts in his hands and caressed them, his touch alternating between rough and punishing, and gentle.

"They weren't you," I gasped out between moans. "You're the only one who makes—" I stopped talking as he licked a line up from between my breasts to my jaw, then sucked my bottom lip into his mouth and bit it gently.

"Oh fuck," I moaned, wrapping a leg around him, grinding myself against him. I lifted the hem of his T-shirt, pulling it off, and the bandana with it. I scraped my nails down his back, and he shuddered, pressing his hard cock into me.

"I'm the only one who makes what?" He released my mouth, rasping the question against my lips.

"The—the—" I couldn't think. "The only one who makes me feel this way."

"What way?" He ran his teeth down the side of my neck, sinking them into my flesh as he bit me.

"Ow." I bit him back, digging my nails into him, and he hissed. "Like I'm on fire. All hot and burning up."

"Good." He rewarded me by slipping a hand into my leggings, and then his fingers were inside me, and on my clit, and I was riding his hand, desperate for more.

"I need you, now," I moaned, and he responded by dragging his fingers out of my wetness and using both hands to tug my leggings down.

"Get these off," he commanded hoarsely, and I kicked off my boots, ripping my leggings and underwear off, careful to stand on my hoodie rather than the stone floor.

I slid my hands up to his powerful shoulders, then down over the hard planes of his muscles, following my hands with my lips, kissing across his golden, inked skin. I licked across his nipples, and he jerked under my touch, groaning.

"Your body's so fucking hot." My voice came out husky and breathless, as I undid his jeans, impatiently pulling them down, along with his boxers. I wrapped my hands around his cock, and he groaned again, so loudly that it seemed to echo all around us. "*Caiden.*" I stroked my hands up and down, and he thrust into my grip, pulling me closer. "I really want to suck your cock."

"Not now," he ground out. "Later. Now, I'm going to pound my dick into you until you forget your own fucking name." With that promise echoing in my ears, he reached down into his pocket, pulling his wallet out and extracting a foil packet. He rolled on the condom, then lifted me and slid me down onto his hardness. I closed my eyes, crying out as he filled me completely.

"Fuck me, hard," I begged.

He kept his promise. We fucked hard and fast, up against the wall, his hands mostly protecting me from the stone; then he spun me so he was behind me and I was supporting myself on a stone boulder, his fingers working magic against my clit. He sent me spiralling higher and higher until I came, the blinding orgasm tearing through me, obliterating all thoughts. As I fell apart, I felt him coming hard inside me, digging his fingers into me, pressing my arms into the stone as he held me in place.

"Wow." That was the first thing I managed to say as he slid out of me and I tried to catch my breath, my heart pounding.

We both started pulling our clothes on, and he gave me a smile that was nothing like the usual expressions he sent my way, and it made my heart skip a beat. "Yeah."

I dropped my gaze. Swiping my T-shirt and hoodie from the floor, I pulled them over my head. Once I was fully dressed, I turned back to him, unsure how to react, hoping he wouldn't act like we'd just made a mistake.

He stared at me for a moment, biting his lip, then pulled me into him, wrapping his arms around me, and kissed my forehead. "Come on. Let's get back to the others."

Relief filled me. We made our way back to the main party, where the bonfire was now roaring, the smell of burning wood heavy in the air, smoke drifting towards us. Cade kept his hands shoved in his pockets, and we didn't speak, but the silence was comfortable rather than hostile. It wasn't like things were going to magically change overnight, but he'd admitted he wanted me, *fucking finally*, and that was good enough for now.

He spotted the boys over by the bar, surrounded by their usual groupies, and we made our way through the crowds to them.

"Did you fuck the hate out of each other, then?" were the first words out of Cassius' mouth, accompanied by a smirk. The girl hanging off his arm gave us a quizzical look, but no one bothered to explain anything to her.

Cade just rolled his eyes, ignoring the question, and headed round the back of the bar to help himself to a drink. Because of course the Four wouldn't wait in line like everyone else.

"Here." He pushed a drink into my hand. "There's only beer left."

"Thanks." I couldn't help the huge smile that spread across my face. I gulped the beer gratefully, purposefully ignoring the smirks and knowing grins that were coming from the others.

"You're so immature, sometimes, you know," I told Cassius, when, after about five minutes had passed, he still continued to wink, nudge me, and basically act like an annoying boy.

"Let me have my moment." He grinned, and I sighed, moving further away from him. Thankfully at that point, the DJ announced that the fireworks were about to begin, and everyone's attention turned to the sea. The fireworks were set up on a group of boats that were anchored just off the coast, so as they began to explode, their reflections danced across the water, throwing sparkles of colour all around.

I forgot where I was, my entire focus on the bursts of light in the sky, showering down on us. When a hard body pressed up against my back, I jumped, so engrossed in the fireworks that I'd tuned out everything else. Caiden's arms slid around me, into the pockets of my hoodie, and I leaned back against him.

"I see you."

There was a roaring in my ears, and the loud bangs of the fireworks echoed all around us, and I wasn't sure if I'd imagined his words.

"What did you say?"

He lowered his head and skimmed his lips over my ear.

"When I look at you. I see you. Not *her*. *You*."

TWENTY-TWO

I knew it would take a while for me and Caiden to act normally around each other, to find new footing after all our animosity. After the fireworks display, he released me with a muttered goodbye and headed off with the rest of the Four while I met up with Kinslee and the other girls I'd come with to walk back to our apartments.

Kinslee was acting shifty and avoiding me, so I cornered her when we were finally alone in our own apartment.

"Kins." She paused in the doorway of her bedroom, her shoulders slumped. "Talk to me. What's wrong?"

"I did something. Something I regret." She turned around to look at me uncertainly. "And I'm not sure how you're going to feel about it."

"Just tell me what it is."

"Um. I kind of kissed James. Well, more than kissed. We might have fooled around a bit, too."

"James Granville?" I raised an eyebrow.

"Yeah. I've always thought he was hot, but he wasn't my type. At all. Then, I don't know, something about him tonight, all dressed down for a change, and the atmosphere and everything...he caught me in the game we played while you were busy with Caiden... Ugh, maybe it was the cocktails we drank before we turned up—"

"Kins. You really don't need to worry. I have no problem with it. I slept with him like one time, and we had zero chemistry. We're purely platonic friends now. Well, we were until Cade and Z threatened him." I rolled my eyes, although, inside, now Cade had admitted he wanted me, I kind of liked that he'd done that.

Not that I'd ever admit it to him.

"Are you sure?"

"Of course I'm sure. Just stay away from Cade, and we're all good." I smirked at her.

"Ha ha. Everyone knows that he's yours. Even his fangirl groupies. Why do you think they try so hard to get his attention when you're around?"

"Because he's fucking hot? And one of the four most influential people on campus?"

"Well, there is that, too." She grinned. "But back to James. There won't be a repeat, I can promise you that. The more I think about it, the more I think it was a temporary lapse in judgement."

"I wouldn't worry about it. It happens to all of us." I walked over to the kitchen area. "Want a cup of tea?"

My phone buzzed as Kinslee and I were curled up on the sofa, catching up on trashy reality TV.

Cass: Pack a bag for tomorrow. Four business. AKA Operation Snowflake.
Me: WTF is Operation Snowflake?
Cass: Codename for our project. Cade's nickname for you.

Me: Right. Who came up with the codename?

Cass: Me. Obvs.

Me: Original. How about NO.

Cass: Better than West's suggestion.

Me: Do I even want to know?

Cass: No.

Cass: We'll work on the name.

Me: *eyeroll emoji* WE won't work on it. What is it you want me to do?

Cass: Just get a bag packed. We'll be at your place at 10.

Me: Fine. See you then.

Me: P.S. I really don't get your obsession with codenames.

"Looks like I've been summoned by the Four."

Kinslee sighed. "Your life is so much more exciting than mine."

"Exciting is overrated. You have no idea how much I'd love a normal life." To have parents that were both alive and loved me, to be able to go to university and get my degree, and enjoy student life without having all this drama hanging over me.

I missed my dad, so much.

As I walked into my room to get my stuff together, my eyes went straight to the collection of star charts and posters of constellations I'd tacked up above my desk, picturing my dad in his work office, poring over the latest research papers while the posters surrounded him. I had so few tangible things to remember him by; these posters had become some of my most treasured possessions.

Below the posters I'd arranged the framed photo he'd

had of the two of us in his office and his crystal ball model with the solar system suspended inside it.

I turned away and quickly packed my bag, before I could be overwhelmed with memories. I couldn't afford to fall apart—I had to stay strong so that I could get to the bottom of whatever was going on in Alstone.

———————

Nine fifty-eight. My phone buzzed.

Caiden: Outside.

This was the first message he'd ever sent me, and seeing his name on my phone gave me butterflies. Why, when it was a one-word message, I couldn't say. Last night felt like it had been a dream; the whole thing was so surreal. I wasn't sure how he was going to act around me today, but I guess it was time to find out.

Outside, I saw him leaning casually against his R8, hood up, his legs encased in dark jeans and black boots.

I licked my lips, nerves and those fucking butterflies racing through me again. "Hi."

His eyes met mine, his expression completely unread-able, and opened his door. "Let's go."

I slid into the cool leather interior and snapped my seat belt into place, sighing as the engine purred to life.

"Did I ever mention how pretty your car is?"

He gave me an unamused sidewards glance as we smoothly slid out onto the road, one hand relaxed on the wheel, the other on the gearstick. "It's not pretty."

"Oh, it is." I smiled and sat back in my seat, stretching

out my legs in front of me. Cade huffed but didn't say anything else.

"So what's going on, anyway?" I ventured, as we shot down the winding road towards his house.

"The boys decided we're going to the hotel to check it out." He continued staring straight ahead, his hand brushing my leg as he changed gear. I shivered.

"The hotel from the photo of my mother? All of us?"

"Yeah. No. You. Me. The boys are checking out other places of interest."

"What places?"

"Talk about it later." His tone was clipped.

"Why not now?"

"Leave it." He glanced over at me, and his expression softened slightly before he sighed. "We'll talk later, okay?"

I nodded, and we lapsed into silence for the rest of the journey.

We pulled up on the driveway, and Caiden beeped once. The door opened and Cassius, Weston, and Zayde piled out of the house, throwing last-minute instructions at each other. Cassius strolled over to us and leaned in my open window.

"Morning, babe. You okay? Recovered from last night?" He smirked at me.

"Fine, thanks." I was hyperaware of Caiden next to me, glaring over my shoulder at Cass.

"Someone get out of the wrong side of bed this morning?" Cassius raised a brow at him.

"Don't start," Caiden warned him. "Let's get this over with. I have other plans for later."

Why did I feel disappointed at his words?

Cassius straightened up and gave Caiden a mock salute, then headed over to his hulking SUV, where West was already waiting inside. They drove away, beeping the horn far too many times for a Sunday morning, and once the driveway was clear, Zayde straddled his beast of a bike, pulling his helmet over his dark hair. Snapping the visor into place, he shot off down the driveway and out of sight.

Finally, it was our turn to leave. I watched the sea as we drove along the coast road to Highnam, the car silent, both of us lost in our own thoughts.

When we reached our destination, apprehension filled me.

I climbed out of the car and stood, staring at the hotel perched on the cliff, where my mother had met the mysterious Littlefinger. A tall Victorian building, it had definitely seen better days. The cream paintwork was dirty, chipped, and peeling, and one of the windows had a spiderweb of cracked glass stretching across it, covered from the inside by what looked like duct tape.

"Okay. Let's do this," I muttered, pushing open the heavy wooden door and walking inside. The man behind the reception desk looked up from his newspaper as we entered.

"Uh. We're here to have coffee?" I eyed him hesitantly.

"Bar and restaurant's through there," he recited in a bored tone, pointing at a door to our left, and resumed reading his paper.

"Friendly bloke, isn't he," Cade murmured in my ear, steering me into the bar area with a hand on the small of my back.

I stopped dead as we entered, and he almost ran into me. "Look!" I hissed. "That's the table she was sitting at."

"You're right." His voice was low. "Come on." He walked over to the table tucked away in the corner and sat down, and I sat opposite him in the exact same seat my mother had been in.

I picked up a menu from the table, trying to appear unobtrusive while scanning the room. I felt really unnatural and like everyone was looking at me, even though in reality, no one was. There were about six other patrons in the room, chatting quietly and not paying any attention to us.

"Act normal." Caiden frowned at me.

"I'm trying. I'm just nervous."

He rolled his eyes. "Relax, will you."

I clenched and unclenched my fists, tapping my nails on the table.

"For fuck's sake." He stood up. "Stand up."

I rose to my feet immediately, and he grabbed my chair and dragged it around the side of the table so it was on the corner next to his, rather than directly opposite.

"Sit," he instructed, folding his large body back on to his own chair. I sank back into my seat, and he leaned over to me. "That's better." He slid his hand onto my jean-clad thigh under the table, and I gasped. He squeezed once—a warning, then moved his hand further up. My nerves disappeared as my whole world shrank to the place he was touching me. "You doing okay, there, Snowflake?" His voice dropped, turning from annoyed to a rough caress.

I could only nod mutely. I took a deep breath and raised my eyes to meet his unreadable gaze. He stared at me, then licked his lips, slowly, deliberately.

Fuck. Me.

I gripped the edge of the table to ground myself as his hand moved higher. He kept his eyes locked with mine the whole time.

"Can I take your order?" I jumped at the cold, intrusive voice.

"Two lattes," Cade barked out, without taking his eyes

from me. I heard footsteps retreat, and then it was just us, tucked away in our corner of the room.

I swallowed hard. His hand stopped, so close to where I really, really wanted him to touch me, but really, really shouldn't in a public setting.

"What's going on?" I managed to get the words out, my voice hoarse.

"I'm distracting you." An amused smirk tugged at his lips.

Why did he have to be so irritating, but so sexy? "Um. Okay?"

Before he could say anything else, we were interrupted by the waiter returning with our order.

"Two lattes." He set the crockery carelessly down on the table, sending coffee sloshing down the side of my cup.

I gasped, my hand flying to my mouth.

"Chill, it's only spilled coffee," Cade hissed as the waiter walked away.

"No." I stared after him, shaking my head. "*No.*"

"What is it?" Suddenly he was right in my face, lifting my chin so I was forced to meet his eyes.

"Him," I said urgently.

"What?"

"Him. The man. That was *him*. Littlefinger."

TWENTY-THREE

F uck.

"Are you sure?" I stared at her, her gaze bouncing around the room, her eyes wide, her chest rising and falling with sharp breaths. "Winter!" I tightened my grip on her chin, sliding my other hand around the back of her neck, and kissed her, hard. She gasped into my mouth, then kissed me back. I pulled away after a few seconds. "Calm now?"

She nodded, looking dazed.

"Good. You sure it was him?"

"I think so. I didn't get to look properly, but I definitely saw that the whole top bit of his little finger was missing. There can't be many other people around with missing fingers, can there?"

"Fuck. Okay. I wasn't expecting this. We need to get photos. West can run them through his facial recognition shit, and maybe we'll get lucky and find a match."

A thoughtful expression crossed her face. "Maybe..." she murmured to herself. Her blue eyes met mine. "Do you trust me?"

Do I?

She frowned when I took too long to reply. "Just give me ten minutes. Please. Trust me, Cade." She widened her eyes, giving me a hopeful look, staring at me from under her dark lashes.

"Okay." I found myself agreeing before I could think it through.

"Good." Her soft expression changed in a flash, a hard look coming into her eyes. "Follow my lead, and don't do anything to fuck it up. I mean it."

Me, fuck it up? What was she planning?

I didn't have to wonder for long.

She gulped down her coffee, then waved in the direction of Littlefinger, who had returned from the kitchen and was shuffling the pages of a newspaper, clearly bored. Four of the other patrons had left by this point, and apart from us, there was one elderly couple, who looked as if they were on the verge of falling asleep.

I watched as he lumbered to his feet, heading in our direction. Tall, built, pale, shaved head, a thin scar on his right cheek, he looked like a stereotypical goon from a crime movie. He flexed his knuckles as he drew closer, and I noticed the gold rings on his fingers.

"Hello." My head whipped around at Winter's sickly sweet tone. *What the fuck?* While I was watching Littlefinger, she'd taken off the hoodie she'd been wearing, and she was now sitting in a tiny low-cut top that showcased her perfect, perky tits. Worse, she was leaning forwards, giving Littlefinger a clear view down her top, batting her eyelashes and twirling a strand of her dark hair with one finger.

I clenched my jaw, grinding my teeth. The fucker was staring at her tits, and from his face, he liked what he saw.

Winter kicked me under the table. Then again. I

breathed in and out through my nose, trying to keep my cool as he openly ogled her.

"What can I help you with, my darling?" He had an accent I couldn't quite place. Possibly Russian.

"Do you have a moment?" Winter indicated the empty chair opposite her. He glanced around him, then shrugged.

"For a pretty girl, anything." He sank his huge bulk into the chair.

"I was just wondering if you could tell me anything about the history of this place, Mr... Oh. How rude of me! I haven't introduced myself. I'm Summer." A tiny, sly smile crossed her lips at this point. "And this is my brother, Barry. And you are...?"

Barry? What the actual fuck? And brother? Yeah, okay, I was technically her stepbrother, but. Yeah, no.

"Petr." He accepted her outstretched hand, shaking it firmly, ignoring me. "I'm afraid I don't know anything about the history of this place. I just work here." His face fell.

"That's a shame." She leaned forwards even further, pouting her lips, and I wanted to haul her over my shoulder and drag her out of there, and punch Petr's leering face simultaneously. "Oh!" she suddenly exclaimed, brightening. "That ring on your finger is beautiful. Is it a sovereign ring?"

"Yes." He beamed, clearly pleased with the attention, as he slid his hand across the table towards her.

"Ooh. It's beautiful," she purred, tracing her finger over it and simultaneously kicking my shin *again*. I could now see his finger clearly, and she was right. He was our man. I picked up my phone, and on the pretence of sending a text, snapped a photo of his hand. How I was going to get one of his face without him noticing, I had no idea.

While I'd been trying to subtly take a photo, Winter's finger was tracing along Petr's knuckles. Both mine and his attention were laser focused on her movements, his with pleasure, and mine...all I knew was I wanted to break every fucking knuckle on his hand.

"What did you do here?" she asked softly, indicating the missing fingertip.

I glanced up at his face just in time to see a hard, dangerous glint flash in his eye, his whole body tensing.

"Sorry, I didn't mean to pry." She withdrew her hand from his meekly, staring down at the table.

"It's okay, my darling. You have no need to apologise. It was a...gardening accident." He reached out and squeezed her hand, his thumb caressing hers, and she raised her eyes to meet his, brimming with faux sympathy.

I needed to break something. Preferably his face.

"You poor man. I'm *so* sorry. You know what, though? It makes you memorable." She actually winked at him. "I'll certainly remember the handsome man who so kindly took time out of his workday to answer my questions."

He preened, pleased with her "handsome" compliment, leaning closer to her, and I clenched my jaw harder. "It's always a pleasure to spend time with a beautiful woman such as yourself." He studied her more closely. "You look very familiar. Have we met before?"

She gave a light laugh that I could tell was forced, waving a dismissive hand in the air. "I always get people asking that. I've been mistaken for a Hollywood actress and a singer before. I guess I just have one of those faces."

"That must be it." Thankfully, he didn't pry any further. If he'd realised she looked like her mother, we would have been in serious trouble. Why hadn't I thought of that possibility? She could be in real danger. Shit.

"Well, my brother and I must be going now." She glanced at me, and her eyes widened as she took me in.

"Um, thank you so much for your time, Petr. Could I trouble you for a quick selfie with me before I leave? I'd love to post it on my social media and make my friends jealous that I got to spend my Sunday morning with you." She winked. A-fucking-gain.

"Of course, my darling." They both stood, and I had to watch as he put his huge beefy arm around her, and she snapped a series of selfies, giggling and pouting while he lapped up all the attention. Then she kissed his cheek, swiped her hoodie from her seat, and strolled off with a wave, her ass swaying in her tight jeans.

I stormed out after her. "What—"

"Don't. Say. A. Word," she hissed through clenched teeth, pulling her hoodie on as she walked. "He might be watching." Then, she added, "Barry," and I fucking snapped.

"Get in the fucking car, and not another word out of your mouth." I slammed the car into reverse and peeled out of the car park, spinning the wheels. Fuck. I needed to pull over somewhere to calm down.

A turn-off appeared to the left, and I threw the car into it, skidding around the corner. Winter fell into the door, unprepared.

"What the fuck, Caiden!" she shouted.

"I'm trying not to crash!" I roared at her, and she cowered back in her seat. Good.

There was an entrance to a field up ahead, and I slowed the car, pulling into the gap and bringing us to a stop. I released my death grip on the steering wheel, turned off the engine, and jumped out, slamming the door violently behind me.

TWENTY-FOUR

Winter

What should I do? And what exactly was his problem? I watched through the windscreen as he stood in the field, clenching and unclenching his fists. He ran a hand through his hair, and for a moment he looked so frustrated, so lost, I was up and out of the car before I knew what I was doing.

"Cade?"

"Don't. I can't." He refused to look at me.

"Caiden." I stepped right in front of him. "What's going on? Talk to me, please?"

"I don't fucking know, Winter." His eyes met mine. "I wanted to kill him and punish you, with the way you were all over each other. Then I was angry because I thought you might be in danger. I just...I don't know, alright!" He ended his sentence on an angry growl.

I stepped even closer and wound my arms around his waist. He stiffened but didn't push me away.

"You realise I was acting back there, right? It literally

made my skin crawl to touch him, thinking that he could be involved in whatever this is."

He moved one of his hands around my back, gathering a handful of my hair and bringing his other hand up underneath my jaw to lift my chin, cupping my throat.

"I don't like other people touching what's mine," he said roughly.

"Am I yours?"

He looked at me, his gaze hard and possessive. "We're fucking, and I don't share, so in that respect, other men better keep their hands off you."

"If that's the case, can I expect other women to do the same? Can I expect you not to be touching other women?"

"I'm not interested in any other women." He rubbed his thumb over the pulse point in my throat, raking his other hand through my hair, making me shiver, then released me.

Oh. "Since when? What about Portia? Jessa?" I bit my lip.

"I'm. Not. Interested."

"Good. Glad we're on the same page," I managed to say.

I stood up on my toes and put my arms around his shoulders, and his body relaxed slightly, some of the anger disappearing from his eyes.

"You called him handsome," he muttered, and I smiled.

"Were you jealous?" I ran my fingers over the short hairs at the back of his neck.

"No." He put his arms around my waist, pulling my body into his.

"You're lying again. I can tell." I kissed his jaw, the stubble scratchy against my lips.

"I'm not." He lowered his mouth to mine, biting my lip softly, before pulling back to look at me again.

I stared at him for a minute, trailing my eyes across the angular planes of his face. From his tousled raven hair, to his stormy grey-blue eyes edged with thick ebony lashes, to his stubbled jaw, and the sexy tattooed body that was underneath his clothes, he was insanely gorgeous by anyone's standards.

"Cade. I shouldn't even have to state the obvious, but I was trying to flatter him by calling him handsome, and, also, have you seen you? You're like—like a sex god or something!"

"That's true," he agreed with a smirk, the remainder of his anger dissipating, and I punched him in the arm, laughing.

Our moment was interrupted by his phone ringing loudly in the quiet field, and he pulled it out. "Cass... Yeah, coming now. Be there in twenty." He inclined his head at the car as he spoke into his phone, and we climbed in to make our way back to meet the rest of the Four.

At the boys' house we didn't even get to discuss the morning's events. Everyone decided they were suddenly hungry, so I offered to make sandwiches with Cass and West while Caiden and Zayde had a quick workout—I heard Caiden mention needing to punch something to Zayde; unsurprising, I guess, after his mood earlier. Speaking of punching, I was kind of shocked that none of the boys had a black eye courtesy of Caiden, after the stunt they'd pulled at the castle.

Sandwiches made, I sat with Cass and West in the large lounge area to wait for Caiden and Zayde. It was a little uncomfortable, to be honest, remembering the last time I'd been there and Cade had been all over that girl and I'd kissed Cass. I cast around for conversation to stop myself being lost in memories I really, really didn't want to be thinking about.

"How much longer will my car take?" I directed my question to Weston.

"Uh. It should be ready tomorrow. I'll phone the garage in the morning to check." He wouldn't meet my eyes, for some reason.

"I don't understand what's taking so long. I know you said they saw it needed new brake pads when they were replacing the tyres, but surely that should be a quick job."

"I said one of us would give you a lift if you needed to go anywhere."

"I know, and I appreciate that. It's not the point I was trying to make, though." Giving up on that line of questioning, I kicked my shoes off, curling my legs under me. "Never mind."

A thought suddenly occurred to me. "Hey, West? How come you don't have a car, anyway?"

"I have an Aston Martin on order. There's a waiting list." He pulled out his phone and proceeded to tell me, in much more detail than I needed, how amazing the Vantage AMS was and how he was having to get it specially resprayed in the matte-black paint that the Four seemed to favour.

After I'd looked at close to a hundred photos and watched no less than three YouTube videos of the car in action on Weston's phone, Caiden and Zayde finally strolled in. Cade had showered—his hair was damp and tousled, and he had grey sweatpants and a navy T-shirt on that stretched across his muscles. It went without saying that he looked so. Fucking. Hot.

His eyes arrowed straight to mine, and he smirked at my blatant ogling. Sauntering over to me, all sexy, powerful male, he threw himself onto the sofa, kicking up his legs onto the coffee table.

"Fooooood time!" Cassius shouted, making me jump, grabbing the tray of sandwiches and brandishing it in our direction.

Finally, after yet another delay, everyone had eaten, and we could discuss the events of the morning.

Cassius, Zayde, and Weston listened attentively as Caiden and I ran through what had happened at the hotel. Or, more accurately, I ran through the events, while Caiden grew more and more tense next to me as I described my harmless flirting, and the others agreed it had been a genius idea. Cass seemed to find it hilarious that I'd given Caiden the name "Barry," but after Caiden threatened to punch him in the face, he stopped taunting him. As I described how I'd touched Petr's hand to get a closer look, on the pretence of admiring his jewellery, Caiden growled under his breath and suddenly tugged me into his lap, putting his arms around my waist and burying his face in my hair.

I froze for a moment, noticing the mixture of surprise and amusement on the boys' faces.

I knew not to read too much into it. He was just possessive. And jealous, even though he wouldn't admit it.

It didn't stop my heart beating faster, though, and those damn butterflies from starting up again.

I finished describing the rest of the morning, minus the part where we ended up parked in a field thanks to Caiden's display of temper, and forwarded the selfies I'd taken with Petr to Weston's phone so he could put them into his computer and work his magic on them.

"Never underestimate a woman," Cassius said, as I trailed off. "I doubt any of us would have been that resourceful."

"Well, unless he'd been gay, I suppose," I mused. "Lucky for me, Petr seemed to like what he saw, and that worked in our favour."

"Course he fucking did," Caiden muttered in my ear. "He's got eyes, hasn't he."

"Was that a backhanded compliment?" I murmured.

"Take it however you want," he said dismissively and started tracing tiny patterns across my stomach with his fingers. I shivered at his touch.

"Anyway, back to business," Cassius instructed, spreading out a printed map on the table in front of us, with several highlighted squares, and ran his finger across it. "Alstone Holdings offices." His finger trailed lazily across the paper to a square marked on the coastline. "Then the docks, where some of the construction shipments come in. They're only small."

He tapped an area marked out on the map, almost directly between Alstone itself and the next town marked on the map, which happened to be Highnam, where Cade and I had been earlier.

"That's the warehouses, where most of Alstone Holdings' construction materials are stored, before they get taken around the country."

His finger moved to the last marked area. "Final place of interest, and the hardest one to gain entry to."

"AMC," Weston told me.

"What? Like the TV channel?" I stared at him.

"Obviously not." He rolled his eyes. "Alstone Members Club. Aka the boys' club. No girls allowed."

"I see." Visions of rich, misogynistic men smoking cigars and dressed in suits popped into my head. Probably not far from the truth, I'd bet.

"We're not allowed to officially join until we're twenty-one," Cassius said. "But we've started working on our dads to try and gain early entry. With my charm, I'm confident I can make it happen."

"If you say so." I leaned forwards, as much as I could with Caiden's arms still wrapped around me, shuffling on his lap to try and find a more comfortable position. "So, what happened?"

Caiden tugged me back and I fell against him. "Stop wriggling," he hissed in my ear. "You're making my dick hard."

"Oh. Shit. Sorry."

"Don't be sorry. Save it for later, though, when I can do something about it, yeah?"

"Uh, yeah. Okay," I mumbled, flustered. Now he'd mentioned it, I could feel him pressing into me. I squeezed my legs together, suddenly needy and aching for him, and he groaned into my hair.

"Snowflake."

Weston turned to me, thankfully either oblivious or choosing to ignore what was going on right in front of him, and I forced myself to stay as still as possible and concentrate on what he was saying. "We split up and covered all the marked areas. Z took the docks and warehouse; me and Cass took AMC plus a quick drive by of the offices."

"Did you find anything?" Caiden and I both listened intently as the boys took it in turns to describe everything. As it turned out, they hadn't discovered much. Security at all four locations was high, despite it being a Sunday. It was understandable for the docks and warehouses, since there was always the threat of theft of valuable construction materials. The offices were closed, and there was no way to get in without being security cleared. As for AMC...no chance. Not unless you were a member. Cassius and Weston had even prowled the alleys to try and find a back way in but came up empty-handed.

"We're not giving up, though," Caiden reassured me. He moved me off his lap and leaned forwards to grab a blunt from the ashtray in front of him, lighting it and inhaling deeply. He passed it to me, and I took a long drag, relaxing into the sofa.

"I'm gonna run those photos through the software now," Weston announced. "If I have no luck I'll have to get in touch with my contact, but that could mean it takes a few days. I'm also waiting on another contact who's going to hook us up with some amazing tech. Once that's here, I'll get everyone together to go through it." He picked up his phone. "In the meantime, I need everyone to use the app I installed on your phones. It means we can track each other with GPS through a secure connection that only the five of us can access. Can't be too careful."

"And I'll pay a visit to my parents today, work more on getting Dad onside for getting into the club early," Cassius promised.

Zayde looked at me. "I'm going to meet with an old friend."

"Are you going to elaborate on that?" I raised a brow.

"He knows people. Shady people."

"Right."

Cassius spoke up. "Everyone clear on what's happening?" No one spoke. "Good. Think we're done here. I'm off to my parents', then." He stood and headed out of the room, Zayde following. I heard the front door slam shut behind them, and I was left with Caiden and Weston.

"I'll be in the computer room if you need me," Weston announced, getting to his feet and stretching. He padded out. Just me and Caiden left.

I suddenly felt awkward, remembering Caiden's earlier comment to Cassius about having plans later today. He was probably waiting for me to leave. "Um... I'm...going to take my bag upstairs and change into something else."

Practically running out of the lounge, I made my way up the stairs towards the guest room, stopping to grab my bag, which I'd left in the hallway.

"Where do you think you're going?"

I turned in the doorway of the guest room at Caiden's voice.

"I thought you said this morning you had other plans for later."

He took a step closer. "Yeah. I do. Your mouth, and my dick, Snowflake."

"Caiden!" My cheeks heated.

He smirked at me, his usually stormy eyes gleaming with amusement. "I seem to remember you saying yesterday, and I quote, 'I really want to suck your cock.'"

Oh, yeah. I did say that.

"And you owe me. Big time."

"For what?"

"Earlier. The hotel." He flashed me a savage grin, and I gulped, suddenly nervous.

"Uh..."

He took another step towards me. Then another.

Then he lunged for me. I squealed and darted into the room, dropping my bag and slamming the door in his face.

He kicked the door open with a loud crash and prowled towards me with intent, and I raced around the bed.

"Why are you running from me?" His voice was curious, his lips tipped up at the corners.

Fuck, he was sexy.

"Because it's fun?" I shrugged, a smile curving over my own lips.

"You can't escape, you know."

He vaulted onto the bed and over the other side, scooping me up in his arms. I put up a token struggle, but I couldn't really resist him.

I clasped my arms around his neck as he carried me out of the guest room and into his bedroom, kicking the door shut with his foot. He laid me on the bed, and I kept hold of his neck, trying to tug him down with me.

"Oh, you want me now, do you?" he drawled.

I responded by wrapping my legs around his hips to drag him down on top of me. "Less talking, more sex, please."

He was totally on board with that plan.

TWENTY-FIVE

I woke to an empty bed. Padding into the guest room, I stood under the shower until I felt human again, letting the hot water soothe my sore, aching muscles. Not that I could soothe the ache between my legs. I shivered. The things I'd done with Caiden yesterday. His tongue...his fingers...oh, and his dick...

Focus.

I had a plan for today. After my morning classes, I had the rest of the day free thanks to a cancelled afternoon lecture, and I was going to use it to meet my mother, if I could persuade the others to help me out.

First things first. I had to call her.

"Winter? Why are you calling so early?" was her greeting.

"Mother. Are you free this afternoon? I thought we could meet for coffee."

I heard her sigh heavily. "I *am* going to be in Alstone this afternoon, so I suppose we could meet. Do you know the Wilson Lounge?"

"No, but I'm sure I can find it."

"Meet me there at two thirty, sharp. Dress smartly, Winter. It's an upmarket establishment, not a student hovel."

Ha. Had she even seen Alstone College? "Yes, okay. See you then."

"Goodbye." She ended the call before I could say anything else.

Step one complete. Next step, see if someone could drop me in Alstone. I couldn't wait to get my car back so I could stop relying on others to take me everywhere.

"Cass, can you do me a favour?" I eyed him hopefully over my bowl of cereal as I sat at the kitchen island. We had a lecture together first thing, so he was driving me to university. Apparently, Cade and Z had gone to the gym. Why, when they had an amazing gym in their basement, I had no clue. "Could you drop me in Alstone town later? I'm meeting my mother. I want to try and get her to talk to me about my dad."

He rose from his seat and came around the island, giving me a quick one-arm hug and dropping a kiss on my head on his way to the dishwasher. "Yeah, course. What time?"

"Two thirty. Actually, better make it a bit earlier so she doesn't complain about me being late."

"Will do. Come on, we'd better get going, or we'll be late." I followed him into the hallway, grabbing my bag, and he shouted for West. He came running down the stairs, and together we headed out.

"Winter?" West leaned forwards from the back seat of the car, and I twisted around to look at him. "I couldn't get any matches for those photos of Petr. I've forwarded them on to my contact to see if he can come up with anything."

"Shame. Thanks, though." My face must've fallen, because he squeezed my shoulder comfortingly.

"Don't worry. If anyone can dig up info on this guy, Mercury can."

"Mercury? What kind of name is that?"

"Code name," Cass informed me.

Of course. I rolled my eyes.

"This isn't just for fun," West told me. "It's way too dangerous for us to give our real names online. We have a policy to never reveal anything about ourselves."

"Oh." That actually made sense. "Are you sure we can trust him with this?"

"Positive. He's always come through for us before. He won't let us down."

His voice was confident, certain, and I relaxed at his words. At the moment, it felt like all we had were a few random puzzle pieces, but hopefully, once we had some info on Petr, we could start putting the pieces together.

———

Later, sitting in our morning lecture, Cassius leaned over and told me in a low voice about his successful dinner with his parents the previous night—how his dad had seemed receptive to the idea of letting the Four join the Alstone Members Club early, after Cass had pointed out that they were technically adults, and some shit about it being good for networking and male bonding or whatever.

We were making our way out of the lecture hall when the TA, Joseph, who insisted on students addressing him by his first name, pulled me to one side. "Winter, can I have a quick word?"

I nodded and told Cassius I'd meet him later, then

followed Joseph to the desk, where our professor was gathering his jacket and laptop bag. He smiled at me, clapped Joseph on the shoulder, and left the room.

Once he'd disappeared from view, Joseph turned to me. "I'm concerned, Winter." His eyes narrowed as he studied me. "I noticed you whispering with Mr. Drummond instead of paying attention to the lecture. You're a strong student—I don't want the bad influence of Mr. Drummond and his little crew of degenerates to be responsible for your grades dropping."

What? The words came tumbling out of my mouth in an angry rush. "Look. I'm sorry I wasn't paying attention today, but my grades are consistently high, and you know that. What's more, Cassius' are even higher than mine. When you've got a valid concern, speak to me then, but don't try and insinuate that there's an issue with my grades when we both know there isn't one. And"—my voice rose—"how dare you call his friends degenerates? Do you realise I could report you for slander? I don't think the dean would take too kindly to one of his star PhD students speaking like that about other students."

He gaped at me, then straightened up. "I think we're finished here," he said stiffly.

What was his problem? Asshole.

I turned on my heel and left without another word, almost running straight into Cassius, who was lurking just outside the doorway.

Oh, no. "I thought you'd left. Did you hear that?"

He stared down at me, his eyes wide and serious. "Yeah. You defended us." His voice was full of wonder.

"Of course I did. I wouldn't let anyone speak like that about any of you."

He suddenly reached out and pulled me into a tight hug,

kissing the top of my head, before releasing me. "I'll see you later, okay?"

"Yeah. Thanks, Cass." I watched him jog away from me, then, shaking off the TA's weird behaviour, I focused on the task at hand.

After going back to my apartment to change into a black wool dress, thick tights, and flat black ankle boots, and wolfing down a quick lunch, I met Cass, and he dropped me in the centre of Alstone outside an elegant white building with a pillared entrance and a smart black door, which was open. "The Wilson Lounge" was engraved in a small plaque next to the door, above an old-fashioned brass doorbell.

Inside I was greeted by a hostess in a crisp white shirt and black skirt, who led me to a small round table covered in a white cloth, next to a tall sash window. As I sat down to wait for my mother, my phone vibrated, Weston's name flashing across the screen.

West: Just heard from the garage. Your car's delayed by another day. Sorry.
Me: It's OK. It's not your fault. I can wait an extra day.
West: You've got more patience than me.
Me: Says the person who's been waiting over 6 months for his dream car.
West: *laughing emoji* True. Some things are worth the wait.

A throat cleared, and my nose was hit by a waft of expensive floral perfume. I dragged my gaze upwards to see my mother eyeing me with disapproval.

Me: Got to go.

I stood and greeted her, both of us with forced politeness —my mother, constantly aware of the presence and hushed conversation of those around us, her eyes darting around the room, and me, because I needed to dig for information.

After we'd ordered coffees, she leaned forwards in her chair, clasping her hands together on top of the tablecloth.

"Did you have a reason for wanting to meet with me today?"

I made a snap decision to go with a direct approach.

"I just wanted to ask you when you last saw my dad." I kept an innocent, bland expression on my face as I continued. "He was going to visit you the day I left for university, wasn't he? I'm sure that's what he'd planned to do, anyway."

"I don't recall the last time I saw him. Not since I married Arlo." Her eyes met mine, glacial and completely devoid of emotion.

Lies.

I knew she'd met my dad—because he'd sent me the text to say so. He had no reason to lie to me, and the only reason she'd be lying right now is if she had something to hide.

Dredging up every bit of self-control I could, I kept my voice even and my posture relaxed. "Did you ever hear anything from him?"

"Winter. I hadn't seen or spoken to him for a very long time. I know it's not what you want to hear, but your father and I didn't part on the best of terms, and our relationship never recovered."

We were interrupted by the waitress with our coffees, and my mother jumped on the chance to change the subject.

"I've been meaning to speak with you regarding your relationship with your stepbrother." She pursed her lips disapprovingly as she stared at me.

"Which one?"

"The eldest. Caiden," she said, as if I wasn't aware of who she was talking about. "I've heard some distasteful rumours that there may be something going on between the two of you. I want you to keep your distance. I shouldn't have to remind you, but he's your stepbrother. And, my dear, that boy is nothing but trouble."

I bristled. "Really? In what way is he trouble, exactly? Please, enlighten me." *Shut up shut up shut up.* Why was I provoking her?

She delicately sipped her coffee and threw me a disdainful glance. "Don't insult my intelligence by playing stupid, dear. He's rotten to the core. In and out of trouble ever since he was a child. It's no wonder his mother took her own life, with a son like that."

What. The. Fuck.

I reeled back, stunned, suddenly short of breath. There was a loud ringing in my ears, and spots danced in front of my eyes.

"Winter! Winter!" I blinked, the room coming back into focus as my mother's face appeared in front of me. "You're causing a scene," she hissed.

"Sorry," I mumbled. I wiped my sweating palms on my napkin and tried my best to get my erratic breathing under control. Swallowing hard, I met her gaze. "What did you say about his mother?"

"She took her own life."

My heart lurched in my chest. "That's awful. I'm so—"

"Coward."

"Excuse me?"

"She was a coward."

"Tell me you did not just say that!" My mouth dropped open in shock. "How fucking *dare* you call her a coward! She must have really needed help, help that she never got, to feel that was her only way out. Bloody hell, Mother, your heartlessness astounds me."

I lurched to my feet, shaking with rage and staring down at her. She stared back, not even a flicker of remorse in her gaze. "I'm leaving, before I say something we both regret."

"Don't tell Weston. Arlo and Caiden don't want him to know. Poor boy," she tutted with faux sympathy.

I have never, in my entire life, wanted to punch someone, but at that moment in time, I wanted to break her fucking emotionless face. I whirled around and stormed out of the building, gasps and scandalised whispers following me.

I had to get away from her toxic presence.

I ran.

Eventually, lungs burning, I sank to the ground where I was, away from the buildings, supporting my back against a crumbling brick wall. Rifling through the contents of my bag for my phone, I pulled it out and scrolled through the contacts.

I pressed his name before I could even think it through. I *needed* to hear his voice.

The phone rang and rang, and eventually his voicemail kicked in. I whimpered, ending the call and dialling Cassius instead.

"Winter?"

A choked sob escaped my throat. I couldn't speak.

"What's wrong?"

I swallowed hard. "Cade didn't answer his phone. Do you know where he is?" I managed to say.

"Sorry, babe, he's off doing some shit with Z. He's probably turned his phone off. He'll be back later. You okay?" His voice was concerned.

The tears came.

"Shit, Winter. What did that bitch do to you? Do you need me to come and get you?"

"No!" I sat upright, trying to compose myself. "I-I don't want to talk about *her*. And Kinslee's coming."

"You sure?"

"Yes," I croaked through my tears.

"Hey, it's gonna be okay." His voice was strong and reassuring. "You want me to get Cade to phone you back?"

"No," I whispered. "It's alright. Thanks, though."

"You know you can call me anytime, alright?"

"Yeah. Thanks." I swiped under my eyes, trying to stem the flow of tears. "Got to go."

I let the phone fall from my hand as I drew my knees up and buried my head in my arms and cried. Cried for the woman who had been in such a dark place that she'd taken her own life, for the two boys who had lost their mother, for the husband who had lost a wife. And instead, she'd been replaced with *my* mother, a cold, unemotional woman, who had no empathy or love to give these people who had had a piece of them ripped away.

Fuck. Cade had this huge, heavy secret that he'd had to carry around, hiding from his brother. Knowing what I did of Arlo, I doubt he would have provided much comfort. Had Caiden been all alone in this? The thought broke my heart. I so, so hoped Cass and Zayde had been there for him. And no wonder Caiden had hated me so much. I would have, too, if I were him. I never stood a chance, not with Christine Clifford as my mother.

Eventually, I calmed myself enough to pick up my phone and call Kinslee.

"Winter?" Her warm voice came through the speaker.

"Are you busy?" My voice was hoarse and cracked.

"Winter? Are you okay? Where are you? You need me to come and get you?"

"Please. I'm not sure where I am." I looked around me, no landmarks to give me a clue. "I think I'm somewhere just out of town."

"Send me your location from your maps app. I'll find you. Be there as quick as I can."

"Thanks."

When she picked me up, she took one look at my face and declared we were having a girls' night in with popcorn, chocolate, and cheesy movies. She didn't pry, just squeezed my hand and said she was here if I wanted to talk.

I appreciated it more than she'd ever know.

Later that evening, lying in my bed, I went over everything I'd discovered from the disastrous meeting with my mother. I had actual proof that she was lying about my dad now. The stuff about Caiden and Weston's mum, though...I didn't even know how to begin to unpack that. If Cade ever wanted me to know, he should have been the one to tell me—my mother had no right to say anything. How was I going to be able to act normally around him, without blurting it out? And even worse, how was I supposed to keep it a secret from West?

My phone interrupted my melancholy thoughts, vibrating across my desk.

Weston.

West: My brother really likes you.
Me: Hi to you too. And ??? Likes sleeping with me?!
West: I don't mean that. He's catching feelings.

Me: What? Why do you say that?
West: He's a bit drunk.
Me: ???

The three dots appeared as I sat on my bed, impatiently waiting for Weston's reply. After about five minutes had passed, maybe longer, I suddenly got a long message from him.

West: Cass told him you phoned earlier & you were upset. Said you were trying to get hold of him. He's worried about you. I can't remember him ever stressing about a girl before. I know he's drunk but he's been talking about you nonstop for the past 10 mins. Not just in a friends kind of way either. Can't explain it properly but if you were here you'd see.

Right. He'd barely admitted that he wanted to sleep with me; I highly doubted that he had actual feelings for me all of a sudden.

Me: Um. I don't know what to say to that.
West: He really likes you. I can tell.
Me: He's drunk. Don't read too much into it. He's worried because he's a good person underneath his asshole exterior. You can tell him I'm OK.
West: Are you OK though? I'm worried too after what Cass told me.
Me: Yes. Mostly. Just more shit with my mother. Talk about it tomorrow?
West: OK. Come for pizza? Z can pick you up. Your car will be ready too.

Me: Finally! No more relying on people for lifts.
Sounds good. What time?
West: I'll check with Z and let you know.
Me: OK.
West: See ya tomorrow.
Me: *thumbs up emoji*
Me: Thanks for checking up on me BTW.
West: I care about you.
West: NOT in the same way as Cade.
Me: Haha. Love you too.

TWENTY-SIX

"Ever been on one of these before?" Zayde raised a brow at me.

"Nope. But it can't be too hard, right?" I eyed the bike doubtfully. I pulled the straps of my small backpack tighter and stepped closer to the huge beast of a machine. Taking in my expression, Zayde gave me an amused smile and handed me a shiny red helmet.

"Wear that. Hold on to me, and lean with me. Okay?"

"I guess so." He straddled the bike, all dark, lethal male, with ripped jeans and black boots and his leather jacket stretched over his biceps. Yeah. Not that I was interested, but he was insanely hot.

And he still scared me, to be completely honest.

Pulling the helmet on, I climbed onto the bike behind him. He reached back and pulled my arms around his waist, then snapped his visor down. The engine came to life with a powerful roar that I felt through my entire body, and I screamed, mostly with excitement but partly from fear as we shot away from the campus and onto the main roads. I hung on to Zayde with a death grip to begin with, but once I got used to the feel of the bike, I loosened my grip slightly, leaning into the turns with him. By the time we came to a halt outside the Four's house, I had a huge smile across my face.

"That was amazing," I told him as I climbed off the bike on slightly shaky legs and handed him the helmet I'd been wearing.

"Give me a bike over a car any day." He jogged up the steps to the house, leaving me next to the bike.

"Hey, wait. Where's everyone?" The driveway was completely empty.

He paused with his hand on the door and turned back around to face me. "Don't know where Cass is. Cade and West have gone to pick your car up."

He disappeared inside the house, leaving the door open for me. I reached the front steps when I heard the distinct low, throaty purr of Caiden's R8 and spun around.

He stepped out, and I drank him in.

"Hi."

"Hi." He was distant, closed off, his face an inscrutable mask.

"Winter!" came the shout, and I tore my eyes away from Caiden's to see Weston grinning at me, standing next to my car.

Except it wasn't my car.

"What happened to my car?" I ran towards Weston and skidded to a halt in front of my little Fiat 500.

"Caiden asked the garage to make a few improvements," he told me in a low voice. "And don't let his appearance fool you—I think inside he's second-guessing himself, thinking maybe he made the wrong decision. What your reaction might be, you know?"

My gaze bounced between Weston, Caiden, and my car.

"How much do I owe for all this?" I whispered to West.

"Nothing. Cade felt bad about vandalising your door. Not just that. Bad in general, I think, for all the shit he did to you. So he took care of it."

My heart started beating faster.

I took a step closer to my car and trailed my hand over the smooth metal, my lips curving into a smile. The scratched and chipped burgundy colour was gone, replaced with matte-black paintwork. The exact same paintwork that Zayde's bike and Cade and Cass' cars sported. I walked around the car, examining it from every angle, noting the tinted windows and the huge shiny black rims complete with low-profile tyres.

Honestly? I think I was in shock.

When I reached the front of the car again, I glanced over at Cade, who was still watching me impassively, and turned to West, who had a huge grin on his face. "Thanks. Can you give us a minute?"

"Yep." He gave me a quick hug and bounded into the house, leaving me and Caiden alone.

We stared at each other.

I moved closer to him.

"Why?"

He shrugged, his hands in his pockets, leaning against the side of his car. "Because." His tone was final.

"Okay. Well, thank you. I don't know what to say, other than I love it. So much." I stood awkwardly in front of him, scuffing my toe in the gravel. He looked at me in silence for a minute, then made a low noise in the back of his throat and grabbed me around the back of the neck, spinning me so I was pressed up against his car.

Then his mouth was on mine, and I was lost in him.

He gripped my neck more tightly, kissing me fiercely, and I pulled him closer, returning his kiss with everything I had. Butterflies were rioting low inside my stomach, and I moaned, gripping his ass as he thrust his growing hardness against me.

"You two gonna stay out there all night, or what? Come on, me and Z are waiting to order pizza." Weston's shout interrupted our moment, and Cade released my neck, stepping back, running a hand through his hair. He looked about as dazed as I felt.

I collapsed back against the car, short of breath, my heart racing, trying to gather my composure. Once my breathing had mostly returned to normal, I moved over to Zayde's bike, where I'd left my bag.

"Come on." Caiden inclined his head towards the house, and I followed him inside. He stopped me in the empty hallway just outside the lounge. "We'll continue that later." Dipping his head, he kissed the tip of my nose, then tucked a piece of hair behind my ear, before strolling into the lounge to meet the others. What were we doing? Were we still just "fucking," as he'd put it, or was West right? Was he starting to like me more? He was bloody impossible to read.

I sighed. No point worrying about it now, anyway. While things were going well, I didn't want to rock the boat.

My stomach growled, reminding me that I hadn't eaten since breakfast.

First priority—pizza.

Hours later, the pizza had been demolished, and we were all lazing around on the sofas, Fast & Furious 10, or whatever number we were on, playing on the huge TV, and the boys were discussing cars while I browsed my social media.

A loud, insistent beeping sounded from Weston's phone,

and he bolted upright. "Be right back," he threw over his shoulder, rushing out of the room.

"Getting a drink. Anyone want one?" Zayde stood, stretching.

"Yeah, JD and Coke, please, mate. Plenty of ice." Cade glanced at me. "You want one?"

I nodded, and he held up two fingers to Zayde.

Cade and I were sitting at opposite ends of the sofa, and when Zayde had left the room I decided to take my chances. I crawled across the sofa and climbed into his lap, straddling him.

He gave me a lazy, sexy grin, his hands coming to my sides. "Hey there, Snowflake."

"Hey." I met his eyes. "I wanted to say thanks. For my car. Again."

"I owed you."

"You really didn't."

"I did." He leaned forwards and gathered my hair to one side, then grazed his teeth down my neck and kissed my throat, before he drew back to look at me again. "I'm not a nice person, Winter."

"I don't believe that."

"You should." His voice was rough, insistent. "I don't have the capability to be nice. I fuck everything good up."

My heart twisted. I ran my nails up his chest, feeling his muscles contract under my fingertips, and his breath hitched. "You're wrong."

"I'm not." Sighing, he lifted me off his lap, just as Zayde came strolling back into the room with our drinks.

"Not interrupting anything, am I?" he drawled.

"No," Caiden said shortly, taking our drinks from Zayde's hand, ice cubes clinking in the glass tumblers.

"Good, because I found a friend."

Cassius sauntered into the room. "Miss me?"

"No." That was from Caiden.

"Yes." Me.

He grinned, a smug, satisfied grin, as he flopped down onto the sofa next to me. "I'm gonna become everyone's favourite person in a minute. Where's West? He needs to hear this."

"I'll find him," I offered, jumping up before anyone else could say anything. I didn't have to go far. I almost ran into him in the doorway, and only his quick reflexes stopped us from clashing.

"I've got news." He brandished a laptop at the room in general.

"Tell us in a minute. I need to announce my news, first," Cass insisted.

"Fine." Weston placed the laptop on the coffee table, then took a seat on the floor, looking at Cass expectantly.

"Are you ready for this?" He smiled widely. "I succeeded in my mission. Operation AMC is a success!"

Everyone stared at him, our expressions ranging from blank to unamused.

He frowned, then tried again. "The board members voted, and thanks to my dad's persuasion, they agreed to let us have a trial run at Alstone Members Club."

"Fuck, yes!" Caiden punched the air. "Nice one, mate."

"Why didn't you just say that to begin with?" I asked him.

"I did." He gave me a confused look, and I shook my head.

"Never mind. Well done, Cass."

"It'll be a kind of probationary period, to see how we get on and if we can behave or whatever," he told us. "But I haven't told you the most important part yet."

He paused dramatically, and both Cade and Z rolled their eyes at him. "Our first visit to the club? Tuesday evening, and my dad told me that Arlo will be there. And what's more, apparently he's there *every* Tuesday."

I gasped. "My dad's notes. This is our chance to find out what's going on."

"My news ties in with this, too." Weston opened the laptop, spinning it around so we could see the screen. "Mercury came through for me. We have our man."

The dossier was short. Petr Ivanov, aka "the Fixer," originally from Belarus. Age thirty-four, suspected criminal ties with several Eastern European gangs. Five arrests and three short stints in prison—all for petty crimes—theft, shoplifting, drug possession. There were several photos including two of his police mug shots.

"It's not much to go on, but it's a start. Mercury's gonna do some more digging, see if he can come up with anything else. We need to work out how he's connected to your mother and to Alstone Holdings. So far Mercury hasn't been able to find any connection, but there's always a paper trail somewhere."

I sat back, thinking. "Well, we know more than we did before. And I can't help but feel that Alstone Members Club is the key."

Caiden took over from me. "Yeah. I agree. We need to go in there with our eyes wide open. Be prepared for anything, but don't arouse suspicion."

Hope sparked to life inside me. Maybe after Tuesday, we'd have some answers. Maybe I'd finally be able to get justice for my dad.

"This all great news. I guess, though, since we're talking about it all, I should mention yesterday. I don't know what Cass said..." I trailed off, looking at him.

"Nothing. Just that you were upset on the phone. And since I dropped you off to meet your mother, I'm assuming she upset you?" he murmured.

"Yeah." I had to tread carefully. I couldn't bring up what I'd discovered about Caiden and Weston's mum. "Basically, she lied to my face, saying she hadn't heard anything from my dad for ages before he died. It all got too much for me—that woman is so fucking frustrating. I can't believe I'm related to her."

"You can be frustrating, y'know. Just saying."

I turned to glare at Caiden.

"So can you."

He grinned, unapologetic. "I know."

Weston yawned widely, then flashed me a quick smile. "I'm sorry you're related to her, but look on the bright side. You get me as your brother."

"That's true." I smiled back at him, and he reached over and squeezed my hand lightly.

"And I guess at least this gives us more solid proof of her involvement. Since you know your dad had contact with her." He scrubbed a hand across his face and yawned again. "We done for now? I'm fucking knackered. I'm off to bed."

"Carly keep you up late last night, did she?" Cass smirked at him.

Carly? I mouthed to Cade, and he shrugged, mouthing *no idea* back to me.

"Maybe." West grinned. He scooped up the laptop and headed out.

"Speaking of, I've got a girl keeping my bed warm upstairs, and she's been waiting long enough." Cassius stood and sauntered across the room. He paused in the doorway, and the gleam in his eye had me bracing myself.

"Hey, Winter. If you fancy joining us, you know where

my room is. One of my areas of expertise is pleasuring two ladies at once." He threw me a cheeky wink as he disappeared around the corner.

Cade growled low in his throat, and I groaned, burying my face in my hands.

Zayde glanced over at us, sighed, and disappeared from the room without a goodbye, closing the door behind him.

I was alone with Caiden again.

He looked at me. "Want to talk more, or do you want me to take your mind off everything?"

I stared back at him, watching as his eyes darkened, his gaze turning hungry. "Option two, please."

He gave me a feral grin. "Come here."

TWENTY-SEVEN

"Will anyone come in?" She chewed her lower lip.

"Nah." I pulled her onto my lap, and she sighed, threading her fingers through my hair, scratching her nails over my scalp as I gripped her hips to line her up with my dick.

"Sorry, forgot my phone." West's amused voice came from the doorway, and I looked over Winter's shoulder to see the fucker smirking at us.

"Can we just go upstairs?" she whispered in my ear.

"Yeah, okay."

She climbed off me, picking up our drinks, her sexy ass swaying as she walked towards the door. I adjusted my dick, already straining against my jeans.

I caught up with her, wrapping my arms around her slim waist, pressing into her back. She carried on walking, laughing breathlessly as I kissed up her neck, then shivering as I scraped my teeth over her skin.

"Cade. We're not gonna make it to your bedroom at this

rate." The drinks in her hands sloshed around, the contents dangerously close to spilling over the tiled floor.

"Careful with those drinks." I couldn't stop touching her.

"Stop distracting me."

"Get up the stairs, now."

"Let go of me and I will." I released her from my grip, and she raced up the stairs, then paused in my bedroom door to look back at me, eyebrow raised and a cocky smile on her lips. "You coming, or what?"

"I will be, soon." I smirked, and she rolled her eyes playfully, backing into the room and putting the drinks down on my side table.

"Ugh. You've been spending too much time with Cass."

Reaching her, I backed her up against the bed, using my weight to tip her backwards. My amusement faded as I straddled her, leaning down to nip at her ear. "Don't mention him. Or any other man," I warned, my voice hard and possessive. "You're *mine*, okay?"

She stared up at me, her pupils dilated with lust, and licked her lips. "Yours, huh?" she asked in a low, throaty tone.

My dick was fucking begging for release as she scraped her nails down my back before gripping my ass and grinding me into her. I stifled a groan. "We discussed this. While we're fucking, you're mine. No one else's. Clear?"

"Clear. Get off me."

"Oh. No. Snowflake, you don't get to order me around."

"You'll like this." She pushed at my chest, and I moved up. Reluctantly.

"Sit against the headboard. I'm gonna thank you properly for my car."

I see.

She didn't have to thank me, but fuck if I'd stop her.

"Okay." She climbed off the bed, and my gaze tracked her as she padded over to the light switch and turned it off, leaving just the dim glow coming from the small lamp in the corner of the room. Taking a big gulp of her drink, she tapped at her phone screen and the intro to "Wicked Games" by The Weeknd started playing.

With a flick of her wrist, she tossed her hair over her shoulders. And then, she stripped for me, confident and unhurried, her movements slow and sexy, in time with the music, until she was just in her underwear, and I was salivating for her.

"Get over here." My voice came out as a guttural rasp.

Fuck, what was this girl doing to me?

"Not yet." She bit her lip, her confidence faltering slightly, and it only made me want her more. "Can you...get your cock out? And stroke it? I want to watch you while you watch me." Her cheeks were flushed, and her pupils were huge as she stared at my erection.

"*Fuck*, Snowflake."

Ripping my T-shirt over my head, I unbuttoned my jeans and tugged them off, then slid my boxers down and groaned in relief as my dick was finally freed.

"Cade," she moaned. "Touch yourself."

"Bloody hell," I muttered, taking my dick in my hand and giving it a tug as she undid her bra and let it fall to the floor. Her tits stood out, high and fucking perfect, her nipples begging for me to suck on them. I stroked my hand up and down my dick as I watched her shimmy out of her underwear, and she was completely bared to me. I hissed through my teeth as my hand moved faster. "Snowflake, get over here, now."

She whimpered and shook her head, her gaze fixated on what I was doing to myself.

Her hand reached down between her legs.

"Don't you fucking dare. Get. Here. Now."

Suddenly she was launching herself across the bed, licking across my IV tattoo, and then my hands were tangled in her hair and she was sucking my dick into her mouth, all hot, wet, suction, her tongue swirling around the head, then her hand cupping my balls while she took me all the way to the back of her throat.

"I'm gonna come," I gasped, and then she was pulling her head away and I was coming, hard and fast, over my stomach.

"Hottest thing I've ever seen," she moaned, falling back on the bed, sliding her hand between her legs again.

"Snowflake. Wait." I stilled her hand. I cleaned myself off, then positioned myself between her spread legs. She was fucking soaked already, and I dragged one finger through her wetness, making her thrash on the bed, thrusting her hips upwards to try and get more contact.

Stilling her with my palm flat against her stomach, I sucked my finger into my mouth, and she licked her lips, reaching for me. Moving out of her reach, I smirked at her and picked up the glass of JD on the table next to us, then tipped the glass so the cold drink dribbled down onto her body, between her tits and down to her belly button. She gasped, and her gasp turned into a moan as I licked the trail of liquid all the way up from her belly button to her tits.

"Cade. Stop teasing me." Her voice was breathless and begging.

"Just for that, I'm making you wait longer." I reached for the glass again and fished out one of the melting ice cubes.

She shrieked as I placed it on her heated skin. "That's fucking freezing, you asshole."

I silenced her with a forceful kiss, sliding the ice cube

onto one of her hardened nipples, making her hiss, before I dragged it away and moved my head down to suck the nipple into my mouth.

"Oh, fuck. That feels amazing," she moaned. I moved the ice cube to her other nipple and did the same, then dragged it down her body, following it with my mouth. I'd never bothered playing with girls like this, but fuck if I didn't want to keep doing it with her.

The ice melted before I got to her spread legs. She was panting by now, reaching her hands out to bury them in my hair, trying to push my head down. I laughed but decided to stop torturing her.

I flicked my tongue over her clit, and she arched off the bed. Hooking my arms around her legs, I flicked my tongue across her clit again, then licked through her wetness.

"Cade. Please," she moaned.

I made her come three times, the third time with my dick pounding into her as she called out my name.

Heading out of the bathroom, I grabbed some boxers from my drawers and a T-shirt for Winter, then turned off the lamp. The blinds were open, and the moon cast a dim strip of bluish light across the middle of the room. I handed her the T-shirt and pulled on the boxers, then slid under the covers next to her.

What the fuck was I doing? The other times I'd fucked her, she'd fallen asleep and I'd left as quick as I could. Somehow, I was now lying with her in my bed, my arm round her, her head on my chest.

"This is more fun than you hating me," she mumbled drowsily, tracing lazy patterns across the ink on my forearm.

"Yeah."

I spoke into the dark room, intending to apologise to her, but instead, the words I'd never spoken to anyone, other than Cass and Zayde, came out instead. "When I was fifteen, my mother killed herself."

I heard her sharp intake of breath, but she remained silent, stroking her fingers over my skin. "Your mother had an affair with my dad. Went on for years, I think. He wasn't exactly subtle about it, either." My fists clenched, the memory of my parents' constant arguments forever burned in my mind. "My mother withdrew into herself. Started seeing a doctor, got prescribed a fuckload of drugs, turned into a shell of herself. Your mother was constantly finding excuses to come over to our house, flaunting her affair in front of my mother, knowing there was nothing she could do."

"Cade. I had no idea what she was up to. I'm so sorry." Winter's voice was low and sad. "Since me and my dad moved away, I've hardly had anything to do with her. He really loved her, you know. It's weird—she seems to be able to get men under her spell, and they'll pretty much do anything for her."

"She's a beautiful woman. And she can charm anyone," I admitted through gritted teeth.

"Not you, though." She wriggled further up my body and kissed my jaw.

"Never. Uh, so one evening—it was a Friday night—I got home and there was no one else around. My dad was out with Paul and Michael—Cass and Z's dads—and West was round his mate's house. My mum had been in bed ill all day. I went up to check on her, and she wasn't in her room."

I took a deep breath, trying to keep my voice steady.

"Cade, you don't have to talk about this," she said softly, running her hand up and down my arm.

"It's okay." I tightened my hold on her, staring up at the ceiling, unseeing. "I had a feeling, y'know? That kind of sick feeling you get where something's wrong. The house was too still, too quiet. I checked her bathroom, but she wasn't there. I thought maybe she was downstairs. Getting something to eat or whatever, since Allan wasn't around that weekend. Something made me check the guest bathroom down the hallway, and when I tried the door, it was locked."

I choked on the words as I rushed to get them out. "I panicked when she didn't answer. I somehow managed to break down the door, and I found her, but I was too late. If only I'd got home sooner, I might have been able to save her. If only—"

"Caiden." She climbed onto me, raining kisses all over my face. "I'm so sorry. I hate that you think that way. You shouldn't. You couldn't have known. You can't feel responsible for what happened."

"I do, though."

She made a pained noise and stared down at me. "You. Are. Not. Responsible."

I had no words.

I pulled her down so she was lying flat on top of me, her head on my chest and my arms wrapped around her, her presence soothing me. Telling her—I hadn't meant to, but it was out there now, and it sounded cliché as fuck, but I felt like a burden had been lifted.

And whatever was going on between us, I trusted her.

I trust her?

Yeah, I did.

We lay there for a while, occupied with our own thoughts, until she lifted her head to look at me, taking a deep breath. "I need to tell you something." Her voice was hesitant, her eyes all huge and serious. "When I met up with my mother yesterday, she told me to stay away from you. And she...*fuck.* I'm sorry, Cade." Tears filled her eyes. "I didn't know whether to say anything, and it's been *killing* me. She told me that your mum took her own life. She didn't give me any details at all, just made it as a throwaway comment, but-but..." She trailed off, the tears now running down her face freely.

I was fucking speechless. And livid. I lifted her off me and shot off the bed, crossing straight over to the bathroom and slamming the door behind me.

"Fuck!" I punched the door, then again for good measure. Sinking down onto the floor beside the bath, I dropped my head into my hands, pain radiating up my arm.

I sat there for a long time, breathing in and out deeply, trying to calm myself.

When I managed to cool off enough that I no longer had the urge to punch something, I headed back into the bedroom, The lamp had been turned back on, and my eyes went straight to Winter, huddled on the bed.

"Do you want me to leave?" Her quiet, shaky whisper cut through the silence.

I climbed onto the bed and scooted up against the head-board. "Snowflake." I pulled her into my arms. "Why would I want you to leave?"

"You were angry with me."

"No. I wasn't angry with you; I was angry with *her.* You've done nothing wrong."

"I didn't tell you that I knew."

"Hey, you only found out yesterday." A thought occurred to me. "Is that why you were so upset on the phone to Cass?"

She nodded.

"Okay. Well, what's done is done. Let's draw a line under it for now, yeah, and tomorrow we can concentrate on finding out everything we can to bring Christine Clifford down."

"Alright." She was silent for a minute, holding on to me, and then she sighed heavily. "Cade? What about West? Don't you think he has the right to know?"

I stiffened. "No. He doesn't need to know. Do you know how much fucking guilt and failure I feel? There's. No. Fucking. Way I want him to feel even a tenth of that."

"He's an adult. He has a right to know."

"Leave it," I warned her through gritted teeth.

"Fine. I'm not comfortable keeping it from him, though." She buried her face in my chest.

"It's not your place to tell him."

"I know," came the muffled voice. Raising her head, she continued. "I won't say anything. Just telling you I don't feel comfortable."

Before I could say anything else, she swung her body round so she was straddling me. "Can we finish off tonight with something happy?"

"Fuck, yes."

All other thoughts flew out of my mind as she rocked her hips against me, and we ended the night the same way we'd started it—with my dick buried deep inside her, and her screaming out my name.

TWENTY-EIGHT

I'd been a ball of nerves all morning. Today was the day the guys were going to Alstone Members Club. The last week, I'd hardly had a chance to see Cade, let alone the other boys, other than in passing. We were all completely swamped with end-of-semester assignments and exam prep, on top of everything else.

My mother had made no effort to speak to me since I'd walked out on her a week ago, and I was in no hurry to reconnect with her after everything. I'd told Kinslee that I'd fallen out with her, leaving out the part about Caiden's mum, and she'd been horrified. We'd ended up talking late into the night, and I was beyond grateful to have her support. She'd had her share of family problems, from the few things she'd mentioned, and I had the feeling that she really understood where I was coming from.

Standing in line to pay for my lunch after a long morning of lectures, I scanned the cafeteria tables and saw Weston waving at me. There they were. The Four, on a central table right by the windows.

I paid for my lunch and walked towards them with a smile. Their faces were masks of indifference, but I could see past the hard exterior now. Somehow, against all odds, we'd gone from enmity and mistrust to friendship and mutual respect.

Placing my tray down on the table in front of the empty seat next to Caiden, I pulled out the chair. His arm shot out, stilling my movements, and I turned to meet his intense gaze.

"Hi," he said, then pulled me into his lap and kissed me, right there, in the middle of the crowded cafeteria.

"Wow. Hi." I stared into his stormy eyes, taken aback by his public display. "What was that for?" I distantly heard Cassius say something, and I felt both curious and hostile stares burning into me from every direction, but all my focus was on the man in front of me.

He shrugged. "Just felt like it."

"Um, okay."

He spun me around. "Eat," he instructed, then buried his face in my hair. "I missed you," he muttered, tightening his arms around my waist.

My stomach flipped at his words.

A huge smile spread across my face. I reached for my plate and started eating, while the boys spoke in low conversation around me.

"Still slumming it, Caiden?" Portia's irritating voice startled me, and I looked up to find her standing at the side of our table, staring at me sitting on Cade, her lip curled in the disdainful sneer she seemed to favour around me. She looked beautiful as always, her perfect red hair falling over her shoulders in tumbling waves, her boobs straining against her tight knitted top, and her artfully applied make-up giving her skin a flawless appearance.

"Insult my girl one more time and I'll make your life hell." Caiden's low, growled threat came from behind me, close to my ear.

My mouth fell open in shock.

Portia's brows flew up to her hairline, and her eyes flicked from me to Caiden in disbelief.

"*Your girl?*"

"You heard me." He leaned forwards so his lips were right by my ear. "You okay, Snowflake?"

"Your girl?" I repeated dumbly, as I noticed Portia storm off out of the corner of my eye. "What's—I mean. We haven't discussed." I couldn't get my brain to work properly.

"*Mine.*" He brushed my hair away from my neck and kissed me once, just under my ear, then carried on speaking to Zayde as if nothing had happened.

What the fuck? I mouthed across the table to Weston, and he shrugged, grinning. I saw him pull out his phone and start tapping on the screen; then he placed it on the table and indicated to it with a nod of his head. A few seconds later, my phone vibrated with a message, and I surreptitiously opened it in my lap.

West: Told you he really likes you.

Well, fuck me. Maybe he was right.

———

I spent the rest of the afternoon floating around my lectures in a daze, basically acting like a dreamy schoolgirl whose first crush had just noticed her. I kept telling myself to get a grip, but Caiden's words played on repeat in my mind. We needed to have a conversation about whatever was going on between us. At some point. Then again, maybe I shouldn't push for anything. Just let whatever was going to happen, happen.

I left my last lecture of the day and exited the building. The day had turned to night during my lecture. I actually didn't mind the dark winter evenings—I liked being able to see the stars. Heading down the path leading to the library, I tugged my coat more tightly around me to ward off the chill in the air.

The library was warm and welcoming after the outside cold, and I removed my heavy winter coat and gloves as I entered, then headed up to the silence of the top floor. Dumping my things on an empty table, I headed into the stacks to grab the books I needed. My plan was to fill my mind with studying tonight so I wouldn't have to be constantly worrying about what the Four were doing at AMC. That was the idea anyway.

"Winter. Can I have a quick word?" The shadowy figure that suddenly appeared around the stacks made me jump back in fright.

"It's just me." He moved closer. James Granville.

"James, you scared me. What are you doing, hiding in the shadows like that?"

"Sorry." He looked around nervously, on edge. "Can we talk for a minute?"

"Um, okay. What's up?"

He shuffled his feet, not looking at me. "I wanted to say I'm sorry how things turned out for us. I hope I didn't cause problems for you."

"That's okay. I'm sorry, too. We could've been great friends."

"But you picked Caiden Cavendish." His mouth set in a flat line.

"James. I-I don't know what to say. I—"

"It's alright." He stepped into the light, and I gasped. His left eye was swollen shut, puffy and bruised.

"Shit, James. What happened? Who did this to you?"

"That's not important," he said sharply.

I reached up to touch the bruising on his face, and he flinched. "You need to get some ice on that. I'm sorry." Instinctively, I hugged him. His arms came around me, and he leaned his head on my shoulder.

"Thanks. I needed that," he murmured, kissing my cheek, and then suddenly his lips were on mine.

I froze in shock.

Then my brain came back online with a roar, and I stamped down on his foot with all my strength.

He jumped backwards with an angry shout. "That hurt! Bitch!" He bent down, rubbing madly at his foot.

"What the fuck do you think you're doing?" I was livid, hissing in his face. "Try that again and you'll regret it. I mean it, James. Don't. Fucking. Try. Me."

"You and Cavendish deserve each other." His mask slipped, and a vindictive smile appeared on his face. "I think I'm going to enjoy this, after all."

Enjoy what? A sick feeling built in the pit of my stomach, and I could only stand and stare as he walked away from me, towards—was that my TA, Joseph?

As he reached him, he held up his hand, and they bumped fists, Joseph grasping a phone in his hand. Then they were gone, and I was left alone, confused, angry, and apprehensive.

I gathered the books I needed as quickly as I could and hurried back to my apartment, on high alert, constantly checking to make sure I wasn't being followed. Kinslee was still out; she'd be at least another half an hour, so I settled at my desk with a huge mug of coffee, books piled around me and my laptop open, to start on my assignment, trying to push James' weird behaviour to the back of my mind.

I wanted to tell the Four. What I didn't want to do was to cause any more drama, knowing how much Caiden disliked James. Would that stop me telling them, though? Fuck, no. Seriously, what had James been thinking? Asshole.

I decided to wait until the boys got back from AMC to tell them what had happened—there was no way I was going to be responsible for distracting them from their task.

Sipping my mug of coffee, I returned to my books. Seven o'clock. The boys would be getting ready to go to AMC. I could only hope that they got lucky and found out who it was Arlo was meeting, or what it was he was doing on a Tuesday night.

As if I'd conjured them up, two minutes later my phone buzzed with a message from Weston.

West: We scrub up well, don't we *wink emoji*

An image of the Four appeared on my screen. All in dark suits, hair styled, tattoos peeking out. Cade had a sexy, arrogant smirk on his face, Cass had a huge grin, West was winking, and Zayde, shock of all shocks, was actually sticking his tongue out at the camera, showing his barbell piercing.

Me: *woman fanning herself GIF*
Me: Bloody hell. I can't handle the hotness. This is now my phone wallpaper.
West: Thought you'd like it. We're leaving in a few. Message you later if it's not too late.
Me: Good luck. I don't care how late it is, I need to hear from you guys tonight.

West: OK. Speak later.
Me: Be careful.
West: Always.

I placed my phone down and started working on my assignment, trying to block everything else out of my mind. As I sipped my coffee, my thoughts went back to James in the library. What was his weird, shifty behaviour all about, and why on earth would he try to kiss me?

I didn't have to wonder for long.

A few minutes later, my phone buzzed with a message from Caiden, then another, then another.

Caiden: Couldn't stay away from Granville?
Caiden: You fucking betrayed me.
Caiden: We're done.

A forwarded video appeared in the list of messages, and I clicked on it with a trembling hand.

No.

TWENTY-NINE

I dialled Caiden's number. Straight to voicemail. Next, I tried Cassius, then Weston, then Zayde. All went straight to voicemail.

"Argh!" I shouted, frustrated, tears filling my eyes. What should I do? Nausea filled my stomach—what if I couldn't explain things? What if Caiden didn't believe me? I couldn't even see him in person to tell him what had happened.

If only I'd mentioned what had happened in the library.

Tapping out a message on my phone, I sent it to him, and hoped for the best.

Me: We need to talk. NOTHING HAPPENED. Check your voicemail. Phone me as soon as you get this, PLEASE.

Then I called him and left a message. "Cade, it's me. Well, I guess you already know that. That video isn't how it looks." My voice cracked, and I cleared my throat, trying not to cry. "James cornered me in the library, and he had a black eye. What you saw in the video was me showing concern and trying to comfort him, and then—" I choked back a sob. "—and then, he tried to kiss me, and I froze. As soon as I realised what was going on, I stamped on his foot as hard as I could to make him stop. Cade, you have to believe me... I would never... I only want you." I was crying by now, and I hung up the phone and buried my face in my arms, leaning on the desk.

Kinslee found me in the same position when she got home. She took one look at me and dragged me into the lounge, where we curled up on the sofa with hot chocolate, and I told her the whole story.

"I can't believe he would do that! Why would he want to do that to you? I know he and Caiden hate each other, but why drag you into it?"

"I can't answer that," I sighed. "I know their dads have some kind of family rivalry, but I have no idea about any of the details. And why was Joseph with him?" I'd worked out —not that it took much deducing—that Joseph had been the one to film us.

"Hmm." Kinslee pursed her lips in thought, frowning. "I know they're cousins. So that has to be something to do with it."

"Cousins? I had no idea."

She leaned over and gave me a comforting hug. "Listen. I'm sure Caiden will listen to reason, once you see him and have a chance to explain things."

"I hope so." I returned her hug, then slumped back on the sofa. "I'm actually pretty fucking pissed off as well, to be honest. Cade should have given me a chance to explain. I thought he'd started to trust me. And yet he was all too willing to jump to conclusions."

"That's true."

We lapsed into silence.

"How hard did you stamp on his foot?" Kinslee suddenly asked.

"As hard as I could."

"I hope you broke a bone."

We smirked at each other. "So violent, Kins."

She shrugged. "What can I say?"

"I love it."

Cass parked round the back of the club in the private parking area, and we assembled round the side of the car. "Let's do this. Phones off, otherwise they get confiscated. Heads down, keep an eye on my father." Everyone nodded, bumping fists, and we headed towards the entrance. My phone buzzed in my pocket.

"Shit, forgot to turn my phone off." Mentally slapping my forehead, I pulled it out and saw I had a message from an unknown number. Fucking spam. I clicked on it, ready to delete, but stopped when I read the message.

Unknown: Thought you might want to see what Winter was up to earlier.

What the fuck?

A video appeared underneath the message, and I pressed Play.

I saw red.

Through a haze of anger, I sent her a succession of messages and forwarded the video to her.

Fuck!

This was why I didn't let myself get involved. Winter had just proved that she couldn't be trusted. I should have known she was like her mother. How could I have been so fucking blind?

Fuck her. I didn't need anyone. I had my boys.

"Cade? You coming?" West called me from the doorway to the club, and I realised I'd stopped in the street while they all walked ahead.

"Yeah, coming." I stabbed the Off button on my phone and thrust it in my pocket, then strode inside to meet the others, my jaw clenched and a pain in my chest.

I stood still while the guy on security searched me, breathing in and out through my nose. The need to punch something was so strong, I dug my nails into my palms to stop myself acting on it. We entered a large, dimly lit wood-panelled room, but I couldn't fucking concentrate on my surroundings, let alone the task at hand.

Why? Why had she gone back to Granville?

"Mate." Zayde gripped my arm. "Back in a sec," he muttered to the others and hustled me into the corner of the room, away from the others. "What's the problem?" he hissed, when we were alone.

"Nothing." I stood, arms folded, looking at him blankly.

"Cade."

"Fucking Winter," I spat. "Some asshole sent me a video of her all over Granville. Today. I knew I couldn't trust her. She's just as bad as that f—"

"Back up a minute." Zayde held his hand up in my face, silencing me. "Calm down, will ya? Don't say anything you might regret. Who sent the video, and how do you know it happened today?"

"Don't know who sent it. It came from an unknown number. It was date-stamped today."

"Show me the video when we get out of here, but don't jump to conclusions, mate. She's really into you—fuck knows why." He gave me a small smirk, then shook his head. "Remember why we're here. Get your head in the game. We can sort this shit out later."

I stared at him in silence.

He levelled me with a hard look—his serial killer stare, as Winter had called it once. *No. Forget her.*

"Okay. Fine. Let's do this," I said, moving past him and heading back to Cass and West.

"Ready?" Cass handed me a glass of whiskey.

Showtime.

Letting my mask drop into place, I pushed everything away. I needed to be emotionless, numb, focused on getting as much information as I could. I scanned the room, taking everything in. It was a proper old boys' club in here, all mutual backslapping and self-congratulatory posturing. A group of men stood to our left, leering at a waitress in a tight skirt leaning over a table to take a drinks order. To our right a poker game was in play, chips piled high in the centre of the table. A polished mahogany bar ran down one wall, red velvet bar stools clustered in front of it. Cigar smoke filled the air, and a low hum of conversation and clinking glasses was a constant sound in my ears.

Two heavy wooden doors led from the room—one directing the way to the toilets, the other unmarked. "Split up and check both doors?" Cass suggested in a low tone.

There was no sign of my father, or any of our fathers, for that matter, so I nodded.

"Cade with me, Z, you go with West." He headed through the unmarked door, and I followed, leaving Zayde and Weston to check the other. We found ourselves in a long corridor with several doors leading off it, most open. At the very end of the corridor, directly in front of us, was a closed door with a beefy security guy dressed in black in front of it, arms crossed and a hostile expression on his face.

"Just our fucking luck if Arlo went through there," Cass muttered, discreetly nodding at the guy.

"We'll try the other doors first."

The first room we looked in was also wood-panelled and carpeted, muted light provided by sconces on the wall. In the centre stood a huge table, with neat lines of coke cut and laid out ready on the gleaming surface, and a pile of small, clear bags in the centre. A balding, suited man was leaning over the table, and a security guy stood against the wall, his sharp eyes scanning the room, missing nothing.

"Can I interest you gentlemen in something?" A woman in the shortest, tightest, skimpiest dress I'd seen outside of a strip club sidled up to me, placing her hand on my arm and batting her lashes at me. "We've got everything here—" She indicated to the table. "—or if you're looking for a more... personal service, I can sort you out. I haven't seen you around here before. I would have *definitely* remembered." She moved closer, curling her fingers over my bicep, her fake tits brushing against my arm. I felt nothing.

"You're wasting your time on him, babe. He's got a girl already," Cassius said in a bored tone.

"Most men here do." She shrugged. "Doesn't stop them."

"I don't have a girl," I muttered under my breath. Cass glared at me. "Not interested, sorry," I said more loudly, plucking her hand from my arm and stepping back. "Have you seen my father? Arlo Cavendish?"

She visibly paled, tottering backwards on her sky-high heels. "Oh, s-sir, I'm so sorry. I had no idea you were Mr Cavendish's son. Please excuse my forward behaviour."

"Uh. Sure." Cass and I exchanged glances. "Have you seen him?"

She shook her head mutely, and I nodded towards the door. As we left the room, Zayde and Weston appeared in the corridor. "Any luck?" West asked in a low voice, and I shook my head. Next room. This one had a heavy, closed door, and as soon as I pushed it open, I was hit by the sound of Beyoncé's "Partition" and a heavy smell of perfume, mixed with sweat and smoke.

"Fuck, yes," Cass groaned under his breath, his gaze fixated on a woman in the corner of the large darkened room, a spotlight shining on her as she swung around a pole on a small stage, wearing nothing but a black G-string. A cluster of men sat around the stage, some watching, others talking in low tones, heads bent close together. Several women were gyrating on men in darkened booths, and three security guys stood on the edges of the room, watching the goings-on with bored expressions on their faces.

"What the fuck kind of members club is this? Strippers? Lap dancers? Best fucking place ever." West stared around the room, a huge grin on his face, and I rolled my eyes. He had a point, though. This was...unexpected.

"Uh, Z, I think that's your dad." Cass had torn his eyes away from the stripper, and we followed his gaze to the middle booth, where Michael Lowry sat with a topless woman in his lap, smoking a cigar while his other hand disappeared under the table.

Zayde sighed heavily. "Let's go."

"You don't wanna talk to him?" Cass smirked, but Z was already heading out of the room.

We ran straight into my father, coming down the corridor with Paul Drummond, Cassius' father. Both tall and imposing, impeccably dressed as always.

"There you are," he greeted us. "You boys having fun? Enjoying everything the club has to offer?" He gave me a smarmy wink, clapping me on the back.

"Yeah. It's not what I expected," I said honestly.

"In what way?" Paul eyed me.

"Strippers? Drugs?"

"Listen, boys. This is our world. We work hard for our money, and at the weekends we play the role of family men. Here...we can blow off steam. Relax. Have our whims catered to. Network. Do you understand what I'm saying?"

"So you're playing at being a father, are you?" Cass gave Paul a hard look.

"Son, you know I didn't mean it like that. You, and Lena, and your mother...you're important to me. We're family. I can't speak for everyone, though..." He trailed off with a shrug and a twist of his mouth.

"Okay. Good," Cass muttered, looking down at the floor.

"Drinks." My father clapped his hands. "Come into the bar—I've reserved us a table."

We sat in a large booth for the next hour, making small talk. My father spoke briefly about a construction contract they were trying to win, and Paul discussed the troubles Alstone Holdings was having with one of their building suppliers. I filed away every bit of information, even if it didn't seem important—as I knew my boys would, too.

Michael, Zayde's dad, joined us after a while and asked if we wanted in on the next poker game. Just over an hour later, me and Cass had both folded, West and the two other guys we were playing with were out, and Z had a pile of chips in front of him and a triumphant gleam in his eye. Fuck knows why I bothered playing poker against him. He had the best poker face I'd ever seen, bar none, and no tells —none that I'd ever noticed, anyway.

Michael had left us to play and gone back to the booth where my dad and Paul were sitting, joined by another three of my father's friends and colleagues. As our game came to an end, I noticed all of them rise from their booth and head through the same door we'd been through earlier. I glanced at Cass, and he gave me a slight nod, and we left the table and followed them through the door.

Keeping back, we headed down the corridor, only to see the men disappear through the door at the very end—the door with the beefy security guy now scowling at me and Cass.

"What do we do?" Cass hissed through the side of his mouth.

"Wing it" was my reply, and we strode towards the door.

THIRTY

I'd been working on my assignment for the past hour and a half, the need to finish my semester with good grades driving me to carry on, even though it was the last thing I felt like doing. It was getting late, and I still hadn't heard anything from any of the Four. I knew, or I hoped, at least, that West would message me with an update, even if Caiden didn't want to hear from me.

Kinslee wandered in, dressed in fleecy pyjamas and fluffy slippers, and came to a stop next to me, leaning on my desk. "How are you still going? It's so late."

"I just want to get this finished before I turn my computer off."

"Fair enough." She picked up the little crystal ball with a 3D model of the solar system suspended inside, that I kept on my desk. "This is cute. What is it?"

I glanced up, a sad smile on my face. "That was my dad's. It's the solar system. He used it as a paperweight in his office."

"Oh. Sorry. I didn't mean to bring up anything painful." She bit her lip, placing the crystal ball carefully back down.

"It's okay. I like to talk about him. I don't have anyone to talk to about him, really."

"I'm always happy to listen, if you want to talk." Squeezing my shoulder, she leaned across my desk to the wall. "Were these your dad's, too?" She pointed at the collection of star charts and constellations I'd tacked up.

"Yeah. I told you he was an astrophysicist, right? He had loads of this stuff. At home, his study was covered in these posters. These are just the ones they sent me from his work office."

"Oh, okay." She leaned even closer, tapping her finger on one of the posters. "Huh. I never knew that was a constellation."

"What?" I was only half paying attention as I tried to finish the paragraph I'd been typing.

"Argo Navis. I never knew it was a constellation. Did you know that the *Argo Navis* was Jason and the Argonauts' ship? You know, from Greek myths?"

"No idea," I murmured.

"It's funny. My brother worked down at the docks last summer, loading and unloading cargo. One of the cargo ships was actually called the *Argo Navis*, can you believe it?" She laughed. "Someone must have really been into their Greek mythology."

I swear a lightning bolt hit me.

"What did you say?" I gasped.

"Which bit? The ship?"

"*No*. This can't be!" My hands shaking, I picked up my phone and opened Weston's app, scrolling to the little safe icon which linked to our secure storage.

It seemed to take forever for the scanned image of my dad's notes to load, but when it did, it was blatantly obvious.

AR(letter missing)O (letter missing)AVIS. TUES NIGHTS.

Argo Navis.

"Kins, I've got to go. I'll be back. Uh, later. Or tomorrow, I guess."

"Are you okay?" She eyed me with concern.

"Yeah, yeah. Fine. Just got to see the Four." I saved my work and closed my laptop lid with a bang, swiped my bag from the floor, stuffing my phone inside, and rushed out of the room. I paused to grab Caiden's hoodie and a beanie hat, pulling them both on, then flew out of the building and into the car park.

Sitting in my car, I sent the same message to all the Four.

Me: It might not be Arlo Davis. I think it could be ARGO NAVIS. A boat at the docks. I'm going there to check it out now. Will let you know what I find.

Text sent, I switched to my maps app and set a course for Alstone Docks.

We reached the security guy. His scowl deepened as he stared us down, slightly shorter than me and Cass, but built like a brick shithouse.

"Can I help you boys?"

"You need to let us through. My father is in there, and it's imperative that I speak with him, right now," Cassius tried.

He stared at us, unimpressed. "Sorry, no can do."

"Don't you know who I am?" I cringed inside as the words came out of my mouth. "I'm Caiden Cavendish, son of Arlo Cavendish, your employer. I don't think he'd be happy that you kept us from him, would he?"

"I know who you are. I'm under orders. No one gets through this door, not without the explicit permission of Mr. Cavendish, Drummond, or Lowry. You can take it up with them later, but you ain't getting through tonight."

"Let us through." Cassius' tone was low and deadly, and I stared at him in surprise.

"Do we have a problem?" The guard pulled out his radio and pressed the button to speak into it.

"No, no problem. Come on, Cass." I dragged him away from the smirking security guy. When we were out of earshot, I turned to him. "We're wasting our time. Let's get out of here." I stepped closer, lowering my voice. "Maybe check that entrance around the back, to see if we can find another way in. We might need Weston's expertise."

He narrowed his eyes, thinking, then sighed. "Yeah, guess so. Let's get the boys and go."

We reached the main room, and Zayde and Weston stood when they saw us, pushing back their chairs and nodding a goodbye to the guys at their table. We exited into the night air and back to the car.

"What do we do now?" West asked once we were all

inside the car, twisting in his seat to look at me and Zayde in the back seats.

"*Fuck*!"

Weston's head flew round at Cassius' urgent shout. "Fuck!" he shouted again. "Fucking Winter!" He slammed the steering wheel, and my stomach flipped.

"We need to get to the docks, right now. Our girl could be in trouble." He started the engine and threw the SUV into gear, peeling out of the parking lot.

"What's going on? What's wrong with Winter?" Weston's voice was panicked.

"Phone," he grunted, concentrating on navigating his huge SUV through the narrow street we were driving down, high stone walls on either side of us. I pulled my phone out of my pocket and turned it on, while Weston reached over to the centre console to grab Cass' phone.

Snowflake.

No. She'd fucked me over.

My voice echoed around the silent car. "Wait a minute, mate. Some asshole sent me video evidence of her kissing Granville earlier."

"Fuck you, Caiden," West snarled, and I recoiled at his tone. "I don't wanna hear it. Stop with your trust issues or whatever shit you have going on in your head. Z, you too, for that matter. Our girl is in trouble. Do you want to be responsible for anything happening to her?"

Zayde and I looked at each other.

Fuck.

Screw the video.

She was my girl.

I needed to fucking remind her of that fact.

I prayed that we weren't too late.

THIRTY-ONE

Pulling my hood over my head, I climbed out of the car, closing the door softly behind me. I'd parked a way down the road from the docks, and my very rough thrown-together plan was to scope out the area and see if I could find this boat. As for anything past that—I'd have to wing it when I got there.

The entire docks area was surrounded by high fencing, and the side I was approaching from had a row of shipping containers stacked up next to the fence, and I could see the tops of several large cranes behind them.

I wiped my palms on my jeans, tucked my phone safely into my back pocket, and inched closer. In front of me I could see the entryway. There was an electronically operated barrier with a white painted guard hut next to it, and a camera mounted on the hut. I could see the silhouette of a man inside the hut, but it was quiet other than that.

Edging around the corner, I jumped back as a pair of headlights swung towards me—a truck, leaving the docks. The driver lowered h is window to speak to the guard, and I took my chance. I ducked under the barrier, around the back of the truck and across the small expanse of open ground to a long, squat building that looked like some kind of warehouse. It was silent, locked up, so I ignored it for the time being, instead using it for cover.

I noted the cameras on high stalks, and the floodlights illuminating the area, but as luck would have it, there didn't appear to be anything pointing in my direction. There didn't appear to be anyone else around, either. I saw two large boats, stacked up with containers, but neither one had the right name. Where was this ship? Had I been wrong in my theory? Maybe the wording actually was Arlo Davis.

No. I was here. I needed to know for sure.

Hugging the wall, I inched around the corner, and there it was.

Jackpot. A small cargo ship bobbed in the water, off to the side of the main docks, in its own berth. The words *Argo Navis* jumped out at me, in faded white lettering on the black hull.

I watched, frozen in place, as three figures emerged from the boat and entered a large stone building on the edge of the dock. The structure itself was in complete disrepair— the roof looked to be in danger of collapsing, the windows were boarded up, and the brickwork was crumbling.

I remained where I was, no cover between the wall I was hiding behind and the stone building.

I waited. And waited.

Eventually, the figures emerged and returned to the boat. I watched, my heart sinking, as it pulled away from the docks and headed out to sea, soon becoming a distant speck.

What should I do?

I was here—I should at least check the building that the people from the ship had spent so long in.

Tucking my hair into my hood, I made a dash for the building and slipped in through the cracked wooden door that hung partly off the hinges.

It was *so* dark inside.

With shaking hands, I pulled my phone from my pocket and switched on the tiny flashlight, then swung the light around me to illuminate the space. There was a corridor up ahead, and shining the torch on the ground, I could see boot imprints in the dusty wooden floor, showing me where the people had gone. I shone the torch all around me and noticed a light switch on the wall, but I didn't dare turn it on, just in case.

I hated the dark.

My breathing was loud in the silence, and the only thought running through my mind was that I should have waited for the Four. I should never have come here on my own. But it was too late to turn back now. I *had* to find out what was in here.

Slowly, hugging the wall, I made my way down the corridor, the old wooden floorboards creaking underfoot.

I heard a shuffling noise behind me and swung the torch round wildly, my heart in my throat. My light caught a set of eyes in its beam.

A rat. It scampered away, and I sagged against the wall, my heart beating out of my chest. When I felt I could continue, I shone the torch on the floor, following the footprints, and noticed the corridor ended at a solid metal door. I was almost there.

I stumbled along towards the door, keeping one hand on the wall as I went, the stone cold and rough under my fingers.

Creak.

"Hello?" I called out, my voice shaky, my heart hammering and every hair on my body standing on end.

Creak.

A sudden "whoosh."

A loud crack as something struck my head.

Then.

Every.

Thing.

Went.

Black.

TO BE CONTINUED...

THAT'S IT...FOR NOW...

Thank you so much for reading The Lies We Tell! Sorry, but not really, for the cliffhanger-type ending. The continuation of Winter and Caiden's story will be coming soon! Feel free to send me any and all abuse/love/comments, and reviews are always very appreciated!

ACKNOWLEDGMENTS

First of all, thank you for reading *The Lies We Tell*. It means a lot to me, and I really appreciate it. I took a chance with this book - it was completely unplanned and unexpected. I was supposed to be writing something else, but Winter, Caiden and the rest of the Four got inside my head AND WOULD NOT SHUT UP. I was completely consumed by them. And that leads me onto my next thanks...

Thank you to Jenny. There is no way this book would exist without you. I'm so lucky to have you in my life, even though you corrupted me and you try to steal my book boyfriends. Thank you for believing in Winter and Caiden's story. You, Claudia and Chris not only had to read my incredibly rough first draft, but have had to put up with an unreal amount of self-doubt and fear from me with this book. I can apologise for the 5000th time, or I can just say, hopefully I will be less neurotic with book 2. Maybe. Fingers crossed! As well as all the emotional support, thank you for everything you've done for this book, too many things to even count. I'm beyond grateful! I suppose it's only right that Z is yours ;)

Thank you to my work wife Claudia, aka The Cocklector. Where would I be without our daily arguments? Thank you for pushing me to do better, and for always being in my corner. Except when we're arguing. Love you!

I never thought I'd be thanking my husband in this way, but yet, here I am! Thank you for being surprisingly enthusiastic about this book, and brainstorming plot lines with me during long car journeys. Thanks for reading all the words, even if you did insist on reading whole passages out loud and putting on random (and completely horrendous) accents for each character, and I forgive you for calling Cade "an angry cunt". Even though I know it was said out of jealousy, because you wish you were more like him. (Haha jk. Or am I?)

Thank you to my amazing betas - Beck, Stef, Amanda and Alley. Your comments and support helped me turn this from a rough story to a finished book. I love you 3000!

A massive thank you goes to the amazing women in my street team. I seriously cannot thank you enough for everything you do. I appreciate it so, so much.

Thanks to my editor, Sandra, for giving me the tough love I needed to make this story stronger - as usual you were right! And to Jeanette, my cover designer - how you always manage to come up with the perfect cover after my nonsensical, completely basic ideas, never fails to blow me away.

Finally, thank you to the bloggers, bookstagrammers, authors, and readers that I've been lucky enough to come to know. Thank you for everything you share, every comment, mention, conversation, kind words...it all means so much to me. And my BBB girls (love you all, thank you for making our group a happy escape from the world), and the Chaddettes, thank you for the daily laughs and encouragement.

If you read all this, THANK YOU!

Becca xoxo

P.S. To the people I've invariably missed, you have my permission to throw tomatoes at me.

ALSO BY BECCA STEELE

ABOUT THE AUTHOR

Becca Steele is a contemporary romance author from the south of England, where she lives with her husband, two kids, and various animals.

When she's not writing, you can find her reading or watching Netflix, usually with a glass of wine in hand.

Join Becca's Facebook reader group Becca's Book Bar or find her via the following links:

facebook.com/authorbeccasteele

instagram.com/authorbeccasteele

bookbub.com/profile/becca-steele

goodreads.com/authorbeccasteele

Manufactured by Amazon.ca
Bolton, ON